These Restless Hills

Joshua Penrod

CATAMOUNT
PRESS

an imprint of Sunbury Press, Inc.
Mechanicsburg, PA USA

CATAMOUNT
PRESS

an imprint of Sunbury Press, Inc.
Mechanicsburg, PA USA

For information about special discounts for bulk purchases, please contact Sunbury Press Orders Dept. at (855) 338-8359 or orders@sunburypress.com.

To request one of our authors for speaking engagements or book signings, please contact Sunbury Press Publicity Dept. at publicity@sunburypress.com.

FIRST CATAMOUNT PRESS EDITION: August 2025

Set in Adobe Garamond | Interior design by Crystal Devine | Cover design by Lawrence Knorr | Edited by Gabrielle Kirk.

Publisher's Cataloging-in-Publication Data
Names: Penrod, Joshua, author.
Title: These restless hills / Joshua Penrod.
Description: First trade paperback edition. | Mechanicsburg, PA : Catamount Press, 2025.
Summary: In 1889, a ruthless and relentless cop chases a labor agitator through coal and steel country. Faced with hostile workers, egotistical capitalists, and demanding superiors, the chase is on through a maze of shantytowns, mills, and mines. Nature's threatening catastrophe provides the backdrop as the tension ratchets higher into an explosive conclusion.
Identifiers: ISBN : 979-8-88819-332-7 (softcover).
Subjects: FICTION / Historical / 19th Century / General | FICTION / Historical / 19th Century / American Civil War Era | HISTORY / United States / 19th Century.

Designed in the USA
0 1 1 2 3 5 8 13 21 34 55

For the Love of Books!

To Jacqueline

"BECAUSE THOU HAST SPOILED MANY NATIONS,
ALL THE REMNANT OF THE PEOPLE SHALL SPOIL THEE;
BECAUSE OF MEN'S BLOOD, AND FOR THE VIOLENCE OF THE LAND,
OF THE CITY, AND OF ALL THAT DWELL THEREIN."

—Habakkuk 2:8

Chapter One

"For the rich men thereof are full of violence, and the inhabitants thereof have spoken lies, and their tongue is deceitful in their mouth."

—Micah 6:12

"I hear you're worth a dollar to the State, big fellow," the man says, looking up at me, his gaze easily sliding off the truncheon gripped in my right fist, glistening with his blood.

"Imagine you're worth even less," I say, my voice quiet, this whole situation and circumstance *too quiet* on top of everything, given the fact that there are at least a dozen or more people watching me—me and Barna, that is—as we play out this little exchange, and they're all so damnably quiet, silent as the new graveyard barely a hundred yards away. It's a steady reminder to the miners here, and all their families too, a background erupting from the mud behind the scaffolding and tumbledown buildings marking the site of the underground coal mine, oblivious donkeys staring numbly at the stray dogs which shriek back at the donkeys and the people alike.

Black and brown dust coats everything, and where it doesn't, there's just mud.

Barna groans, settling down on one elbow, his legs crossed at the ankle, as if enjoying some languorous and sun-dappled afternoon on a riverbank. He's tall, over six feet, and maybe even taller than me, though he's not got the same bulk that I've managed to acquire over the decades.

He groans again and manages a smile, loose and crooked teeth crimson. "Just another Cossack, just like in the—what do you types think we call it? Oh . . . the *old country*."

I wave the truncheon at him. I can hear his accent; it comes and goes, it seems, as it pleases, sometimes that thick Hungarian, other times just enough touch on the English to let everyone know he's not from here, but still that he's been around for a *while*, and nothing is truly *new* for him.

"We hung up the Maguires," I say, smiling, breaking his stare, and looking up at the crowd, still so silent and motionless, while I think about those bodies dancing and jerking, hanging from the rough rope. "Strung 'em up all over Schuylkill and Luzerne and Carbon and wherever else we had to string them up. You never seem to learn. None of you." I raise the truncheon, pointing it at them all. "And here we're not going to broker with all of that bullshit that such types whispered into your foreign fucking ears in God alone knows what language."

Barna winces and groans, rolling his head around on his shoulders. He again spits blood out onto the dirt. His common cotton shirt, once white and now saturated with sweat, dirt, and blood, draws my eye. It's so similar to my own.

He spits again, coughing as he hitches in a ragged and deep breath, and he looks up at me and says: "So what do we do here then, Boss? You going to take us all in?"

"No." I let the truncheon down, stepping one small step forward as I did so. I looked at the crowd, and then back down at Barna, who seemed to relax when I said that single little word.

That lie, that is.

"Just you," I continue. I stab at him with the club, hitting a nipple, then cracking it off the side of his skull just as he started to yell about the quick jab that I had given him.

Then I hit him again, on the shoulder.

Again, the upper arm.

Exposed ribs as he curls up and I truncheon him again and again, cursing at him.

I hope he knows it's not about him; it's about the next generation of Molly Maguires that he's trying to recruit in whatever Hungarian form he's trying to fit. None of the coal companies are going to let that happen;

he *has* to know *that*, just as *they* have to know too. They've already seen and heard too much about the red flags flying in Britain, and they'll have no truck with it here. This is business.

I've no pleasure in what I'm doing.

But a man gets paid for doing a job. I could be laying bricks. Picking coal.

I hit him again, in the side of the knee, and he squawks like a wounded bird, suddenly clutching at his leg.

I breathe hard, my chest heaving, sweat pouring down the back of my neck, my scalp, my torso on this cool May morning.

I stop at last, and Barna lays there, nearly motionless except for his weeping against the pain.

I raise the club again like a pistol, shoving its point at the crowd. "All of you, every single sodding last one of you . . . *fuck off* back to your shitbox shanties."

I don't speak Polish, Lithuanian, or most especially Hungarian, or any other twisted Polack tongue but the gestures and the tone of my voice was enough to convey my message.

The crowd—the women, the men, the children, faces far and near and streaked with grime and they are all faces I've seen before, in every town and on every battlefield—shuffles, uncertain, sullen, glancing at me before their eyes again drift back down to the mud and dirt and coal dust and manure and the Almighty alone knows what else tramped into this sad patch. The unsettled pairs of feet shuffle in all different directions. I stare at them all as they move slowly away. I search for any that look back at Barna, but none do.

Good.

"Come on," I said, gesturing to the still-reclining *organizer.* "On your feet."

He wasn't reclining so much as he was, perhaps, recovering. He tried moving, but only groaned.

"Not hard enough to break any bones," I assured him. *Except for maybe one or two of those swings. And maybe for the smaller bones, the fingers . . . or the eye socket, or something.* "On your feet," I say again.

Barna rolls onto his stomach, gathering his arms and legs and pushing himself up. He spits a gout of semi-clotted blood out onto the mud, the same mud clinging to his hair and his fingers and face, and the same mud that I can feel under my feet and smell deep in my own being, the smell of sulfur and coal and metal.

Barna's on one knee, and I seize him under a single armpit, pulling him to his feet. He staggers for a moment, swooning. "I think you cracked my skull," he croaks, dizzy.

"Then there's even less harm done," I respond, shoving him forward. He surges, stumbles, somehow catches his balance.

He stops, looking back at me, and I see that his right eye is nearly closed, an angry purple, black, and red balloon of blood swelling around it. His gaze drops from my face to the Pennsylvania Coal and Iron Police badge on my jacket front. "You're going to burn in hell, all of you, one day," he says.

I clap the shackles on his wrists and look right into his eyes—as much of them that are still open.

"I'll see you there."

Indeed, where we will return. Dust and blood, the full circle . . . I've no illusions about my mortality, and all who know me know I've dealt it out more than most. I think of the Book of Exodus: *Behold, I will smite with the rod that is in mine hand upon the waters which are in the river, and they shall be turned to blood.*

———

"Well?" Jonas Ogden's only word to me comes out as a spitted spike of contempt, it seems for both Barna and myself.

"He confessed," I say, shoving Barna forward against the clerk's desk, sending a cascade of papers drifting to the floor and rattling the thin glass window barely held in its frame.

Barna chuckles, rueful and quiet, and finds a chair. He throws his head back to stare up at the ceiling, most likely in an effort to try to staunch the gurgling stream of his nostrils.

"Look at that!" Ogden screeches, a tremulous finger extending towards the disorganized sheaf of papers on the floor.

"Gravity," I say. I move over to the larger desk, Ogden's desk. I rifle through its papers for a moment, ignoring his own beginning squawks of protest.

I, Thomas Harris Houghton, do hereby sign and witnesseth
the confession of one Markos Barna, late of Indiana County,
Commonwealth of Pennsylvania. Mister Barna did on one
occasion and averred to more than one occasion in the past
attempt to form an unlawful labor combination. Under
Pennsylvania Act 228, I, TH Houghton, CI324, Pennsylvania
Coal and Iron Police, doth swear it in the presence of Ogden,
day shift supervisor, Pine Hill Coal Company, Mine 11, Indiana
County, Commonwealth of Pennsylvania; Tuesday, 28th of May,
the Year of Our Lord 1889.

I extend the sheet to Ogden. "Sign this."

"You're a man who takes great pleasure in his job." Ogden looks down at the paper, his faced pinched in disgust. He pulls a pen from another spot on the desk, dips it in fresh ink, and signs his name with a flourish. "What do I do with him?"

"Put him in there," I say, pointing to the small iron cell in the corner. "And then the sheriff will come get him. Or not. Hard to say."

Barna's assumed a new position of extreme rest and tranquility in the chair, his head lolling all the way back as he looks at the ceiling through swollen eyes.

The only hope for the doomed is no hope at all, I think, Virgil's *Aeneid* popping into my recollection.

I know Ogden's type, all too well. They like to butter up the superiors, anyone that's a little bit above them in the company. Here, he's a mine manager but probably hasn't been in a shaft for years, maybe never has. His neck is thin, his arms bony, his spectacles tiny. He's got a wisp of a mustache and grease in his hair, tamping it down against the scalp of his tiny skull. It's the same type, the *clerks*, running about on all of their busyness at the railroad offices in Harrisburg, Philadelphia, Altoona, or wherever. These types never set foot on a train other than in the most sumptuous railcar afforded by their privileged position within the Pennsylvania Railroad. Ogden's the same; just biding his time here in the mud and woods and rocks of Indiana County until he gets a new posting or a different job in a cleaner place.

They leave the dirtier jobs to me, and I'm one of the most hated of the most hated. I'm the Coal and Iron Police, and I'm not sure who possesses the greatest degree of contempt for me; the ones who hire me, the ones who I'm hired to deal with . . . or what I have for myself. Not that I had that much of a choice in the matter. It fell to me after my release from the services of General Grant and the Army of the Potomac, whom I had joined by signing up in Philadelphia in 1861 and then, when I got back to Philadelphia four years later with the Negroes all freed and the country in one laughable piece, my time in the Army had run out, and I needed something new to stop from sliding into an almshouse residence . . . or into a gutter. Both have plenty of ghosts waiting to visit time and again.

That's when at a gathering it was implied that I was good with my fists. And with just about everything else, including anything with a blade or a bullet from the Reb, had made sure I had those skills, in spades, and then when I finished with those Rebs, I was fully persuaded by an intimation at that gathering that the C&I would welcome someone like me.

Welcome, they did. And now, more than twenty years later, times spent in foundries and at camps and in the mills and in the mines and on the Pennsylvania Railroad, they all wanted rid of me.

Refuse, back to the refuse pile. The unwilling to be buried, the willing to be led and protected, as in the Book of Mark, I will smite the shepherd and scatter the sheep.

It's not been getting any easier in this line of work, I must add. Thought it had been over with the Maguires, but things have just gotten more involved even as things grow and grow and grow. There's just one choice, just one set of two directions things might go—either the discontent can disperse and lose strength among the many; the other choice is that the message is so necessary and compelling that it swarms through the larger masses like wildfire. It gets worse every year; we are all headed somewhere, but we don't know where or what.

Some of us couldn't care about that, the proximity of the grave well known to us.

The events around the world had once been a pagan celebration; the new pagan celebration is now that of the laborer. The weeks leading up to and away from May 1st rise to a new level every year; what had once been a dance around a pole for Beltane is now a day of anger, marching, and chanting. Demonstrations in the streets, starting in Chicago, but certainly now in other cities, like Pittsburgh and New York and Philadelphia, all the way out to the smaller and more isolated mine sites, like this one. My betters—of which they are legion—seem to think that this is something that can be licked just by sending me or someone from my cohort to crack some skulls, break some limbs, and put the fear of God into these immigrant types . . . except not so much as to send them packing back to wherever they came from. Drums beat, their cadence starting and echoing, pairs of hands feeding oats to the herds, filling the hands of their illegitimate babies lest the papers begin to roar the headlines, and the drumbeats pound on, and on, and on . . . and on all sides. The numbers for the money are bigger on one side, far from poor on the other, but the money numbers have the lower body numbers. The combinations all have bodies, but despite this, they're riven by their own tendencies, mirroring the moth to the flame. They can't stray far from their own action, as that is *all* they have.

That's the advantage that I have, of course, which is that there's really nowhere for them to go. They left for a reason, after all, so there is temptation to join in those marches and riots, from the Haymarket in Chicago three years ago all the way through to the rumblings I've been hearing coming out of Pittsburgh. I'd already had enough to do with the Maguires; now, the new ones pop up everywhere. My many betters don't seem to fully understand this, not the same way I do. Ultimately, this is good for me as well, as it keeps me paid and on the tracking trail. It's not like, after all, that they can't go back home, home to the Old Country, as some of them do. I've been surprised from time to time about how much traffic I hear about going back and forth from here to there and back again, bringing more family members back with them, or staying over there with their sudden American fortunes. Still, more of them stay and then send for family who do the crossing themselves . . . the way that industry, here in Pennsylvania, but also in New York, Chicago, and places further west, continues to grow, the country will be importing thousands, even millions, of them from the Old World. I have wondered, from time to time, what the new West must be like? I will likely never know. But if I stay here, stick around long enough without a bullet in my brain, it will start to look like not the country that I was born into or the country that I fought to preserve. I feel the pain in my knuckles as I clench my fists.

The front stoop of the shanty headquarters squeaks as I step back out onto it and light a cigarette, hacking out the first inhale. Not as bad as the hack that all the miners have, to be sure, but spend enough time around dust and coal, it's going to get you at some point. The cigarettes helped, sometimes, but one can't smoke all the time, and they do tend to get in the way, especially when engaged in work, up-close.

A group of children, maybe 4 years of age, run and chase each other and draw up short when they see me on the porch; they wait for a beat then all turn on their heels and beat feet back whence they came, the little shits.

I'm not a monster, any more than anyone else is. It's just my job, is all, and there are times when I can embrace it more than others.

I spit out a draining load of snot from my sinuses, cursing the irritation I feel.

I hear footsteps behind me and turn my head just a bit to see the little malformed mustachioed string bean, Ogden. I peer at him from the corner of my eye.

"Well," he says, sighing, "Barna's locked up."

I nod.

"Where you off to next?"

I can't help but notice he's got a bit of a hopeful note in his voice as he asks that question.

"Back to the main job. Back to Magursky." No harm in telling him; everyone in the vast web that is the Pennsylvania Railroad knows, even if most of them think that Magursky himself is something of a myth.

"And where you going to find him?"

I take off the bowler, smoothing my remnants of hair back. "Johnstown," I answer. I look up at the sky, again spitting raindrops. "You know it?"

Ogden nods. "It's a busy place, a boom town."

Perfection. I look over at Ogden, whose comportment seems to have improved considerably when the realization finally dawned within his thick skull that I was not intending to remain anywhere nearby; indeed, he seemed about to rotate in excitement.

"I met Daniel Morrell one time a few years ago," I say.

Ogden frowns. "He died a few years ago."

I pause. "That is true, Ogden. I met him prior to his death."

Ogden's turn to pause now, but I wasn't in any hurry to attempt another conversational gambit with a suckerfish like him.

"He was a great man," Ogden says.

I draw deeply on the cigarette. "Another fucking Quaker," I respond.

———

I was pleased—as pleased as possible for me—to find that my horse, a sturdy, smart steeldust American Quarter named Amos, had been brushed out and fed, just as I asked. The young man minding the small livery and stable saw me coming and hurried to get the saddle cinched back onto Amos, along with my bedroll and other accoutrements. Oftentimes I would take the Pennsy to the various spots where I had been assigned a task, but given the difficulties I had expected at the outset for my next task, I had decided a horse would expedite the flexibility and, just perhaps, other needs that I would encounter on the way.

I double-checked the cinching and flipped a coin to the stable boy, swinging one leg over the cantle as I settle in. I had ridden much over the past few years, and I found that while I easily remembered the approach, I sometimes had difficulty in getting the muscles to obey my desires. Part of that was practice, the other part age and wear.

I turn Amos down the path leading out of the mine equipment and buildings, intending to cover half the distance to Johnstown in the remainder of the day and set up a small camp comfortably distant, back in the woods that this part of the state offers aplenty. It reminds me of my youth in some little way, in the woods and under the stars, away from the dirt, mud, and coal dust.

I keep my mind as empty as I can for the first mile, letting any various and sundry get the impression that my lurching slouch meant just another tired traveler. If anyone wanted to stir up some trouble, I was happy to oblige with a response sounding in mayhem. Most times, my demeanor and size alone are enough to keep away all but the worst, most idiotic, or most desperate, but one never really knew. All the more reason to camp out under the stars and trees in this late springtime and avoid any cheap inn on my way to the next job.

Amos, a fast horse as befits the breed that he is, trots along at a pace congruent with my need for peace and solace. I had not wanted to beat Barna, but compared to what could happen to him in the future, I let him go with only this slight dust-up. If such a situation would manifest that would require my return, Barna could be assured that his next stop won't be to the cell in the mine office. It would be to the infirmary, or even to the dirt. The Coal and Iron Police are not here for parades or to break up fights among drunken foreign louts. We are, instead, to instill and keep order along the giant of industrial enterprise spreading around the Commonwealth, from Philadelphia to Pittsburgh, from Scranton to Erie. I've had two careers so far, one as soldier, and the other as police, and I could feel the weight and history of both settling in my elbows, knees, and neck. How much longer I was going to be able to . . .

Stop.

There's not much point in speculating what's next for me in this life; I don't expect to make it to 50 years of age anyway, which is not that far away. Some have wondered, openly, and even to my face, what my career and lifetime will account toward in the hereafter, with some even going so far as to suggest, like Barna had said, that I'll burn in hell for my deeds. That would probably be the case if I had thought that anything happened beyond moldering in the grave and supplying ample gristle for the worms and bugs.

I've seen the bodies strewn across the fields of Gettysburg and Chancellorsville and dozens of other places, and I can tell anyone who's interested that is all that happens. We live, some for longer than others, and then we die, and then that's the end. Barna, myself, and even the various Presidents of this great nation just turn into lumps of rotting meat when the vital force expends.

I close my eyes, thinking of the sensation of striking Barna. I can still feel it, and it's not just due to the age or the wear. I feel it the same as I always did, back through my fingers and palm, my elbow, my shoulder. My jaw hurts under the stress of such clenching, my rear teeth crooked and at least one or two cracked from the experience of my own deployment of power, much less the times when I myself had been socked in the face. I squeeze my hands into fists around the reins and then relax them, the aching, cold pain oozing from my knuckles and wrists.

Still, that impact, that finality of the motion satisfies. It always has.

Still, that impact, on Barna, is but a minor one in comparison to the man I'd been pursuing for more than a year now and not had more than a glimpse of in that time: Istvan Magursky, he of the Hungarian enclave in the Old Country, supposedly, and now over here in America. From poor immigrant to cheap laborer to working in the coal mines to a "laborist" active in the iron and steel combines, from Steelton and then to Johnstown.

I wonder what that Quaker would have thought of all this, had he lived long enough to see it.

Amos strolls down the road for some time longer and my eyes remain nearly closed, both collecting my thoughts and clearing my head. *Will be in Johnstown midday tomorrow. Hotel or camp? Who to see first?*

A smile, somehow, manages to play on my bruised lips, thinking about camping tonight. Yes, I'd accrued the seniority within the Coal and Iron Police to have a reasonable expense allowance, but I'd also saved up somewhat over my time, due to my proclivities for spending time in the woods under a mild shelter and with a thin bedroll. Some might think that would come from my days in the Army, but it was really how I started life, on a farm in Fulton County, not far from where, ironically, President Buchanan—who could be thought of as the actual father of the war with the South—was born as well. I can't speak much for his background— knowing he was a lawyer tells me quite enough, in my estimation—but my own family brought me into the world on their farm near McConnell- sburg, on the other side of the ridge from the birthplace of Mr. Buchanan. My earliest memories are of the great valley between the twin ridges, hazy fields, the smell of cowshit, and rolling landscapes of farm and forest.

That was a long time ago now, and it seems like even longer, espe- cially when one would go to a place like Philadelphia or Pittsburgh, or even one of the smaller cities such as Johnstown. Coal and steel replaced trees, made manifest by the fires and the smoke of industry, and the iron and steel monstrosities crossing to and fro in the Commonwealth replaced much of the horse and wagon. Good for all that, is what I say.

More changes came from the needs of the dozens of boomtowns in the Commonwealth, drawing more people from the Old Country to cross the ocean with the intent of doing great activity here, either to start anew, collect enough for a grubstake and continue the journey westward, or to return to Europe as a new man, pockets heavy with the gold of the New World.

Some charge to the mines in Arizona and Nevada, visions of gold and silver dancing and swirling about. Some fly to the open spaces of Texas and Montana—the newest state—with pictures of thousands of head of cattle and horses to be bred and sold. Some escape to the West to find their own liberties for their houses of worship, far away from the eyes of the politicians and established churches.

And yet here, in this hilly and difficult Commonwealth, a handful amass *true* fortunes. I've heard that someday we'll all see such largesse and that the privileged few who have access for now will become the privileged many. I've not seen that yet. I doubt I ever will. That's not the fate for a man like me.

I rub the metal badge then tug my topcoat over top of it once again, hiding it from view.

Some have called the Coal and Iron Police vindictive, and that is true. We are as vindictive as our masters command us to be. Those others whom we've attacked express their own vindictive desires against us. It tempts all such path-takers into escalation, and it's been my experience that one can find enemies anywhere, especially when one has made them everywhere.

I consider my options, knowing what I know of the town and its politics. For the better part of the past three decades, the centerpiece of Johnstown's booming status has been that of the Cambria Iron Company, among the largest in the state. The company became an early leader in the development of the entire industry, particularly after the War Between the States, and was probably as responsible for the railroads—via making thousands upon thousands of miles of iron rail—as the railroads themselves.

I'm used to company towns, but Johnstown is a *big* company town. Population nearly triple what it was just a decade ago, and with the way the nation needs steel, the place won't be going anywhere but up, not for a long while, even with the booms and the busts, the steel up, the coal down, the gold up, the silver down, the trade up, and the trade down. Thousands may be out of work. There will always be thousands more in it. Cambria Iron is a national force of nature; God alone knows that my most regular employer, the Pennsylvania Railroad, has depended on it for years for its tracks and various others of its many needs, for its cars, its locomotives, its everything. Steel for the new buildings in Chicago, wire for the railroads and farms, and pieces for the new Brooklyn Bridge in New York City. I've not been to Johnstown, but I can picture it already . . . smoke, sooty stacks, blazing fires with waterfalls of sparks and molten metal pouring from ladles the size of a locomotive.

Another fucking Quaker, I had told Ogden.

The truth is, there was more to it than that. Daniel Johnson Morrell was a well-known man, an outright Pennsylvania hero who started from being a Quaker stock boy in a store in downtown Philadelphia to the head of the largest iron works in the state and then a Congressman in DC. Should have called him *another goddamn politician,* I suppose, but one can't always be on track with one's thoughts in the aftermath of administering a beating. Truth is, Morrell turned Johnstown into an industrial center for the state, for the country. He really *was* a great man. Johnstown may not be here without him, and that means he is an author of the reason I'm riding into Johnstown today. He was such a great man, it seems, that he can control my fate from beyond the grave.

Amos ambles along, as do my considerations of the nature of the world today. When I'd been born, the only possible way from my hometown to where I'm riding now would have been a few days of difficult and even dangerous travel under some conditions, riding through woods on old war roads from the Revolution and even before that, during the wars with the red man, or, at best, some connections along with the statewide canal system. Then, in a hurry, came the railroads and with them, it seemed, holes plunged deep into the earth and enormous steel structures pouring out more of its own making, molten skeletons and shells for the country, for the tens of thousands of ants working in them, at the same time while making the machines that dug the fuel from those deep pits, which, in turn, fueled the fires and the locomotives.

I let out a long slow breath, remove my derby, and scratch my head. And now, some forty years later, I'm riding to Johnstown to investigate one Istvan Magursky, as much a product of this new world as I am . . . just from different sides of the ocean, different upbringings, and far different views of the world. I'm sure there's disagreement there on what things could be. That question never really did much for me, a pointless fucking exercise. The way the world is, that's it. That's all it ever is.

As I turn a bend in the road, the mountains to my right divide into a type of gap, looming over a deep river valley, high shoulders to block light but for a few hours during midday every day.

The Conemaugh River's running high in this valley, northwest of the town. With any luck, it won't even take me four hours tomorrow to find my way into the town.

I pat Amos's neck and lead him slowly up a gentle slope, looking about to make sure no others' camp might be nearby. I find a spot in the far corner of a meadow, half a mile from the road. Here, I can build a small fire and cook something, and here I'll stare into that fire and then I'll lay back on the bedroll and stare up at the stars pouring their light down on us.

I'll think of the battlefields. And when I try to stop thinking of the battlefields, I'll think of Mary Elizabeth . . . my eyelids drift close . . .

"Mary Elizabeth," I whispered. She shushed me, touching my face with her light fingertips. Her skin was radiant and smooth in the moonlight, almost as if it were absorbing it and reflecting it back twofold, a beacon within the room glowing greater than the nighttime light outside.

"Thomas," she said. It was always Thomas—never a diminutive or the "Tom" nickname which her own mother referred to as "vulgar."

"What has happened to you?" she asked.

"I don't know."

I start awake with a snort . . .

I prefer to think of the battlefields.

Chapter Two

Entering Johnstown unfolds as I expect. I can see the smoke from far away, and the trains run along the river in and out of the town with a pace that can only be thought of as nearly constant. Coal, people, agriculture going in. Steel coming out. Always, always steel. The thundering trains on the rails echo up and down the narrow valley, carrying transformed earth in every direction, to every stop.

Of course, there's wagon and horse traffic as well on the narrow roads carved into the mountainsides and some others further below down in the valley. I stare straight ahead, left hand on my hip, right hand holding Amos's reins; the positioning of my left hand is enough to move the side of my topcoat away to reveal part of my badge glittering in the partial sunlight beating its way through the smoke and morning mist.

The badge, I confess, is probably not the first thing drawing the eye; even the dusty, dusky scabbard can't fully conceal the stock of the Winchester lever-action. Nor the stock of the 12-gauge side-by-side coach gun. And then, if they see those, they're going to be looking more closely at my person which, as I've learned through difficult times and extreme trials, is best served when adorned with twin Colt Peacemakers in .45, a stiletto, and a couple of other blades secreted around my body. And two that make me smile the most—two Remington .41 rimfire twin-shot derringers, one up my right sleeve and another held in my left boot.

The sun cuts through the cover in patches, warming the air and then my body, nearing discomfort. I consider removing the coat but just the shirt and badged vest wouldn't be appropriate for any type of official entry into the city. The letters of facilitation and access, signed by

Governor Beaver himself, I hold in a satchel draped across Amos's neck and my coat, and then there was the objective of somewhat concealing the full complement of my carried armory.

There's more traffic, it seems, with each of Amos's steps, moving around me, toward me, with me, on foot, on donkey, on horse, on machine. Wagons and solo riders, some exchange nods, some exchange conversation. At least one wagon of freshly dead hunkies, killed by the yellow fever. At least one pair of men further down the way, doubled up and squared off, exchanging punches. I had a notion to oblige myself to join them, but there would be time enough for that after bringing the Magursky issue to a successful and exceptionally final close.

The smell of a city greets my nostrils as I get closer as well—certainly there's the underlying presence of horses, along with cattle and pigs moving to slaughter, magnified far more than what one might experience anywhere else. The sulfurous tang of burning coal screws into my nostrils, along with the outgasses blowing upward from hundreds of assorted stacks, the smells of steel and iron searing through one's awareness. At night, of course, one will be able to see the ever-present red-orange glow of the hot fresh metal being made, the showers and cascades of sparks, the cajoling of the foremen and shouted communications in a handful of different languages, among the men on the mill floors. The steam pours from the two hundred feet-long red brick boiler houses and the black painted and sooty locomotives as they rumble by with their loads of coal and fuel and metal, pounding weight into the beds of gravel underlying the tracks, occasionally a stuck brake shrieking with ear-busting volume as they grind past.

What a spot for enterprise such as this. I study the high walls of the hills looming over the valley as I get closer into town, the hulking brick boiler houses greeting the passersby, the start of the sprawling Cambria Iron Company, again huddled along the river with any number of other buildings—houses, businesses, churches, shops. The further I go toward the actual downtown, known as Milltown, the higher and steeper the sides of the valleys reach until I arrive at the spot where the Conemaugh and Stoney Creek rivers combine, a scaled-down version of Pittsburgh's geography but with a location more forlorn location and taller hills casting it in shadow, capturing and jailing the smoke and mist.

What a spot indeed. The full size of the Cambria Iron Company is apparent now, as I've already been riding past various buildings and outposts of it for the better part of fifteen minutes as I round the bend to see all of the plant and, just beyond it, the crowded buildings and homes of Johnstown. Homes rise up to my right as well, workers' and families housing stacked atop one another, but it's the steelworks across the river that captures my attention.

That, and the fact that the tops of all these tall hills are denuded of trees, some having been removed to make room for coal and iron ore, whereas even more were removed due to the choking gases congealing over this valley in a mix of smoke and mist.

I had, of course, thought of Mary Elizabeth last night, decades in the ground now. Then, I also thought of the battlefields, also decades past, and yet, so much more vivid than those memories of her. The smoke and the dust remind me, though, as it always does. What does it say about a man who prefers the visions of hell on earth to that of his one missed chance at a different and better life?

Still, as Amos trots past the length of the Company, I see massive steel barns festooned with pipes and stacks and other, smaller, brick buildings holding administrative offices and other shops for machines, tools, and various other implements that a steel company might need. I hear the low roar of the blast furnaces, the machinery grinding, from within the buildings. Further along, more buildings of the sister operation of Gautier Steel operate in much the same way. One can hear the low thuds of heavy steam hammers and the deafening ringing of steel rail and billets slamming against each other and the ground alike. The hammers are so much like distant cannon, my palms sweat.

Growing up on a farm ninety miles to the east, among quiet bubbling streams and breeze moving across the tops of the grass and in the waving branches of Fulton County, I couldn't imagine being here all the time. Or rather, I couldn't have at one point in time, if I hadn't already lived through the much louder, the much bloodier, as I heard cannons detonate and watched men torn apart by cannister and explosives and bullets, clouds of the sky replaced by splashing clouds of blood arcing through the air and splattering across my face, my uniform, my hands.

The bridge spanning the Conemaugh River was a solid one, as might be expected from my ever-more-prosperous employer. The Pennsylvania

Railroad is not one to spare an expense, at least when it comes to equipment. Personally, like any one of us, I could do with a more profound number of coins to rub together in my pocket.

While it's a boomtown now, the place now known as Johnstown did not factor largely in on the map of opportunity but for a few happy circumstances. This is a steel and coal valley town surrounded by these high hill walls. With water power, ore, and fuel all located near one another, it all started with a few isolated furnaces and being the eastern terminus of the western branch of the Pennsylvania Canal. Supposedly his little lordship himself Andrew Carnegie got his start in business here, being a telegram message runner for the Canal and the over-mountain railroad that connected the eastern and western Canal branches. Then a sleepy inland port town, with the establishment of the presence of ore and fuel, Johnstown found itself to be at the very beginning of the growth of the Republic.

Driven by the needs of the Union during the Civil War, Cambria Iron makes the world's finest railroad rails. Morrell, the Quaker, had come in at the right time and saw how to make a ramshackle foundry business turn itself into the world's largest iron company. Of course, a lot of this was bought in the barter with blood, both sons of the North and the traitors to the South, but the country itself was born in blood—by the colonists coming from England and Spain, by the whites and the red men already here first, and now between the races and the new types coming over from Europe every day. Everything this country has ever done took root in and sprung from soil and clay soaked with the blood of thousands. Now more than ever before, that blood seeps in from the ragged edges of the machinery, from the points of the picks and the edges of the axes.

The instruments change, the symphony stays the same.

Everything is both new and filthy here; from the town's start as a canal and railroad port it remained sleepy for decades, with the first iron furnaces a start-and-stop affair, short on capital and likely even shorter on brains and will, but the factors that led to why the town became what it did were easy to see and find. The rolling hills, covered with thick carpets of timber stretching as far as the eye could see, contained the ore for the iron, and then once the timber was gone, the other hills and valleys had plenty of coal to dig out.

One can feel these things in the ground, in the air, in the waters, and one can feel the weight of the ancient earth pushing upward to reach the tunnels of the workers and the banks of the capitalists. It spells times from long ago, before people were here, before the animals that we would have recognized were anywhere near.

As far as the bridge, though, the four arches span the river just at its conjunction. A dwarven version of Pittsburgh, the three rivers cut channels through a set of steep hillsides. The bridge is stone, and it looks as if it had always been there, erected a thousand years before and bound to be here for another thousand.

I snap free of the reverie. It's almost as if Amos knows exactly where he's going. I steer him along, or at least give him general suggestions, as he eases into the pace between and among the other carts and horses, the ringing and thumping of the mill more subsumed here in comparison to the noise of humans doing commerce. The grocery store, the dry goods, all of the rest. I tip my hat to several people who make eye contact—not that there are that many—and they tip theirs in response to my greeting. I note a few who look at me and whose eyes go flat, sliding from my face as if I were a ghost that they had to pretend wasn't real. At times too, those sliding glances paused again when they saw the Coal and Iron badge.

———

I let Amos off to ponder his own questions and enjoy some fresh oats at a livery from which I can see my eventual destination, a hotel by the name of the Capital, constructed by who else other than Cambria Iron Company. A newsboy shouts about the latest from President Harrison, thrusting the daily sheets at any and all passersby. The red brick four-story looms ahead of me, the welcoming staircase wide at the bottom and contracting to a smaller entrance one story up. I have to splash my way across the street, several inches of water from recent rains overwhelming the gutters. A pair of draft horses pulling a brewery wagon clatters past me, nearly splashing my not-so-fine attire, as I mount the steps, badge prominent, my small overnight bag in one hand, other tools of my trade obscured but hardly hidden.

This way, I doubt that I would even need to leave a message with anyone. Word will get through soon enough: the scarred, ugly, big bastard from Harrisburg is here, showing off.

Certainly, one doesn't need to see far into the future, especially when it all happens at once.

"Ah, you must be Mr. Houghton." The clerk glances up at me for a moment before returning to his desk to shuffle through a set of cards.

"I am," I respond.

"You are . . . expected." The glance lasts a little longer than what I'm comfortable with and I consider for a moment the sap in its special sleeve within my coat.

I avoid the inevitable polite response to smile. Instead, I stare at him, unmoving, unblinking.

After a moment, he looks down once again and announces, "A-ha! Here we are. Yes, Inspector Houghton. Pennsylvania Coal and Iron Police."

As if a blanket of silence were thrown by an invisible spirit frustrated with the bustling noises in the lobby of the hotel, the idle sounds of clinking plateware and conversations nearly stunned into silence.

I clear my throat, still holding my stare, and say, "Why don't you announce that a bit more loudly, friend, and we'll see how many people I have to shoot and sap over the course of my stay? Why, you might even earn a mention on that list."

He whirls about, hiding his movements as he goes through yet another register. How fucking difficult could a hotel welcoming procedure be? I reflect on the possibility of just having camped during this stay, but it was hard to turn down the opportunity to stay in a hotel.

"Here it is, sir!" he whirls round again, urging a key toward me, along with a sheaf of papers. "Your room number is written there, sir." He nods again, smiling, the obsequious little bastard. "Do you need help with your bags, sir?"

"No." I turn to move away, eyeing the staircase.

"Oh, sir! The *elevator* lift is on your right! The only hotel in the City with one!" he calls. The hotel staff member that operates it nods at me and gives a nervous smile.

"I prefer the stairs," I reply without glancing back. The "elevator," a box with no escape and an idiot operating it, lacks appeal.

I open the door to my room and throw the valise on the bed, framed with brass. The place has running water, along with apparently hot water.

None of my superiors need to know this, however, despite the per diem allotted to me. There's an oak chair and a small matching table below the window cowering between the heavy drapes. I part the drapes and open the window, reclosing it immediately after being greeted by a four-fold increase in noise from the mill a few hundred yards down the river. Hotel staff obviously take great pains to wash the tobacco stains from the glass inside and even the grime from the mills on the outside, but it's a constant and losing cause. The glow from the window illuminates the rose-colored ornate wallpaper decoration and the matching pile carpet. This is one of the cleanest rooms I've ever stayed in; it must be factored into the cost of that massive stone bridge crossing the river.

I can see the confluence of the rivers from my view, rivers running murky and a bit orange from the flow of materials from the nearby mining operations. I look northward, following the Little Conemaugh; I know that up that way, somewhere, there is a rumored private retreat for all of the fat cats around Pittsburgh who seek to escape the filth and din of their own making in their own city, and they can shoot imported animals behind fences and parade around with parasols among many mansions on the shore of a manmade lake supported by a huge dam.

The goddamn rich, I think. And I dare not look myself in the mirror, recognizing who puts the pittance in my own pockets. The look that I give back to myself in the midst of such dark thoughts elicits evil feelings, enough to stoke the rage. That will all come in due time. For now, I cannot.

I ignore the note on the floor, one that had been slid under the door-way, impending upon my arrival. I look out the window instead.

Smoke belches from the stacks and the furnaces at Cambria Iron; the PRR trains roll incessantly by on that new bridge. It's not ancient, though. It's brand new, and only the Pennsy could do it this way, building it brand new and making it appear as ancient as Cairo. The trains, like nearly everything else, operate on what seems to be a continuous basis. I had passed under the bridge on the way here, and now I can look back and see, from this elevation, the path that I had taken on my way into the town.

I sit back in the chair and ponder it, making some adjustments to the various implements and weapons hanging from my person. The houses on one side of the river, packed and jammed together, for a mile or more down on my left, hug the western side of the valley, clinging to the hill-side, while the Cambria works have spread out over the flat areas that could be found between the eastern side of the river and the hills further in that direction. Various parts of the works had also begun the inevitable creep up those hills, carving away at them, placing buildings and other structures on them, as the needs grew and grew and grew for the product of the furnaces. The greater the amount of that product, the greater the need for space for the raw material coming in. Ore piles, mountains themselves, tower over the men and the railcars; the same with the vast hills of coal. It's almost as if the minerals and ore and slag were the same as piles of silver and gold—in the boardrooms, the gilded mansions, the finest homes, the churches, the banks, the halls of the State Assembly in Harrisburg, and the national Congress in Washington. I recall the Book of Matthew: *"My house shall be called the house of prayer, but ye have made it a den of thieves."*

The Pennsy train ends just as another one trundles through from the west; I could only wonder what this town would have looked like forty years ago—within my own lifetime—when there were but a few homes around a sleepy Pennsylvania Canal stop and the over-mountain Portage railroad winching its way up and down the steep faces of the ridges to the east.

How do people live here? I think. Not that it's any better, not in Pitts-burgh or Steelton or Scranton. The houses are stacked atop one another, the people stacked even more deeply. Languages as far as you can get from English. I sit up straighter in the chair as I confirm what I'm seeing below—black-clad Jews with their own odd hats and side curls, moving along the half-flooded muddy way to some store or another around the corner from the hotel.

What drove you from your own home? I think. I think often of this question, of those summers and winters near the great Central Valley of Pennsylvania. A town like this, and I think of the sound of the insects buzzing in the high grass, the fireflies at the edges of the great forests. A city like Philadelphia, and I hear the gaggle of a dozen different lan-guages, pushing and tugging throngs. Same with Pittsburgh and now, same with Johnstown, topped off with a gray and brown choking haze.

My eyes drift closed, letting in only the smallest sliver of the smudged light. I consider having a smoke, just for a bit, because it's in these quiet moments of alone amidst the dirt and the grim and the din when I remember the 71st Pennsylvania. I remember being at the Angle, and then being on the receiving end along with the 69th facing down Pickett's charge, with men on both sides being blown to pieces in clouds of smoke and fire. I remember the screams and the deafening cannon and the crack of rifles. Squinting my eyes against the burning smoke while I fire minie after minie downrange. The truth is, only a small fraction of the men on either side actually fired their weapons.

I always did.

Coughing, seeing the tattered Rebels drawing closer and closer, hearing their yell, our own Philadelphia shouts bouncing right back to them and giving them the what-for.

I start awake, eyes wide, drawing in a deep and straggling breath. I hold it in for a moment, then let it go all at the same time. More than twenty years ago now, more than a quarter century, in fact, and yet those are the memories that are always the closest to me. I don't want them, but I've no choice. I roll up my unbuttoned sleeves, my eyes lingering just for a moment at the jagged patchwork of flesh on my left arm from elbow to the base of my knuckles, sutured together by what appears to be their own type of railroad tracks, laid and surging in different directions. Some of the skin glows an angry red, some white, some pink, a hash that formed beneath the bindings and thread when I somehow fought off a fever and the stinking seepage from my dying limb.

And then one day it stopped bleeding green and when I cut the bandages off on my own, this is what remained. Still functional, with strength and some mobility, but little flexibility and utterly bereft of any aesthetic.

I cough again, as if still lost in the smoke of Gettysburg and Antietam, the meat grinder of what they call the Overland now as we drove deep into the heart of Virginia. At least I'd not thought of Mary Elizabeth, the look on her face when I told her of my enlistment, nor the pain when I'd received her letter telling me of her new fiancé. No one knew how short an engagement that would be.

I slap the side of my face, shaking my head to clear it. I roll a cigarette and check my pocket watch. I had just enough time for coffee downstairs before I would get to work.

Still, I can hear the screams and smell the gunpowder. Mostly what I smell is the smell of the blood and the charred meat that used to be men.

I light the cigarette and watch the smoke drift upward into the ceiling, feeling the smoke in my chest, tasting the spicy burn as I release it back into the air. *That is me. Just another furnace.*

Someone of fine old English extraction, as one of my aunts would have said, should look around and see what our people hath wrought. Fact is, our family had moved up into the great valley from Maryland two generations prior to my birth and the other fact is that we had not felt so fine old and English when General Washington needed troopers. I should feel proud about that; I should feel proud in looking around at this new country. I do, some days. I do, when I head back to Harrisburg with the notes of conclusion of a specific job for the Coal and Iron Police. Not that I'm under any illusion as to what they are. It also means plenty about what I am.

The war taught me to find pride in a few other things that perhaps civilized society does not exactly find with the same approval. There is no mystery or magic here. Instead, I know that the white-gloved types of that world sneer at me, more than a fresh hunky even. They do not want those precious white gloves too dirty, even whilst building the country, about which they endlessly crow and prate.

And it still seems that way to me, even with—or especially with— carrying the Reb's shrapnel in my forearm. I'm still hazy on how or what hit me. It hadn't been a ball or cartridge; instead, as near as what the field sawbones could tell, some shell had hit the muzzleloader of one of my regimental fellows and the pieces of that got blown into my arm as it exploded, both metal and wood. It could have been worse, even for the arm, and Christ knows I saw enough men on both sides blown to pieces. I could feel the metal still in there, though, beneath the hard and leathered skin covering the muscles and sinew. Some of the metal would move from time to time, working its way against the bottom of the skin, sometimes in the muscle. The pain is constant, varying in level but never its presence, with the pieces that were closest to the bones, which would drag and scrape the surface of the bone. Worse still might be the thought that there are *other* pieces buried in my wounds, flung there by ripping explosions and reduced to bits of body and blood. In this way, I still carry some of my battlefield brothers with me.

I administer the beatings because I'm told, because that's the way forward for the country. Or it could also be that this is what I'm paid to do, like it or not, by the Commonwealth and by the railroad, and by the coal and steel barons. One gets to a point where one cannot tell the difference between any of them. Certainly not how they act, at least to me, and not to the new groups of people that we see flooding into the country.

I stab out the cigarette in its crystal grave, the ashtray catching the reflection of a hundred tiny red sparks. My eyes again drift to the hulking structures of the Cambria Iron Company. In there, I know, there are men like me and men not like me, all vying and fighting for their own spots and spaces in this world and in their work.

I cough out the last of the smoke, leaning back in the chair and setting about re-arranging my various implements of will imposition and harm. My eyes go back to the note that I had intentionally ignored, left for me by some anonymous, creeping, cringing fool in the middle of the carpet.

I stare at it for some moments and sigh, hauling myself upright to retrieve it.

The note reads: THE SONS AND OTHERS ARE WATCHING YOU.

Good. I certainly hoped that they were; there could be little doubt in my mind who the Sons were. In this case, the Sons of Vulcan, who were also the fathers of all the labor conflicts that I could find in the Commonwealth today. They were themselves the only true force in Johnstown, and they had also been the first force in Johnstown; the Quaker had found a way to choke them into the darkness.

Would that he could see this State now.

And a simple enough note.

The eyes had been watching me since before I'd arrived; this much was certain. I realize I'd been sending messages, but of course other messages had been sent before I arrived, sent by others.

The Sons of Vulcan were long gone, sucked into the much larger "unions" and other movements that had taken form over the past decade. Some of them still owed fealty to that old brotherhood, however, and to know that they still had deep roots here, in this city, and an awareness of when I entered it, is more than enough proof for me that I'm indeed on the right track.

They might have thought they had pure motives, but mixed them with their own self-interest, particularly those leading the groups themselves. Everyone's on the take; everyone is owned by someone else. It's always going to be that way; the difference is that I've learned to accept that. And I've been fortunate enough to be blessed with enough attributes to allow me to go in somewhat of a different direction. And fortunate enough not to have been torn to shreds on the battlefields.

Still, the note gives me a different message. The clerk at the desk? The concierge?

It doesn't matter; the information made it here, even before I did. Eyes in the crowd in Indiana County as I leveled the beating upon Barna or any number of eyes seeing the badge beneath my lapel as I trotted Amos into town.

I smile.

As I do so, I look up at the ceiling, and from the corner of my eye, a shadow flickers from the light seeping under my room door, along with a creak of the wood.

Interesting.

I lean gently forward in the chair, transferring my weight to my stockinged feet as I stand, then crouch, sap in one hand, a .45 in the other.

I slow my breathing, drawing in all the detail around the door. It could be nothing. It could be something. It could even be the local constabulary coming to say hello, or it could also be the local constabulary making an attempt to see me off with a hurried farewell. It wouldn't be the first time such an attempt would be made and probably wouldn't be the last. Most have found a change of heart after the first few moments of such an attempted exercise, and I generally found that I would be welcomed into the community after all.

I flex my fingers around the grips of both the pistol and the sap as I creep forward, still concentrating on the door and my breath, one step after the next. I pause, watching the light filtering under the door, trying to detect any movement again from the other side.

A small envelope crinkles and rustles as someone pushes it under.

Then, a pattering of feet beat their way down the carpeted hallway.

I curse, lunging for the door, seizing the bolt and throwing the whole thing open. "Son of a—" I growl as I just see the doorway at the far end of the hallway close, leading down the back stairway.

"Well, my *word*, I just *never*—"

My eyes are drawn then to the two *other* people in the hallway, on the opposite side, a corpulent couple of a certain age, the female half featuring a hat so laden with colorful and enormous feathers that I find it instantly distracting and an irritating reminder of displays of the privileged. For just a brief moment I entertain myself with a vision of sapping them both to the floor, but I tear my gaze away and run down the hallway in my stockinged feet.

I round the corner to be met with another hallway, empty. I whirl around, tearing open a closet door where I'm met with nothing more threatening than a pile of clean linens. I turn again, moving back part of the way I had just come, seizing open the door for a corner stairway. I charge through, then draw myself up short.

Just listen.

My heart thuds in my chest, and I slow my breathing. I ease forward, peering down the staircase, and then back up.

Nothing.

I throw the door open with yet another curse and I see the older rich pair of twats still standing in the middle of the hallway, mouths agape. I holster the .45 revolver and move the sap into a less threatening position.

"Did you see someone? Skulking outside my door?" I point to my room door.

"I'm afraid we had just come from the lift and rounded the corner," the old "gentleman" states. "And then just a moment later when you came charging out of there like a bull, and—"

I hold up a hand. *Their getting off that contraption scared off whoever had been listening at my door.*

It is possible that these two had spared me a potentially dangerous situation, but I avert any feeling of gratitude. Gratitude is dangerous.

"I'm Houghton," I tell them. "I'm from the Coal and Iron Police and an employee of the Pennsylvania Railroad." I breathe out again. "You're sure you saw nothing?"

They both remain mute, shaking their heads as one.

Society types, I think. *Jesus wept.*

"Smells? Sounds?"

Still nothing from the rich, as per usual. I sigh. "All right. Carry on about your business."

"Are you . . . are you allowed to carry . . . such weapons?" the woman queries, her voice trembling. I wonder if she sounds that way constantly, or if it's just my presence. Or my appearance. I notice their eyes drifting to my disgusting and scarred forearm.

My hand freezes on the door frame, and I look back on them. Her husband makes to shush her and move on down the hallway, and I say, "Coal and Iron Police, madam. In case you didn't hear that the first time."

"*Coal and Iron Police, dear!*" the man whispers, his voice hoarse, his tone urgent. "Good day to you sir," he says to me as they shuffle past. He nods, with a tip of the cap. I smile thinly back at him, returning the nod to this man who wouldn't hesitate the steal the shirt from my back to throw on the ground so that his shoes might not become bespeckled by the mud and besotted by the horseshit strewn about in the streets below.

When ordinary measures of politeness fail, one moves to forced respect. If forced respect fails, one moves on to brute intimidation. Invoking my employer is, as usual, more than enough to keep things moving in a direction that pleases me.

I study the time on my watch. *Time for that coffee. And then I will proceed with my questions.*

Chapter Three

"Mr. Houghton! Houghton! Over here!" the voice yells from the far side of the restaurant, above the clinking glass and dishware. I wonder for a moment why they didn't just hire a marching band to play Mr. Souza's new number to greet me as I enter the room.

Judging by my meeting partner's body language and facial expression, I had betrayed my own irritation with my own deportment, and he sits quickly, chastened, I hope.

"*Sorry,*" he mutters through gritted teeth as I come to the table. "I'm Strickland, your liaison to what you might need around town."

"Might you also be a liaison to some discretion, then?" I couldn't let it pass, no matter how chastened this thundering jackass might appear to be. I stand at the table, looming over him. I look at the polished silverware, the spotless white linen. *This is where the betters dine, while the men in the mines and mills wouldn't be able to pass a tablecloth like this without sullying it. By their presence alone, in the eyes of some in this town, I'd imagine.*

Then again, it's not like the people in here actually have to worry about those types venturing in either.

"Apologies, sir. Apologies." He gestures again at the chair. "Please, please! Sit!"

I stare down at him for a moment longer, drawing in a deep breath and slowly releasing it before I settle my bulk into the chair. I study Strickland for a moment, this scrawny man with a thin black tie pulled tightly round a stiff and equally spotlessly white collar, his impeccably trimmed mustache barely darkening his upper lip.

"Drink?" he asks. I'm impressed with the squareness of his teeth and might even be somewhat dazzled by their spectacular whiteness had I not wanted to knock them out, one by one. I cannot believe they have sprouted from his own gums. The way his lips twitch around the teeth in some kind of grin looks far too similar to the few men I've seen hit with electricity to be comfortable. As if I, too, might catch that look.

My teeth, however, are far from that pretty.

"Coffee is fine," I reply. Strickland snaps his fingers at the waiter, and I grit my teeth at that action.

"Coffee, young man, for the good sir here."

The waiter's eyes flash to me and then slide away. He inclines his head and body, nodding in understanding and silently shuffling away.

"I'm looking for Magursky," I tell Strickland.

I'm unsure as to whether it's the fact that I've elided all small talk and come straight to the point, or that I had uttered the name of the devil aloud. He looks at first as if he doesn't hear and then leans forward and then back.

What the hell is he waiting for?

Strickland laughs nervously. "Ah, so, yes, indeed, ah." He quietens when the waiter approaches once again with two cups and a steaming silver pot of coffee, pouring each cup without comment, leaving the carafe, and shuffling silently away once again.

"Magursky," I say again, seizing my cup and blowing some of the heat from the top. Strickland makes no move toward his own, but this time nods.

"Yes, Magursky is one of several of the miscreants in this area that you might have the poor fortune of having to encounter, Mr. Houghton."

"There are *miscreants* everywhere, Strickland. I'm only to find and apprehend Magursky. He's wanted in connection to any number of problems, not the least of which is a series of assaults on mine managers and a member of the Coal and Iron Police." Willoughby. Clement Willoughby from Chester, not even yet thirty years old and already a charge of the charitable home near his place of birth. Could no longer speak, could no longer see after his skull had been shattered like an egg as Magursky and his thuggish cohort stomped and kicked him until the point of death and been reached and then surpassed. Something else had kept Willoughby alive, though not by much, trapped in a chair, pawing at the air, and making sickening mewling sounds, like so many still left from the War Between the States, clinging to their own shredded remnant of their lives. My right hand massages my left forearm, throbbing in sympathy.

"Of course, of course. Magursky is the worst of the lot to be sure, and we were quite hopeful that we would avoid his attention here in these peaceful valleys."

I raise an eyebrow. While it's true, Johnstown hadn't seen as much agitation as other parts of the state—the famed Quaker Morrell had been unusually effective in ensuring that such things didn't occur within the walls of Cambria—still, outlying mines and anything connected by the thousands of miles of Pennsy roads could erupt. I take the fact that Johnstown is a little bit outside of the main areas of concern keeps it hidden from many problems. For years, my attention had been devoted to the Molly Maguires on the opposite side of the state, but industry's industry, labor's labor, immigrants are immigrants, and greed is greed.

I scratch my chin, flicking at the stubble, and sip the hot coffee, feeling its rejuvenating effects spearing through my tired mind.

"There was an attempt earlier," I tell Strickland, carefully watching his face.

It's his turn to raise an eyebrow.

I regale the events of the previous hour to him and he frowns. "I'm quite sorry about that, Mr. Houghton. I'm quite surprised. There are a limited few who were aware that you were coming here. Of course, the Coal and Iron Police are hardly unknown here—I'm sure you'll see some colleagues around."

"No, I believe word of my presence and my arrival came either from one of the places I'd visited prior to this one, or the ones who had initially requested assistance from the Pennsylvania Railroad to begin with. No one else is aware that I was coming."

"Ah. Well, then, that will be a happy surprise for them."

"I am sure you're correct." *And they say I've no tact.* I work at the kinks in my neck, rolling my head about, my stray whiskers scratching against the collar.

"Are you going to be interested in linking up with your colleagues during your time here in our fair town?"

"I doubt it. We'll see." The one man that I had had a pretty good idea that was going to be in town was Jimmy Welsh, another man I had known from the war and who had a disposition that was, if anything, even worse than my own. And Magursky himself, in all likelihood. I had only caught a handful of glimpses of him over the years I've pursued him. Not just I, for that matter, had him as a quarry, and he belongs as a ghost to more than half of the Coal and Iron constabulary. Presumably, he would know me by sight.

"I'm sure we'll be able to find them if need be."

I nod.

Another pause descends atop the table for a few moments while I consider more coffee.

"You sound to me to be an educated man."

"I'm not." *Except for the renowned college of butchery located in Gettysburg, Antietam, Fredericksburg, and everywhere else.*

"And yet?"

"And yet my grandfather was the educated man. He had been educated in England, came to Philadelphia and then joined cousins in the farmlands, first in Maryland, then Pennsylvania. In what was then the frontier. I continued my education as best as I could. I have read some books in my time, but there's certainly no trail of glory behind me." *Perhaps a trail of bullet wounds, cracked heads, and broken limbs. Such is my true legacy to this world.*

"You're English then?"

"I'm American then. And now."

Strickland paints a perfect white, indulgent smile across his wall of condescension. "It's a time of great change, Mr. Houghton," he says. He leans back in his chair, pulling his tight vest more tightly around his skinny torso. "Much changing in the nation, in the Great Commonwealth, and certainly here in the heart of these mountains. Never has there been such a great industrial expansion in the history of mankind, and, of course, Cambria leads the way."

I sip the coffee. I'm of a mind, thinking of the Book of Ezekiel: *They drink wine and praise the gods of iron.*

"Such frantic expansion and improvement takes a lot of resources. Of course, this is not strange news to you, seeing as much of the

Commonwealth as you have. But . . . there are social aspects to this that I do not think any of us understood. Numerous new types coming from all parts of the world." He smiles a wan smile. "You understand this, of course."

I sip the coffee.

"Houghton," Strickland says, looking up at the ceiling, eyes drifting over to the chandelier. "Houghton, of English stock, for sure."

I incline my head.

"Yes, well, the English, Scots, the Germans, even the Irish—Ulster Irish, of course, more than the Papist Irish, though there are plenty of those now as well. These are not the problems. The problems are the *people* from the countries that are not so well acquainted with the blessings of virtues such as courage. Along with intelligence, drive, and discipline. Or even hygiene." He sniffs, as if the memory itself were painful and rife with smells of its own.

I sip my coffee. *This is exactly the type of horseshit that's worse than what covers your shoes.*

"You agree, of course?" Strickland pauses, looking out the window at the pedestrians passing to and fro, and again with another group of black-garbed Jews making their way into the doors of a bank across the walk from the hotel. "And those . . . *Jews*."

"Mr. Strickland," I say, putting down the coffee and leaning forward, shooting my cuffs. "Have you ever been in battle, sir?"

"Many, many battles, Mr. Houghton. In the boardroom, even on the shop floor."

"Hmmmm." I tap out another cigarette from the case, replacing it in my pocket, twirling the fresh cigarette between my fingers. "I mean real battles, Mr. Strickland. Battles with musketry and cannon."

"Well, no, of course not. I was just born in 1859 . . ."

"Then spare me any notion you have about courage and whatnot. I'm not an educated man myself, not like you, but I can tell you that you wouldn't have been worth a bucket of pigshit at Chancellorsville." I light the cigarette, tossing the smoking matchstick in the crystal ashtray, thinking about how the expensive things all seem to look the same. I grit the tobacco between my lips, blinking the blue smoke out of my eyes. I think of the smoke from the rifles and the cannon then as well.

I rub my forearm.

"It wasn't just the fighting, you know? It was the graves detail. Where we stacked our own men and those of the rebels in pits and covered them with a foot or so of soil. You think that's enough to keep things out of the eyes of the passersby, of the farmers in those fields?" I laugh, not a shred of honest mirth. "No. The fields themselves would be roiling with the rot of the hundreds or even thousands of bodies within the soil. Roiling back and forth as if the bodies themselves were pushing out of the ground of their own accord. Like an unknown underground ocean of the dead."

Strickland appears to me now as if he is as pale and light green as the rotting soldiers.

"I don't mean to offend you, Mr. Strickland, but I'm here to find Magursky, to apprehend him if possible, and if not, to put him down. I'm not impressed so far. I feel like I should be working and I'm not, and I'm deeply troubled by the fact that you seem to think this is working. It is not."

Strickland looks deflated, weak, twisted, his face sallow and slack.

"I'd like you to conduct me to the first place you might find appropriate for my inquiries. It makes no difference to me, be it iron, coal, or rail. Your town here seems to have all three quite close to each other."

He brightens a bit at that stiff and remote compliment—if that is what it was. "Indeed we do, sir! Indeed! A concentration of industry and power in such a small area, where the rivers meet and the mountains come together."

I pour another cup of coffee. *Christ, this man is a first order swindler. No wonder he's so prosperous while still so young.*

I drink it down, hot steam pouring from the corners of my mouth and my nostrils as I exhale against the hot liquid. I barely taste it, I barely smell it. When I think of the burials, I lose my taste and smell, and the scalding coffee does nothing to erase it from my memory, the back of my throat, the top of my tongue.

Strickland doesn't hold my gaze; instead, he ponders the pressed tin design of the ceiling, the chandelier, the fine linen tablecloth. Finally, he says, "I think the most convenient for you, at least now, is to visit some of the administrative offices of the Cambria plant. From there, I can introduce you to some of the men in charge, and also connect with the men connected to the mining activities."

"That sounds quite promising, Mr. Strickland." I push the cup forward and slide my chair back away from the table. *I've no need of a so-called liaison.*

"Let's begin."

———

In the late afternoon, the mills thrum with activity and, what's more, noise and racket. It amazes me that men work in these conditions, most of them quite willingly, even if they would readily agree to an improvement to their lot in life. The battering, tooth-crunching sound, as loud as a battlefield but only without remit, the punishing heat and what must be, for those outside in the Pennsylvania winter, an equally punishing freeze. As Strickland and I walk closer to the mill, the sounds seem to grow louder in a disproportionate amount for each step taken. I study the Pennsy's Stone Bridge again as we move toward the mill, Strickland kind enough to have shown me several of the more important structures and homes nearby the Capital Hotel, no doubt with the staying power to be here forever and for generations of the families to live in such places.

"Any number of immigrant groups from different parts of East Europe," Strickland was saying. "You'll see the signs as you go to different places, things written in five, six, or even seven different languages. You're even starting to see Italians now too, God save us from wog Papistry."

He stops short. "You are not . . . a Catholic man, are you, Mr. Houghton?"

"God left me on the battlefields." *Probably long before that, if I am to be any judge at all.* I light a cigarette and study the towering steel structures of the buildings and furnaces, brick and metal. "I don't know what that leaves me." Truth is such that I hadn't seen a Catholic Church in my life until well into my teens and then only in Philadelphia, signing up with a mostly-Irish regiment. Some within that regiment found my English ancestry both unsurprising and infuriating. Arguments about ancestry go back with the Irish at least as far as ancestry itself.

We cross the iron bridge over the orange-brown and churning Conemaugh River, foaming with angry runoff from the near-constant rains, and push through labor's well-used turnstiles, stalking past the clerk's office and directly to another closed room within an adjoining brick building. He leads me behind a counter to find another waif-like man with a clean white shirt and drooping mustache; the new man's look of irritated surprise at this interruption morphs quickly to concern when seeing Strickland—probably this late in the afternoon being the larger surprise—and then his face grows slack and pale when he sees me, my badge shining and pronounced.

"Mr. Zimmer, this is Officer Houghton from Pennsylvania's very own Coal and Iron Police. He's looking for a specific . . . miscreant named . . ." he stutters for a few seconds, which I watch with delicious interest, and then I interject:

"Magursky."

Zimmer's stunned countenance shifts focus from Strickland to me and back again. "That name does not sound familiar to me, though with so many thousands of new men working—" He throws up his hands.

"I doubt he'd be using that name, Mr. Zimmer."

As if in perfect punctuation to that sentence, an echoing *boom* vibrates through the floor, rattling shelves and desks. Then another, then another, then a rapid-fire *boom boom boom boom boom* that suddenly pushes me toward the far wall.

I'm not prone to flights of fancy or attacks of the nerves, but the twenty or thirty seconds of that protracted racket was enough to nearly send me back to any number of adventures of my youth, the foremost in my mind the Mule Shoe at Spotsylvania . . .

"Mr. Houghton?" Strickland leans forward with solicitous concern. "Those are the very large steam hammers we have here at Cambria, Mr. Houghton."

"I see." I try a wry smile. "Much like cannon fire in my experience."

They both blink, one after another. "Oh, indeed? Well, please don't be alarmed, Mr. Houghton. I can assure you that there are no cannons firing here in the City of Johnstown. But there are going to be a lot of noises from that hammer and others like it."

"I had heard about the hammers. I thought that it had been exaggerated."

Zimmer smiles, a flickering look crossing his face. "The hammer is ten thousand pounds, Mr. Houghton. It poses a challenge to exaggerate when it goes beyond description itself."

"I will bear that in mind."

THOOM THOOM THOOM THOOM . . .

"Yes, indeed," Strickland says, tugging on his lapels. "The hammers have such a deep resonance through the earth that for miles around, the underground coal miners—"

"Can hear it, yes. So I've heard."

Zimmer shuffles some papers on his desk. "We tend to keep work crews together because of the same language. Same jobs, same familiarity. Increases efficiency. Doesn't hurt the injury rates either, for that matter."

"I understand the mining crews are similar, at least, that would be as I would have seen throughout much of the state."

Zimmer hands the papers to me. "That's likely true. But I don't know about coal mining. I just have the payroll manifest here."

"I'd like to see the floor."

Zimmer and Strickland exchange worried glances. "Well, we don't precisely go *onto* the floors, so to speak," Strickland says. "Mr. Zimmer here is deeply busy here with his clerking and related activities, and I am among the administrators a floor above us—"

"Go get a foreman. I want to see the works, at least to have a look this evening. Don't worry. There will be plenty of opportunities later, especially since I do not expect to find Magursky here. Not today, at any rate. I have to talk to people."

"How—how many people, exactly?" Strickland asks, hands clasped, face openly cringing.

THOOM THOOM . . .

I smile this time, appreciating the added voice of the steam hammer. I lean forward, into my answer, "Let me be as clear and as direct as possible, Mr. Strickland. I am going to find Istvan Magursky, and if I have to personally *interview*—in my own way—every fucking person in this city in order to do that, I will."

Zimmer shrugs, looking at me above his pince-nez. "That's well and good, Mr. Houghton. I can assure you that there is no Istvan Magursky on the payroll here at Cambria Iron Company, nor has he ever been on the payroll here. That is not to say that he has never been here. There might even be a Magursky or two in the area, but he would be foolish to use his own name, would he not? I believe both of you gentlemen already alluded to this."

Even in my time working the Molly Maguires, with the C&I working together with the Pinkertons, I've not had occasion to be overly impressed with any lack of foolishness. There's been plenty to go around, not the least of which among our own ranks. Or, even occasionally, what I've seen staring back at me from the mirror.

"Most of the Hungarians in this area are invested in the mining labor force," Strickland says, hands still gripping his own lapels. His eyes stray to the clock. "There are several groups among the various sites at Cambria and, from what I understand, Johnson Steel a few miles that way." He points upriver. "But you would be especially likely to find them among the miners."

"All in good time."

"Indeed." His eyes flick to the clock again. "We'll be moving toward the second overnight shift very soon. We, of course, operate twenty-four hours per day."

"Of course."

"I assume you'll want a discreet spot of observation? Though I can assure you, the foremen keep our work crews very tightly reined."

As if on cue, a big man, my size at any rate, his face blotched red with heat and smeared with soot, enters the room, looking about with what can be described only as a look of total bewilderment.

"No," I reply. "I'm fine being seen."

"This is Auberger," Zimmer says. "Call him Fritz."

Fritz removes his cap, bowing his head to me, mumbling out a greeting and shaking my hand. His hands, as one might expect, are huge and calloused, scarred with burns and healed cuts and tears. He rounds his thick shoulders to make himself smaller, stooping slightly as well. His heavy mustache is streaked with grime and sweat, and plasters some of the longer stray hairs to his cheeks; I imagine that his face, beaten with years of heat and cold and fists, probably can't even feel the ticklish irritation that would have most people clawing at their skin.

As I shake Fritz's hand, the knuckles too, I see, have had some recent work.

"Ready when you are, Fritz," I say.

I follow him outside toward the sprawling facilities, filled with the glow of molten steel and the showers of sparks from pouring ladles. I smell the hot metal, the burning coke fuel, the hot brakes of the railroad hoppers and skip cars that transfer the fuel and the ore from site to site. Gray and white curtains of mist and rain cloud everything. The rain pours down against the searing heat of the buildings, steam rising from the metal and joining with the puffs of steam from the locomotives at idle and the various joints in the pressure systems leading from boilers and reservoirs to the plant itself.

It takes only a few brief moments for the rain to soak through my hat, and we're still some distance from the buildings.

"I see now that I've found the rainiest area of Pennsylvania."

He grunts in reply, shaking his head. "It's been a horrible spring, sir. Rain, rain, rain. Everything is dirt, right? Except that the dirt turns into fucking mud, and everybody's in it past their knees."

Except for the rich, I think, picturing the servants pulling at their precious footgear as they enter their mansions. Daren't soil the expensive rugs from Turkey and suits from London.

As if reading these dark thoughts, Fritz chuckles and shakes his head. "Everybody who's got to work for a living, that is."

"I guess that's most around here."

Fritz just rolls his eyes. "Always got the bird sitting on the shoulder, telling you what you're doing wrong."

I smile. I've had that from time to time in my own life, but I also had to recognize my own rather strange life that allows me some sense of solitude.

Not that I've not earned that in other ways as well.

"The crews around here are good, Mr. Houghton," Fritz says. We walk past an octagonal brick building which seems to be the home of the booming hammers, thankfully at a bit of a pause in their work. We enter a rolling mill to the right, climbing a cascade of steps to a catwalk, just as a ladle the size of a house pours its yellow-white molten steel into a vast mold. The air shimmers with the heat blowing off the poured steel, white flames licking around the edges of the ladle. Showers of sparks pour from all sides, hurling onto the floor. The crew watching stands back with what I judge to be a reasonable amount of prudence, though even from my vantage point up here, I can feel the searing heat of the metal reddening my face and the backs of my hands. Steam rises from my clothes, water evaporating from the drenched fabric.

"Reputation of our workers goes nationwide. Part of the problem is that the training is so good here; a man learns at Cambria, he can go anywhere in this nation and teach people how to make steel."

I had heard of this before as well, but I also had to wonder why, if the plant was so good, why so many were eager to leave, other than the lack of organization to the labor in this town.

"No leaflets? Nothing laying around with recruiting notions?"

Fritz laughs. "In what language would they be written, sir? I've got Poles over there, Hungarians here, a mix of English and Germans all over the place. Not even to mention the Ukrainians and Slovaks and whoever the hell else has been coming around." He motions me to follow, and we continue down the catwalk in a building so large, one imagines one can see the curvature of the earth itself in the contour of its floors and structure. "Finding literate men is . . ." His voice trails off, and he punctuates the unfinished phrase with a shrug.

Assuming even he can read, that is. "All the immigrants?"

Fritz shrugs, nodding affably at the same time and rolling his heavy shoulders. "And the darkies to boot. I don't envy them, sir, not at all. Traveling all that distance to a place where they don't know the language, don't understand the ways . . ." His voice trails off as we continue along the catwalk, our steps above not drawing any attention from those below, or moving across the catwalk toward us, brushing elbows and shoulders as we pass.

If there's anything faster than the telegraph, it's the way information gets passed around among the hunkies. It was clear that by the time Fritz and I made it to the far side of the mill, my presence, and perhaps even my purpose, had been noted, detected, and this information distributed through the work crews. A cadre of them had formed up at the end of their shift just as the new ones were coming in, a group of thin men in smeared and scorched skin and clothes, mustaches and grubby caps, stealing glances at me and yet either unable—or unwilling—to be able to fully stop themselves from staring just a moment too long; when I meet the gaze, their gazes fall away, off to the side, tracing out a new spot on the ground.

None more than the others, though. Nothing other than the normal challenge that I would get from a group like this. I was waiting for the gaze that's held.

That would be the next man I would approach.

But there's no challenge here; just an all-pervading and sullen resentment flashing through the stolen glances at me—the Cossack. Isn't that what Barna called me? Is that not what they *all* call me? It comes and it goes, like any fashion. I use it as a signal to let me know that my presence is, indeed, felt.

Fritz calls one of the men over, a name that I didn't catch, and in reality, probably couldn't have pronounced anyway.

"Houghton," I say, pointing at my chest, and then my index finger moves slowly to the badge. Everyone knows the Coal and Iron police, whether they know English or not.

"I'm Jan," says the man, eyes still averted, looking to the ground. "Last name Kwiatkowski."

I laugh. "Say that again?"

His eyes flash up to mine, and even against his heat-seared cheeks, I can see the color rise. *Good. Try something here, let me make an example of you in front of all your friends.*

"Kwiatkowski."

"Queen what-ski?" I wave my hands at it, batting away the so-called Old Country. "I'm looking for another ski. All the skis are the same to me, but I presume you might find some important differences among your own." I stare at him. "Do you understand me, *Yon?*"

He nods. "I do, sir." His accent is indeed pronounced and here I see that he is actually far younger than I thought, barely into his twenties, by the looks of it. He would have picked up the language on his own in a hurry, particularly if he wasn't born here.

"Magursky," I say. "Ist. Van. Ma. Gur. Sky."

He shakes his head. I'm not keen on the fact that he's pretending not to know; everyone knows the names, even if they don't know them in person. Hunkies, however, know all the hunkies, even if one's Polish and the other Ukrainian or Hungarian or Slovak. Pick one's poison.

Fritz looks at me, then looks at the man. Without warning and not too much slower than the strike of a cobra, Fritz cuffs Kwiatkowski right on the back of the head. The young man shrinks away, picking his cap back off the ground. "The last thing I need is trouble on this fucking floor, boy. You understand me?" Fritz growls.

The young man, in a hurry to agree, nods so quickly that his cap starts to slide from his head once again. I study him carefully, then look over to the group of workers following this exchange.

I move past the burly young man and approach the work gang. "You assholes speak English?" I yell.

They look at each other, side-eye gazing, back at me, then to the floor, to the wall, to the beckoning doorway and the path it represents to leave the mill.

"Magursky," I say, louder than necessary, but perhaps not for all who might be listening from the shadows. "Any man who helps me find him will be rewarded by the Pennsylvania Railroad." *And any man who doesn't help and is found later to have knowledge, will also be rewarded . . . in a different manner.*

I reach into my coat, the big hogleg pistol dangling in plain sight for all to see. I withdraw a folded flyer with Magursky's likeness on it, unfolding and holding it up for them to inspect. I pause as I direct it toward each and every one of them, my eyes steady and watching their own for any widening, and aversion.

A couple of them return cockeyed grins to me and one man looks at his friends. A five and a half foot tall piece of wire and sinew—this is the most dangerous type of man, even if he's well into his forties. Perhaps even more dangerous as a result of that further small fact. He clears his throat and jabs his thumb into his chest. "Me speaken ze Ingells," he says.

I look at him. "What's your name?"

He looks to his companions, most of whom stare down at the floor, still shuffling towards the door, inch by inch. Fritz glowers.

"Name is—" and then he finishes with something that I can't even come close to pronouncing.

"I didn't catch that. Say it slowly and loudly, so I remember it."

He raises his chin and looks me right in the eye. "My name's Jones, you fucking halfwit!" he bawls into my face.

The rest of them erupt into gales of laughter. Even the young man that Fritz had hit a few moments ago fails to suppress his grin.

I can't help but to admire the humor, personally, and if I'd been on the other side, I'd have felt the same way. But, for better or for worse, I'm not on that other side.

The sap had been in my left palm, my hand cocked so the rest of them couldn't see as it slipped down my sleeve into my grasp as I showed them the flyer. I bring it over to my right and flash it across Jones's face, a sickening crunch of jaw and bone and cheek. The man goes down without a sound, as if God himself had cut his strings.

I stand over him, looking down. The pool of thick red blood spurts from his smashed mouth. I take another step toward the group.

"That was funny," I say. "Which one of your dead-eyed fucks is next going to try my sense of humor?"

I stare at them—one, then two, then another and still another, pausing at each of them with my gaze. If only for now, the ill-concealed mirth has vacated.

"How about we give him something, just to make sure he remembers?" I lean close, brandishing the sap, and then cracking it into the man's elbow. I'm not sure if I just broke his arm or not, but he's going to have a hell of a problem for a while.

He doesn't stir.

Even the rugged and experienced Fritz stares at me, a little too much white showing around the eyes, a look I've seen so many times, in combat and in the police.

I approach them, looking each in the eye as I walk down the line, poking several of them in the chest with the end of the sap. "Istvan Magursky," I say. *Poke poke poke poke poke* with each syllable. "Has anyone seen him? Does anyone know about his whereabouts?" I pace slowly, the stare continuing, the sap still in my hand, waving it under their noses. "Anyone know anyone else who might know where Magursky is? I know he's here in Johnstown, somewhere. And a shiteyes like him doesn't come into a shitheel town like this without all of you other motherless shits knowing that he's here." A few more paces, then I turn round and head back up the other way. "Making all kinds of promises, talking about how much fucking better life would be if you'd all just listen to him. No? Just a *goddamn* ghost that no one's heard of or seen. Fine." I stop, raising my voice another notch. "Fine indeed. But let me add one more thing to your knowledge, since I'm *here* and this *Magursky* isn't. He's filled with horseshit and his promises mean nothing. His paradise doesn't exist. You all fucking know what will happen."

I raise the sap, pointing it distinctly at each one of them again, a constant reminder. "You'll be out on your goddamn arses, you and your families in the county poorhouse, because you'll lose this." I swirl the sap around, pointing at the mill's vast expanse. "*Do you hear me?*"

Some of them look away, some of them mumble.

"I'll be back. Maybe some bright light among you will have a sudden memory of important information that I'd like to know. I would urge you, most seriously, to consider that. Now. *Fuck off.*"

I look back at Fritz who's helping his man Jones back up to his feet. Another gout of blood erupts from his broken mouth, and he cradles his elbow.

"You certainly did fuck this man up, Mr. Houghton," Fritz says, mouth working with some effort at holding something back.

"I don't take kindly to prevaricators, or those with the smart mouth, now lately broken. This fella, it seems, has both qualities and that is a dangerous combination to deploy in my presence."

Fritz grimaces, holding the man up by a single armpit. "I assume you want to talk to some of the other men?"

"If the movement of news around this facility is as efficient as it seems, I expect to have some type of response very soon."

"Yes?" Fritz's tone suggests one of great hope.

I pause, the THOOM THOOM THOOM and then a sequence of double impacts, smaller, but quicker, come through and echo even above the roar of the nearby blast furnaces, steam vents, and moving ladles. A whistle sounds, signaling the shift change.

"Yes," I say, staring up at the ceiling and willing the steam hammers to stop that cursed sound. My own forearm throbs in sympathy with every one of the impacts. "I think I'll go back to the hotel and consider my next steps. You've been most helpful."

He looks at me, then to the blubbering and still bleeding Jones, then back to me, signaling between the depth of his new problem and of his desire to be rid of me, posthaste.

"I'll find my own way out, Fritz, thank you."

The rain still falls heavier. It tends to keep the smoke and the dust down and diluted, just a bit. That translates into a handful of other things, namely mud and squalid water flooding down the streets and walks, the ever-present smell of dung and urine mixing with the smoke of wood and coal, the hot stink of searing, sintering metal. I pull my hat low over my eyes and hold up a hand to the brim. The works never sleeps, and I watch the skip cars and steam engines moving ore and coke, the black and gray blanket of the mill's smoke mixing in with the rain and the fog. The gas lamps and electric lights from various buildings and homes around the city cast an extra yellow glow with the fog and the rain. Shambling, shadowy figures move in and out of gloomy, sooty fog as the rain pours from the sky.

I trudge back through the mess, splashing the mud and water on my boots and trousers, thinking that I might just find my travel allowance from the Pennsy enough for the fine hotel to do some of my laundry—not that there was that much to do. I feel the grime under my layers of clothes, the stink of the fresh steel, and my own sweat mingling and offensive in my nostrils.

I keep my hands free, arms swinging, as I leave back out through the administrative building. Strickland's nowhere to be found; I am confident that he found his way up to one of the higher offices where he's performing his widely-known duties as head bootlicker, and God alone knows what else.

I exit the building but stand under an overhang at the furthest corner, watching as the shifts change, hundreds of pairs of eyes with the potential to look in my direction, men in overalls covered in grime, jabbering at each other in their odd tongues, some laughing with each other, more tired and drawn. I light a cigarette, blowing the smoke out slowly into the watery air and feeling the tobacco help clear my head. The weights of the various tools of my trade hang heavy off my body as I wonder what I'll have to use next. I think back to the look in Fritz's eyes, all fine in helping me attend to my duties as long as it only requires some harsh words and maybe even if, from time to time, he decides to get his fists involved. Fritz's role as a group foreman may have come from his acuity;

it's just as likely that some of his acuity was informed by his ability to handle the more willful of the immigrant lot.

But when *I* hit one of his men, suddenly the game changes, the look in his eye completely different. Almost the same look, I imagine, as the look in the eyes of a slaveowner and his property. Some of us put a stop to that, only to be placed in this new situation where we see the same men, only instead of the Negro, who were brought to this land against their will, we have hordes crowding in through Castle Garden and Philadelphia and so many others, being driven to feed the machines that have grown up everywhere since.

The Statue of supposed Liberty stands in New York Harbor now, built a couple of years ago as a gift from the peace-loving French, those same lovers of peace that precipitated the war on this continent to begin with.

I walk slowly back to the hotel, eyes alert under the brim of my hat, pulled closer to shield their direction. The weather, however, this Biblical rainfall going in this smoky valley, makes observation largely worthless; even listening for the sound of a follower or even an attacker is futile, against the sound of the driving rain, the water coursing through the streets and in the ditches, and the larger nonstop din of a town cluttered with clattering wagons and locomotives, mills and mines, steam engines and whistles. I take some comfort in knowing that anyone set to attack me would have to also brave this driving rain. What would it mean for that damned parade they planned now? I wonder what it means for those same sodden masses coming from only God knows where in the supposed Old Country. I mount the steps to the Capital Hotel, grimly thinking about the likelihood that any number of them wouldn't be resting in this lap of luxury this evening.

And here I am, enjoying the same finery as the capitalists themselves. I relish the simple irony of the name of the inn at which I've chosen to rest. For some reason, my damaged brain produces thoughts of Jesus Christ; had I ever believed, surely Chancellorsville killed the dream.

The boom town is forever busy, tortured with heavy noise and smoke over all and through all, and, at least on these recent days, an inordinate amount of water, running in the gutters and streets, falling from the sky. It collects grit and dust and smoke on its way to the ground and deposits even more of the grime on top of the people walking about, the animals, and the machines. The mills groan and thunder with activity while the streets teem with hawkers and vendors, businessmen of all stripes and colors walking about and making money.

There are many, many sets of eyes in this city. I'm under no illusions about that, and nor would I expect it to be any different here than anywhere else in the Commonwealth. The difference, as I've discovered over the past few years, has been that the chain of whispers that connects all of these sets of eyes doesn't just go through a household or even a neighborhood, but stretches all over the state and even so far as to the Old Country itself.

This damned rain.

The downpour makes it harder to see who is truly looking at *me* as opposed to just looking around. There are plenty of things to see if one is interested in grime and industry; just as it is easy to find the things of interest related to vice itself. It's not hard to find a card game or some dice, and even easier to find gallons of the rotgut whiskey and the rough tobacco and even more potent nostrums that are as easily carried by the Pennsylvania Railroad and by wagon. Some gin here, some hashish there. Some moonshine there, carried under a blanket and cradled with the delicacy and reverence of the newborn infant in the crook of an arm, and a small fragrant box with a paste of the poppy in it, all the way from San Francisco. If one truly wishes to explore, the fact that the same stuff came from the hinterlands of the Pamir Knot. Certainly, Johnstown is not noted for Asian kin, but at the same time, it is on the same web of iron rails that connects it to New York City and Philadelphia in a matter of hours, and even with the far West Coast in a few days. If the spider's web to do such things can be managed through the exchange of currency over thousands of miles of ocean and continents themselves, then the idea that something that allows an escape from this constant parade of smoke and grime cannot be held to be any less likely.

I suppose I could understand it, at least some small part of it, even as their language and their ways seem so utterly strange to me. The one thing that all men—even all living things, as near as I can tell—is that desire to get away from circumstances that doesn't agree with where they are in life. The deer has the freedom to flee, the fox has the freedom to hide and then to pounce. What does the trapped man have? When one is a slave to the issuers of the pittance that allow one to barely avoid starvation? Well, the few coins that are left over allow the pathway to escape, into a bottle or inhaled from a pipe.

I pause for a moment, shaking my head so subtly that it was likely only I who had noticed the motion. The sensation starts with a tickle, perhaps at the back of one's neck, or an itch invading one's earlobe. Then, a slight twist in the stomach. These are the non-vision sensations that one develops when one has been in the game of predator and prey for one's entire life. The skin feels the weight of the penetrating gaze of another, someone who believes themselves to be a predator.

I see at least two of them watching me. However, one does not assume that the eyes one knows are there are the only ones watching. I did mark these two: one who looks much like any other shop clerk, observing the foot traffic in the rain, the hat tidy and straight rather than that of the man with the hat marked with soot and grease, and another one, slight and young, a boy of nine or perhaps ten years, flitting about as a newspaper hawker, but doubling as a pickpocket and a lookout. *Talented lad,* I think.

But not that talented.

So the mice are at play while the cat isn't away. *Good. Very good indeed.*

———

If it's not the ones watching from around the nearest corner, it's the ones watching from more than a hundred miles away to the east who create far bigger problems, of a species of stupidity that must be experienced to be believed. At least I know what the ones outside, the closer ones, lurking in the shadows of the corner with a pistol or a stiletto, are about. I prefer that game. Instead, the political ones in Harrisburg, casting lots amidst the finery of silk embroidery and the piles of paper created by the furnaces, continue to get worse, and then worse still. It's always the same, these politics, and I have just never been able to reconcile it. I can see why people want to avoid the truth, myself included. I just have never been able to understand how trading in bullshit could be some profitable. I missed the train on that one. When I look into the eyes of those trading this, I see weakness. I see expulsion of will without the stones to back it. I see whining lunatics, the lot of them.

As Homer said, one suffers with too many masters.

There was a time not that long ago where I would savor each telegram that I would receive. They were, without fault, irrelevant, insane, and sometimes dangerously stupid. There had been a golden age, just around the time when I started working on detail specifically for the Pennsy, that my direct boss was also a veteran, a grizzled man that I had fought with years before in the GAR, who, among other habits, maintained a tendency to conduct every conversation by shouting at the top of his lungs and spraying tobacco juice upon everything, including the people facing him. But, even with that inconvenience, he managed to keep my lanes clear. Until, one day, he died of paroxysm mid-shout, and his purple face never lost its hue anymore than his eyes, wide with fury, ever recessed back into their sockets.

In later years, however, I had been ruled by a succession of imbeciles who largely mimicked Boring's methods, if not his salubrious outcomes. This allowed me to have a pause to be ready for any means of idiocy from Harrisburg communicated to me by the fists of the telegram operators, also employed by the Pennsylvania Railroad, tap-tap-tapping out these wise missives for hours on end to whomever might be on the receiving end.

I had made several other stops, checking around, making my presence known and felt and the object of discussion; this spider's web of talk throughout a town with more languages than Babbel. I visited the cobbler, I visited other boarding houses, I visited workmen's victual establishments; the homes, the elderly, the working washerwomen and those mothering at home, the small children and the sullen ones sent to work.

Nothing, or at least nothing yet. A pain knocks gently at my temples, my teeth clench as I glance down.

This one reads:

TO: HOUGHTON, CAMBRIA
FURTHER CIP PERSONNEL IN AREA STOP WELSH NEARBY
STOP SUGGEST REACH HIM FOR ASSIST STOP HE ALSO HAS
TASK STOP REPORTED SUCCESS EARLY STOP ENGAGE I.M.
STOP NO MISTAKES STOP YOU HAVE FULL SUPPORT OF
PRR STOP ADVISE RECEIPT STOP

I crumple the telegram in my hand, right before the hotel clerk's very eyes. He glanced at the motion, then retrieved a small wastebasket from under the counter.

"Sir?" he asks, his voice hopeful.

I toss the missive in the trash, look him in the eye one more time, and say, "Thank you."

I only allow myself the slight crooked grin, a single upturned corner of my mouth, the slightest tinge of satisfaction at throwing it out flushing through my system, once no one was studying my features and I routed myself to the stairs. *Advise receipt*, I think. *Fuck off.*

I return to my room just in time to see yet another parade marching its way through the sloppy downtown streets running with equal parts dung, rainwater, and the dusts of industry. *How many times do they intend to celebrate this weekend?* I wonder as I light a cigarette and sit next to the window, the sun threatening just enough to limn the edges of the clouds jostling for position with each other as the rain comes down. As near as I could tell, any number of celebrations were ongoing here; the English and the Irish for being in far better economic straits than the strange people with odd tongues jabbering on and between shifts. Perhaps that was why there was more than one celebration this weekend. They came in shifts and drifts, just like the armies of workers themselves. Droves driven to the beats of the drums, ears tingling with the excitement of the brass instruments shimmering in the rain running down the window panes of those, like me, watching from inside. Still, the crowds gather along the streets, twirling small streamers and noisemakers in their hands, greeting each other with their odd and jabbering tongues. The Hungarians, like Magursky, smooth their mustaches while the women crowd about with each other, the twenty-year-olds identical to the seventy-year-olds with the so-called babushka wrapped around each of their heads.

Ukrainians. Poles. Slavs. Only they could possibly tell each other apart, as I surely could not.

I shift in my chair, pulling one of the .45 hoglegs from its resting spot at my hip and placing it on the small table. Anyone observing me might assume that I was contemplating the possibility of taking off the top of my own head with the revolver, a single shot echoing, barely heard, against the piercing brass and the thumping drums and the crooning cacophony of the mongrel crowd. They'd be wrong about that, however; I was not the type for self-immolation. Not that it mattered so much, for I knew that I wasn't terribly long for this world anyway, living as long as

I already had amidst the human rubble that I had seen in my fewer-than-fifty years on the earth.

What does it take, I wonder, *to pick up from all you have known and cross an ocean to a new world that you have only heard about through others' telling of it? What does it take to leave all you know and do this?*

Why have they come here? I ash the cigarette and roll my head about atop my shoulders, feeling my neck pop and crackle against the strain that I'd been accumulating. I put the cigarette in the ashtray and do the same with my knuckles, watching the single trail of smoke from the burning end of the tobacco float its way to the room's ceiling.

To leave what you had, however small, and to come here, where you are hated, but where this is now your country too?

I grunt as I lean forward to get the cigarette again, and I take a long drag.

Magursky.

I smirk again at the thought of the telegram and fantasize just for a moment about what I am more than capable of doing to the person of the sender.

The marching band plays on in the rain. Onlookers wave their flags and twirl the noisemakers as the parade passes.

Christ. I have to get out of here.

But first things must come first. I'll start by visiting the closest mine. One mill at a time; the seeds that I had planted there may yield fruit. One must have patience, at least from time to time. One mill at a time and then one mine at a time. Johnstown's many blessings included having many things of use immediately to hand, and this coal mine is only a few hundred feet away. Oddly as well, it is some distance skyward, into the side of the hill across the river, hundreds of feet above the city. This river too looks angrier and angrier as the rain continues to fall.

I close my eyes, still sitting upright. The pain in the temples is not abating, but not worsening. *Rest quickly,* I think. *Rest first, just for a moment.*

———

I lay flat on my back, staring at the ceiling. The hotel is quiet, even the subtle sounds muffled by the heavy carpeting and the arrangement of the rooms now silent. I can hear my heart beating and feel my own ragged breath coming in and out of my torso. My right hand clasps my left forearm, an odd fixation on the bumps and lumps and misshapen flesh; something that feels wrong to the touch and yet somehow also generates an irresistible tendency to want to touch the deformity again and again and again. I can feel the pieces of metal and lead, perhaps even pieces of my own bones and the bones of my comrades who were blown into pieces of shrapnel that are now lodged deep in my own flesh. A ghoulish notion, perhaps, but having seen personally what men are made of when taking the field of battle, it seems rather slight by comparison.

My fingers probe at the bumps, the unnatural smoothness of the scar tissue in comparison to that of the living skin, the portions of the arm no longer with any type of hair, nerves, or any sensation at all. I've fancied that I could hold my forearm out over an open flame and feel nothing. I've done it a time or two with candles atop a table, but for what it might be worth, the smell of the smoking, cooking skin is always enough to put me off that, just as it too brings back substantial memories, those memories enough to push away those of Mary Elizabeth.

I hear my breath coming in, going out. My chest rises, and falls. *What keeps it going?* My life has not been one marked by excessive comfort; staying in a place like this is not only unusual for the allowance we would normally be given, but also out of character and habit for me. Never mind that, however; I'm here, in absolute luxury, and I cannot sleep because the only thing that I can think about is the fact that my body draws breath—it cannot help but to draw breath—when I've seen hundreds and even thousands of men die on the field of battle, and other men die at my very hands when enforcing the rights of the companies of the Commonwealth.

Interdict, disrupt, and/or destroy all industrial action . . .

It seems like more than my lifetime ago that I would listen to my grandfather reading books to me next to the stone fireplace in the farm in Fulton County. Only ninety miles to the east, that farm is, but it might as well be as far away as the moon given the great distance into my past. My grandfather is, after all, dead now for thirty years or more. I've not seen or written to my parents except under the most rare of occasions, as I know that my sudden darkening of their doorway would occasion far too much concern and a dim red anger coming from some place only Providence could explain.

Eventually, I learned to read those books left behind by my grand-father, at least until the winter when we needed the paper to start the kindling in order to have a fire. It was well before I went away to seek my fortune—such a laughable turn of phrase, especially seeing how my life would turn out—and before I went to fight in the War Between the States. Sometimes, I might sound like an educated man, despite my desperate attempts not to appear as such. I never made it past the sixth grade, as the needs of the farm would take over and if anything developed more than my brain, it was my shoulders, torso, and thighs.

Though my grandfather's books helped, they never assisted in me making better decisions.

I rub my knuckles, feeling the scabs and scars. Oh yes, these fists had killed men just as that single finger had when pulling the trigger on a pistol or rifle.

The ceiling turns to a landscape, a sprawling depiction of cannon fire, smoke, and parts and entrails of men strewn about, underfoot and overhead.

My existence, my legacy is a war record buried deeply in some office in Washington, DC, and the payroll record of the Pennsylvania Railroad and the Coal and Iron Police. That would be the sum of the practical tally of my time on earth. When I eventually did shuffle off to the next world—more than likely one with flame and burning pits—the tally would likely be counted far different, and at that point, the flames of the battlefield would be the flames in which I would spend eternity.

I hadn't been man enough to ask her, even after the first time we had made love, about how she had gotten her own scars. We were in an upper field high on the mountainside over the ridge from where President Buchanan—the man whose cowardice had delayed the War and then made it that much worse . . . though having delayed it, I was able to participate in it—had been born.

That was long after I had seen Mary Elizabeth's scars, etched on her otherwise flawless skin between her shoulder blades. I learned later that she had been beaten for stealing peaches as a little girl. Stealing, that is, from her family's own tree and when she was but nine years old and her drunken lout of a father, a brutal and vulgar man, had stripped her to her waist and taken a switch to her while her mother and siblings had watched, faces unchanging as the stone beneath the rich soils that had given the peach tree such life.

I run my fingertips gently down one of them and she shivers, pressing close, then pulls away. "Stop," she says. I pull my hand away. I hadn't even really been aware I'd been doing it, not suspecting that I was touching on her own type of trench warfare of the type I'd see in the months to come. I look to her face. She sits up then, her hands in her lap as her dress falls off a single shoulder, her skin glowing in the afternoon sun. She stares down to the grass and I can see the shimmering to tears in her eyes. She wipes them away, all of a sudden, angry with herself, with me, with everything, just as she gets to her feet.

"I have to go," she says.

I'm still leaning back on the ground, propped up on a single elbow, my own contented smile still frozen on my face. I'm not sure what is happening here; my world is reeling. I had known Mary Elizabeth for years, we had grown up together, but I had never known this . . .

"Mary—" I say.

"Stop it. Don't talk. Not right now," she says, shaking her head and turning away, tugging her dress back into place.

I hadn't been man enough to ask her or help her—to show her that there might be other ways for a man and a woman to converse. I left for Bull Run one morning, though I hadn't known that at the time.

But then, once I came back after Appomattox, Mary Elizabeth was gone, cold in the ground for two winters by then. That'll teach me, I thought at the time, except that it had taught me precisely nothing at all; it had taught me to never speak of such things, not even to think of such things. Such things had bad habits of reappearing unbidden, against all of our wishes.

Sometimes in life, things that you don't want to reappear will never; I think this happens when we tell ourselves repeatedly that we don't want to see them again, that we don't want to have to relive all that, except that deep down in our heart of hearts, we actually do. *We lie, to ourselves, to others, to whomever might be willing to listen to us regaling them with our tales of woe, missed opportunities, and the unrequited possibility, an avoidance of the gaze when the gaze would mean a promise.*

It's hard to hold the gaze when its buried in six feet of Fulton County clay, and my absence from it before that also belongs to the claims of the dead.

Even then, I walked more among them than the living, and I think Mary Elizabeth somehow knew that, and here, all these decades later, with all of the graves that I've personally escorted others into, she calls to me from hers, though I never answer.

Perhaps the day that I do will be the day that I really do join them all. And her.

My eyelids spring open.

I listen for movement beyond the room door, cursing the heavy carpeting lining every surface in the structure. My hearing, like so many other things about my body, is not what it used to be given the amount of not only gun and cannon fire I've experienced, but also years in the proximity of screeching train brakes, heavy machinery, and all other things loud have muffled what surely once was a decent pair of ears. I've even eyed up an ear trumpet from time to time, but can't seem to bring myself to go to the expense, on something both so evocative of and compromising toward vanity.

And even an ear trumpet now would do little to overcome the silence induced by the carpeting.

My breathing, however, seems absurdly loud by comparison. It's defiant, in a way. It is almost as if I'm breathing louder to compensate for the silence in the room and out in the hallway, a reminder to anyone who might be listening to give their best attempt to stop that breathing. Please. I'll entertain you for that dance.

Just let me see you come into the room.

It brings a little, profound smile to my face. I drift off to sleep, to join the battle and see departed comrades again torn to shreds by grapeshot and other bits of shrieking, red-hot metal.

Chapter Four

I squeeze my hands into fists, stretching my fingers against the pain in my knuckles. Pain has been my constant and growing companion for years. This forever friend, particularly in the mornings, stands as yet another reminder of the fleeting nature of life, and how so much had been given when younger and unappreciative, only to have it taken away as one ages, taking stock of one's diminishing faculties. The Bible ascribes only three score and ten to the span of the years of man, and, in truth it seems to me, one is mighty lucky just to make it to three score or a little beyond. I can see the final horizon now, much more than what I would have as a youth except for those times on the battlefield, but then the horizon disappeared soon after it would loom before me. Now, the horizon marking the boundary between this life and oblivion sticks to me, in the corner of my eye, edging closer every day; some days, it seems to have elbowed its way to a place of great prominence before my eyes.

The squeezing and relaxing, however, serves a few practical purposes. One, it helps sharpen my sense of alertness, particularly as I also draw on my morning coffee. Two, it reminds me of the things that I've done and still paid to do—to seek out, engage, and finish conflict with those targeted by the companies and, ultimately, my social betters. Third, the motion itself brings a sense of rhythm and peace to my mind and soul, an anchor to the day's tasks ahead.

It is going to be a long day, and first I would need a fortifying pot of coffee and a cigarette. Which I would not be getting in this hotel; the actual first order of the day was to avoid the dining room as I had an intuition that Strickland or one of his type would be waiting for me downstairs as a "guide." I am not entirely sure of his purpose, but my general lesson over the years is that if I've been assigned a guide, I'm being steered. Being steered is not in the interest of an investigator.

Why. The ever-present question. *Why* would I be steered? Certainly having Magursky lurking in the shadows of the town was in no one's interest, except for perhaps the pockets of the misled types for whom the English language is still an impenetrable mystery. *Why* is the word that the investigator uses: how and what are more easily ascertained. *Why* is the question that develops the arrow of truth.

Why is Magursky reportedly in Johnstown? To answer this question is to answer what he's doing here and his means. I know roughly why he's in this city; for the same reason he would be in any city in the Commonwealth; so as to sow discord among the laborers and to get them to engage not only in some type of labor action, but perhaps something far more militant and violent. *Red flags flying in London.* I had had my taste of this over the years, and the Molly Maguires swinging from the gallows, where I put them, are memories that I'll take to my own grave. Along with others over the years that have drawn the ire of the great industries, with the latter's instrument of reconciliation being myself.

Why has Johnstown been a bit slower in terms of labor unrest than many other parts of the Commonwealth? It could be that Cambria, for example, was better with its workers, but my remit expands beyond Cambria Iron and into the surrounding town itself, to the smaller shops and to the mines and, of course, the Pennsylvania Railroad. It could be; yet, every place I visit is both the same and somehow different. It gradually occurs to me that they are all different at the same time and not too different from each other; it's just that things are changing so fast around us that it's happening everywhere. Which brings me to another consideration of what the network of thugs that Magursky has left in his trail and therefore upon the path before me: it seems clear that my arrival in this city was well-anticipated.

I stare at my reflection in one of the many mirrors in the room, arranging my tools of persuasion and donning my coat, which dried out overnight. I know the staff would want to offer me a parasol as well, something that I could consider as another tool of my trade. Call it instinct wrought by long experience.

I pause at my room door, my fingers ready to turn the key and pull the chain free, but I just listen, just for a moment. My shoes are to the side, waiting for my feet, and I stare down at the footwear with a grim smile.

Silence on the other side.

Some morning, I think, I will do this and there *will* be someone on the other side. I look forward to that day and hope it comes sooner rather than later.

———

I close the fire door quietly behind me as I emerge into the alley separating the hotel from another brick building. The stink of rotting garbage mingles with the gray water puddling and sluicing down both sides of the alley. I pull my hat on, along with the best smile I can muster. This will, with any luck, be the first in the long line of actions that will teach the people who had been "guiding" my quest a bit of a lesson. This wasn't unusual in and of itself, but it was a bit unusual in the arrangement that had been made.

I hurry the length of the alley away from the main entrance of the hotel. There's always a chance that they would have someone behind to watch for this, but by the time the message reaches the rest, I'd be long gone.

Horses. Coal. Dust. Smoke. Steel. Flame. Still, the rain falls in great sheets, and I deploy the parasol. It courses off the fabric as though being poured from some great opening in a pipe, but I've learned, on far too many occasions, expressing any dismay about the weather is just a waste of time and breath. There's absolutely nothing to be done about such factors; weather is what happens when you're outside, to be certain, and also sometimes when one is inside as well. One has to do one's job, no matter the conditions.

One also has to be ready, no matter the conditions, which the young man in front of me, peering around the corner, his back to me, does not know . . . and is about to learn. I had spied him earlier, and I easily realized his inexperience.

I wriggle my fingers around in the brass knuckles, padding toward him on the sides of my feet.

He's a slender lad, certainly not yet in his twenties but playing a man's game regardless. Twenty years before, his type'd have not stood out in the battle lines as being unready for the task based on his youth.

I'm several feet away from him, listening and watching. I ease closer, my movement and the sound it elicits masked by the noise of the falling rain and the rushing water.

I tighten my grip on the parasol handle. I pause for a moment when the young man leans forward, again peeking around the corner.

I withdraw to the left, his same side, and push myself against the hotel's basement bricks.

He waits there for a moment, his eyes scanning about. My eyes drift to his right, observing the possibility of a confederate there, taking another angle to watch the front of the hotel.

The smell of the refuse clustered around the kitchen entrance of the hotel is almost enough to water one's eyes, another distracting force that could work either for or against me. The youth is dressed as one might expect for these times and this town; grubby woolen clothes, well-worn with attempts to keep them in reasonable order. At the same time, he's not noticeable. He would blend in with any of the grubby thousands about, shuffling to the mills or mines, or collecting the alms from those more fortunate.

Is this the same one I'd espied before?

Sadly, for him, already being unfortunate was not going to prevent him from an accelerating descent into greater misfortune.

I inch forward a bit more, then, still silent, I lay the parasol down atop the filthy alley bricks. I flex my fingers in the rings of the brass knuckles. I see that the young man is even more slight than I had originally thought, his body made larger by the fact that he also wears an old, worn, oversized cloak drawn about him.

He pulls back, tightens his cloak. I can see the rainwater soaking in through the fabric of his cloak. He's soaked to the bone. I think I can hear his teeth chattering.

I get another step closer. I keep my eyes on him but refocus so that the distance looks clearer for a few moments. I listen carefully, inclining my head in an effort to assist my damaged hearing. I move my eyes to the side, pressing closer to the brick wall. Testing to see if yet another figure follows me along the wall and creeps up behind me.

No one; just the sounds of the early morning rainstorm in the alley.

I shift my eyes forward once again, drawing myself up and stepping away from the wall. The young man leans forward, again peering around the corner at the entrance of the hotel.

I reach to him with my left hand, grasping his shoulders.

"Looking for me?" I ask, my voice absurdly loud and out of place.

The youth whirls about, eyes widening in recognition, mouth widening in surprise. His hands fumble for something beneath his cloak.

My right hand, reinforced by the knuckledusters, flashes out and crashes into the center of his face. His head snaps backward, hat floating toward the street, his wet and matted hair flying and whipping about from the impact.

I hadn't hit him with full strength—that likely would have broken his neck.

The one thing I didn't calculate on, despite the fact that I'd been using the knuckles off and on since the war, was the back of his head hitting the brick wall with the same force.

The youth's wide eyes cross and roll up to the perfect whites as he slides slowly down the wall, thick blood coursing from his broken nose and turning thin and pinkish with the onslaught of the falling rain.

"Ah, shit," I say. *Going to be difficult to get some answers this way.*

I reach downward and grasp his combined collars of shirt, threadbare coat, and cloak, and drag him back out of view. I feel for his wrist; his heart still beats strong, at any rate. Problem is that I'm not sure who the kid is or whether he's going to wake up. If he does, I hope it isn't too soon. If he doesn't, well, he'll just be another ghost lurking through my sleepless nights.

I look at his hands, his fingers, which carry the standard amount of dust and detritus one might expect from a laborer. It appears to me that he's spent a lot of time around the coal mines; I'll keep that under advisement until new facts bear some greater weight.

Having situated my erstwhile combat partner, I press again into the wall, taking off my hat and barely peering around with a single eye. I can see two other men, comporting similarly to the way this young man had just been, but I also know these are just the two that I can see. The rippling curtains of rain, and the misting from the drops hitting the soaked streets, spell for an impossibility to attempt to make them all out. I should assume that there will be at least one beyond the two that I've found.

I also expect someone watching the other side of the hotel too, for someone leaving the back of the building and presumably, the now-sleeping alleyway assignment counted on him being aware of his surroundings. Fortunately enough for me, he failed in his job. He'd certainly realize this when—and if—he eventually awoke. Which would also likely be with the worst headache of his life. These shadows, whoever they'd been hired by, should have been warned about the Coal and Iron Police; it wasn't me especially, as I knew at least a dozen or more men with the CIP that were easily tougher and more violent than I am, some men that wouldn't have bothered to leave the hotel quietly. Some of the men I know might now just be leaving the hotel as fire consumes it down to its sticks and bricks.

I could certainly have done that, had I wanted, and that time might still come, as I well knew. I've learned that it might be better to be possessed of a greater retinue of skills beyond merely cudgeling someone. Not that anyone could readily tell the slightest degree of difference.

Now deprived of the ability to listen to the youth speak, I'm not at all sure as to whether he's one of the webs of watchers observing me for the benefit of my employers or my enemies—as if there were any difference at all.

Funny to think that, considering what you just meted out upon that young man.

I slide away then, retrieving the parasol and shaking off the filth, retiring to the opposite side of the alley, and round the corner to the left, leaving them all looking in the wrong direction.

———

Coal and Iron Police have plenary arrest powers throughout the Commonwealth. We are known to be peacekeepers more than investigators, however, although the former term is a farcical one even under the best of circumstances. Certainly, my mission here in Johnstown has been disguised as a path to a most desirable outcome, the prevention of sedition and social unrest. Truth is, that is true largely to the extent that's been what has been written by the Governor on my letter of authority. Yet, even the Governor's signature is one largely told to him by the Railroad and its various clients. A big farm boy like myself, of "original English extraction," has about as much hope of getting information from these floods of jabbering immigrants as, it seems, the hope one might have that the sun will ever shine again in this city. Still and all, Magursky's features are etched into my memory more firmly than the poster of his likeness I bear with me; I'd seen him more than a decade ago, during the railroad strike of '77. He had not yet been in his twenties yet during that, when we had gotten word from Martinsburg at the outset of the uprising; I had been detailed to Pittsburgh to quell what I could, and he had been marked out as a new leader of the discontent. From afar, I saw him glare at me and stalk away as his bravery faded in the vision of what would be visited upon his little clan of laborists. They faded away, scuttling like rats under the glare of the sunshine, but for whatever reason I had become entangled with this fool, and it attracted my notice whenever his name arose in the reports over the years.

I skirt round the far side of the building and cross the street again, splashing through the surging water, well over my ankles at this point. My feet have been soaked for days now, it seems, and even I have new blisters forming among the calluses. One might think I'd have been used to such discomforts by now, but there's been something about the entire excursion that has been giving me a fundamentally ill feeling. Certainly, I'd been looking for Magursky off and on for a number of years, and this is not the first time I've been in a prolonged hunt. I cut my teeth on that with the Maguires years ago. Such situations are always dangerous and frustrating.

And nor is this the first time I'd been in a company city. Many a company town have rolled out its own form of welcome to me over the years, just as it had happened before my entry into Johnstown. There's the same self-importance from every minor industrial player, the same sulking and suspicious looks in the eyes of strangers to this country, the same stink of molten metals and ores, burning wood, coal, charcoal, and coke. The same smell of animals and people and their waste in pits and dishes, children silent and fearfully watching. The screeching, thrumming, and chattering of trains as they charge between the hills of this valley at all hours. The sight of the houses stacked atop one another in neighborhoods with language borders as real as any of the borders that they would have found in their homelands, which is still more of the sight of the ruined hilltops and hillsides, killed by the smoke and by the industry of men.

Even still more with company cities, although there were perhaps none as single-company as Johnstown. Given its relative isolation from other parts of the state and its historical inaccessibility, it grew up a breed apart. Of course, with the Pennsy, the separation really had disappeared over the past fifteen years or so, and every day, trains with fresh arrivals from the eastern seaports and even from those coming upriver via Pittsburgh, would arrive in Johnstown. Same thing with those that would leave town, as told to me yesterday; the reputation of Cambria was such that it was a garden and finishing school for those skilled in steel and iron, and men could write their own tickets to anywhere else. Some went back home to the Old Country, with fancy new threads and a pocket watch, while some—most, perhaps surprising even themselves—broke with that history and stayed close, here in this spot, where they made their new home.

And still, this incessant, pouring rain. I could barely get a third of the way through a cigarette before it would become hopelessly soaked, and I felt a fool trying to preserve a paper-wrapped tube of tobacco by cowering under some overhang. The alternative is to go inside at the risk of being seen or perhaps even recognized.

———

I think about my next steps. This goddamn rain is unrelenting too, and that's just about the kindest estimation that I could think of. I rode into town under the last remnants of blue sky that this place would seem to ever experience. There's always more in between the words that come rolling out of men's mouths than what the words themselves contain. I don't believe a fucking word he said, for example, about the recent immigrants to the area. Tis true, I'm no fan myself, but I was born just a simple farmhand, fought in the War Between the States, and have been a skull-cracker for the past two decades. The only thing I can see in front of me is more of the same, no road out. At least the men and women from overseas have a chance to get out, to make something better than what they've got. I cannot boast the same.

Yes—my cigarette is soggy, frustrating my morning's purposes even further and adding to my irritation, scraping against my concentration. So when I see the young man standing in front of me, staring idly through a shop window, I feel like shoving him through his own reflection. As it is, however, as I approach, he turns to look at me with a slight, gentle smile which drains more quickly than the water and mud sluicing on the ground. Rain pours from his own bowler as he steps out of the way and tips it.

Why not.

"My name is Houghton, and I'm with the Pennsylvania Coal and Iron Police. I'm here performing an investigation, to find and locate a specific individual. I'd like to ask you some questions."

The young man hesitates, glancing back at the display in the window—a selection of timepieces—and then back to me. He nods once, his friendly demeanor now somewhat guarded. "I'm Vic Heiser," he replies. "I live with my parents on Washington Street." He gestures with his head, more water pouring from its small brim.

"How old are you, Heiser?"

"Sixteen."

Sixteen. And the lad isn't working in a mill or mine.

I look to the sky, the interminable rain still falling through the smoke and soot of the stacks of the mills. I edge closer to the window, trying to obtain shelter from the meager overhang. I pull out an increasingly smudged and wrinkled paper, unfolding it and showing it quickly. "Do you recognize this man, Mr. Heiser? Undoubtedly, he looks a lot like many of the other newcomers to this city."

Heiser leans forward, peering at it just for the slight moment that I have it out. An enormous raindrop hits the depiction of Magursky's face, a narrow face with narrow eyes and a prodigious mustache. I wince and dab at the water, refolding it and placing it back in my pocket.

Heiser shakes his head. "I'm sorry, sir, but no, I've not seen him."

I smile. "Looks like everyone else, does he?"

Heiser shrugs. "I'm not sure I would say that, sir. It's just that the drawing isn't very good. And it's not very clear."

I incline my head, taking my turn to shrug. "What are you going to do with your life, boy?"

He smiles, turning his gaze back to the timepieces displayed in the window. "I think . . . I think I'm interested in being a watchmaker, sir." His eyes fairly glow with the notion as he takes in the view. At first, I thought it might have been that glimmer of avarice that shimmers from so many in their new land. It isn't that; the skin around his eyes is softer, not pulled tightly into any slitted glare. Instead, his wide-eyed willingness, his own effortful attention shows ambitions beyond the mills and mines. There's something else out there in the world for him. *That makes the first person I've met here with that.*

I nod then as I see a cop making his own hurried way down the walk toward me, splashing violently with every step. I brush back the coat from my left breast and expose my badge. "You have a good day now, Mr. Heiser," I say. "And good luck in your quest to become a watchmaker." I had almost said 'another damned tinkerer' but there was something so astonishingly earnest about the young man that even I couldn't bring myself to that degree of incommodiousness. He nods at me, smiles, then continues to ogle the objects of his affection through the window.

"Mr. Houghton! Mr. Houghton, sir!" calls the copper, feet splashing violently in the sluicing rain. He waves at me too, as if I didn't see him. *Why don't we just find the marching band for yet another goddamn parade as well, since we're coming up on the holiday . . .*

I wave subtly back at him with a nod, then my wave turns into a motion insisting that he quell the enthusiasm. Not that I'm inconspicuous by any stretch of the imagination, even on my best day, but having another sizable, uniformed copper yelling my name and hailing me from the middle of the walk borders on the ridiculous.

"Ah sir!" he says, half smiling, face red and breathless. "Good that I found you, sir." He pauses, catching his breath.

My eyes roll slowly upward under the brim of my cap to give a visual cue to my awareness of the constant rain.

"You found me, all right." I look around, the streets and walks gaining in traffic with every passing moment, it seems. "Just out looking around to see the town early."

"I understand, sir. Would you like to come to the station house with me, sir? We understand you've been making inquiries and were looking to talk with some of us regarding your investigation."

"Happy to," I say.

He nods, grinning, squinting at me through the driving rain. "I'm Davidson, by the way. It's an honor to meet you." We shake hands.

"Lead on, Davidson," I say.

He nods again, turning on his heel and marching us down Market Street, and he looks over at me. "There was an urgent message for you at the front desk of the hotel, but I am supposing that you didn't get it."

"I had to leave out the back," I say without offering further explanation.

"Yes, sir. Well, sir, it appears that some gentleman named Barna died last evening. I guess in a jail up in Indiana County. It was a telegram from the Pennsy brass addressed to you."

"Ah."

I enter the police station like I own the place which, in a way, I like to think that the Coal and Iron Police do. Or, at least, those who own the coal and iron, along with their police, also own the municipalities in the Commonwealth, including public agencies such as the police force. In my estimation and limited experience so far in this town, Johnstown of all places seems to represent that state of affairs as well as any other town of similar size in Pennsylvania. Still though, not as bad as some of the coal patches that I'm familiar with. At least in Johnstown, you *can* use the United States dollar to pay for things rather than the scrip supplied to the miners and the families by the mine owners. And one can go to stores other than those owned by the mine owners themselves, while the owners sit in their big mansions up on the hill overlooking everything else, myself included. Perhaps especially myself.

But . . . there it is. And such thoughts are completely pointless.

I follow the patrolman, Davidson, up a set of wooden stairs. The banister feels freshly oiled as I head upstairs, and I imagine that the granite steps are as solid as they've been since the day they were formed.

Much to my surprise, Davidson escorts me right through an outer office and through the open door of the larger office, that of the Chief of Police.

"Mr. Houghton, sir, it's a fine, fine thing to finally have this opportunity to meet with you." Barnabas Clay, the Chief of Police, beams widely at me, rising from behind his oversized and overly neat desk, smoothly extending his right hand to me. "We like to think that we extend every hospitality to other members of law enforcement throughout the Commonwealth."

I incline an eyebrow as I shake his hand. "Even the Coal and Iron Police?"

"*Especially* the Coal and Iron Police," he replies, not missing a single beat, his smile attaining further broad measurements across his jowly face. "Your force is highly regarded, highly decorated, and highly . . ."

He appears to be searching for a word.

"Feared?" I provide.

Clay spreads his hands. "Your words, not mine." He pauses this time and looks at me. "You look as though you're capable of instilling a bit of fear yourself."

My turn. I spread my hands. "I do my job."

Clay nods and smiles. His eyes drift in the direction of a knock from his office door. I incline my head slightly while Clay gestures for the man to enter the office. "Ah, Patrolman Eldridge!" Clay exclaims, "come on in."

I watch as the officer enters, his own face smiling brightly. He's a younger man though not as young as I had first estimated, perhaps a decade less than myself. Of course, not having gone through the war can also shape a man. It allows one hope.

Clay introduces me as I stand to grasp the younger man's hand. "Houghton," I affirm. "Coal and Iron."

"Inspector Houghton is a *special* officer of the Coal and Iron Police," Clay says. I stay impassive, ignoring the man as best as I can without being overt about it. I need to get on with this; my nerves are firing with the coffee and agitation at the thought of being delayed in my pursuit of Magursky. "He's on orders directly from Governor Beaver himself!"

Eldridge's eyes darken a bit as he looks at me again after the Chief's description. I swallow down another wave of irritation, though I can't avoid a fleeting sense of pleasure at the imagery of me cracking some sense into Chief Clay's thick skull with my handy sap. Already, however, with a bit of a problem involving the comity of our various jurisdictions, such a fantasy, if acted out, would have hardly added to any attempt at a harmonious unification of efforts.

Instead, I give Eldridge a thin smile. The fact that my visage was a study in scars and mismanagement would immediately give the lie to such efforts. In the end, I therefore can only work with what I had— scaring the shit out of whomever it was that I was interacting with, even if another lawman.

"And quite the decorated war veteran, as I understand it. *Quite* a decorated veteran."

I say nothing.

Eldridge nods then turns his attention back to the Chief. "Some kind of rain we're getting here, Chief Clay. I'm a little worried about this."

"You talk to anyone out in town that shares those concerns?"

Eldridge shrugs. "Everyone's used to having some water in the streets, I guess."

Clay's grin never falters as he nods. "I don't think we've much to worry about then."

"Yes sir."

I light a cigarette and give a small wave and a nod to Eldridge as he exits the room. "Seems like an energetic officer," I observe.

Clay sighs, settling behind his desk once again. "They always are. Until they reach some point, where they just get tired of removing the refuse. The hunkies, Mr . . . *Houghton*." There's a sense of relief to him as he remembers my name as not being that of an immigrant population. "The hunkies, the wops. God alone knows there there're going to be coming next. Probably be repelling a flood of niggers soon. Surprised in a way that it hasn't happened yet. Oh, we've had a few, for sure, but not like other places . . . not like . . . *out there*." He waves, a vague expression on his face, in a random direction from the window.

I smoke the cigarette. "I'm not sure I can help you with any of those concerns, Chief. About the only thing I can say is that I am searching for this one particular man, Magursky."

"Ah! The rabble rouser of all rabble rousers! His reputation precedes him, as yours does you. It seems only fitting then that you two would be squaring off."

"He is wanted for questioning by the Pennsylvania Coal and Iron Police. I've been sent here to detain him and bring him back to Harrisburg." *Sent here by the owners of every coal mine, iron mongery, and the mighty Pennsy itself, including all of its subsidiaries, partners, and competitors. And the governor himself, as Chief Clay so kindly and roundly points out to one and all.*

From one of the many interior pockets of my coat, I pull out the now-wretched, wrinkled, and water-spotted parchment with Magursky's likeness and the notice of the possibility of award for information as to the whereabouts. I slowly unfold it, watching Clay's eyes widen just a little bit with each new display of the paper. Of course, his eyes to me look to be focused on the REWARD element, rather than the photo proper, or its accompanying information.

I lean forward, handing the paper to him. "Have you seen this man, Chief Clay?"

Clay looks at the parchment that I hand to him. He studies it with some intensity, narrowing his eyes. He glances up at me. "These hunkies," he says, shaking his exasperated head, "these mustaches of theirs. Makes them all look alike. You think that's intentional?"

I shrug. "I can't tell you that, Chief." Intention about one's facial hair isn't an important matter of detection to me, other than the possibility that it either represents an avenue for identification or a method for disguising it. It isn't lost on me that the Chief himself has something of a mustache of his own.

He sighs again. "They all look the same to me. The Brits have it right about that. Wogs I think is what they call them."

I stay silent, my gaze even and steady. I cross one leg over the other knee and fold my hands in my lap. "Take your time," I say, my voice quiet.

Clay seems to find that fact itself a bit of a distraction as he glances up at me in between studying the elements of the paper.

REWARD: $500.

I'm not sure what Johnstown pays its chief of police, but there's no question that it would make for a nice extra summertime windfall for the good Chief and his family. I also can't get quite past the fact that my own employer parades this award amount to some jackass like him and, in the meantime, pays me a pittance for difficult and violent work.

Chief Clay studies me. "You seem to have a habit of leaving injured and dead behind you, Mr. Houghton."

I incline my head. "That sounds like a compliment to me, Chief."

"It is not."

I shrug. "Don't try to walk in my shoes, I won't try to walk in yours."

Clay sets his grin into something more redolent of iron fence rather than mirth. "It is true that the Coal and Iron force does tend to go about things more differently than a local constabulary."

Indeed. And that's precisely why I end up traveling all over the goddamned Commonwealth to straighten out these messes. All of which are messes that I didn't make.

"This man. Magursky." I point at the paper with his likeness, using only my eyes. "The sooner I can find him and get him out of your city, the sooner you'll see the back of me, Chief. And all of us can go on about our business."

Clay leans back, pressing his fingertips together. "I fear for our country, Officer Houghton."

Jesus Christ. Is this "lawman" going to get behind these efforts or is he going to continue to muse about things not relevant? "Did you fight for the Union, Chief?"

A beat, then another. "No, I did not. I was a bit too old, I'm afraid."

Horseshit. Maybe he's ten years older than I am, but there had been plenty of men his age, and younger even than myself, on both sides of the War. I somehow manage to bite that particular word—horseshit—back, but what I say instead is barely more diplomatic, "Then you'll have to take my word for it that there have been worse times." Even as I carry the Governor's words to all whom I meet.

He bangs the flat of his hand against the top of his stupidly oversized desk. I wonder then too if he had been sitting behind that desk when the blood and innards of men had rained down on me, my ears ringing and numb with the roar of the cannon and the rifles' crack.

"It's different, Mr. Houghton! It is far different! I was a member of the constabulary then as I am now, and now that I've achieved the pinnacle of my career in police work, I can see it especially from this vantage point."

Ah. Not really a surprise, though to be perfectly honest, this man reminds me of plenty of the officers that I encountered during my time in the GAR. Small men, small minds, and of small courage when the

Minie balls tear through the air's fabric like linen. Turning tail, turning turtle, even turning possum—and then striding for the horizon opposite the violence. *Poltroons, all of them.*

"Well," Clay says, handing the likeness flyer back to me. "I wish you luck in your search for this . . . gentleman."

I can imagine him using the same inflection on the same word when, outside of my earshot, he speaks of me.

Poltroon.

"I am also asking you—please—to not kill any of my men or, in fact, any more citizens of Johnstown on your quest to rid the Commonwealth of labor unrest." He gives me the same picket-fence smile. "Unless they deserve it, of course!" He laughs a belly laugh, clasping his soft midsection. Somehow, I don't think anything is quite as funny as he just made his own remark to be.

"I'm hopeful that your men don't stand athwart my investigation, Chief. In fact, I was quite hopeful that I could count on your assistance when such time becomes necessary."

And still, no answer about Magursky. Onto the next idiot.

———

"Mr. Houghton!" exclaims Cyrus Ferguson, already up on his feet and marching around the sizable expanse of his desk. He extends a hand, shooting his ivory cuff links as he does so; I also note the ivory pin in his tie and some other type of contraption holding back a perfectly yellow metal watch chain; there is, in fact, no mistaking it for anything but gold.

"Mr. Ferguson," I acknowledge, nodding, returning the handshake. As I do, he invites me to sit down in one of the wingback chairs facing his desk. I pause for a moment; he takes this as reluctance—which it is, but for different reasons than what he likely had imagined—and indicates for me to take the seat once again. I do so, sitting straight up, then, thinking better of it, I lean further back into the overstuffed chair and put on some type of relaxed air.

So. Is he the banker?

"You've already been making quite an impression around our humble town," Ferguson says, smiling so much that it even reaches his eyes, his old skin well-rutted with crow's feet. "I understand that you're living up to every inch of the considerable reputation exuded by the Coal and Iron Police."

I incline my head but say nothing. *Perhaps he's the lawyer.*

"Well, I am here to tell you, that you are most welcome here by those of us who concern ourselves with ensuring that this fine young city remains a place of industry and prosperity for years to come. The engines of industry and commerce are, as you can see, thriving here. New ways of working, new inventions abound here. And this is why I'm uncommonly grateful for your presence, along with the organization that you represent." He reaches forward and pushes a crystal tumbler towards me, gesturing with his eyes as he picks up a bottle of whiskey.

"I'd appreciate that," I say, nodding. Perhaps a little toot of the whiskey would at least help make the time go by more quickly for me as this rich bastard drones on, even with most of society still breaking their fast at this time of the day, to the extent that they are able to afford to do so.

"The growth has not been without consequences, you know." Ferguson finishes the pours. He attempts the subterfuge artfully, but you won't be able to put much past a copper of twenty-odd years; his helping is much more abundant than the one he poured for me. Well, it is his booze, to do with as he might wish. Still, it's a tell, and true to the word, a tell gives me a king's ransom of facts.

He sniffs daintily at the glass, half-closing his eyes, a small smile traced on his features. He sips at the whiskey.

Banker and *lawyer.*

I toss mine back with a gulp and then place the tumbler down on his desk; I don't smash it, I don't hurl it, but I'm none too gentle either. I give him my own best attempt at some type of bland smile, enjoying the whiskey tones in the back of my throat and nose.

His eyes widen a bit and his smile grows a bit nervous—the reaction most people might have to one of my actions. It's just taken me a different route to get there with Ferguson. Just me, quaffing his expensive stuff like tuppence rotgut.

He says, "Ahh." Then he clears his throat. "Yes, indeed, consequences, to the country, to the state, and to our city here. And I mean immigrants, sir. The whole lot of them is nothing but problems, but they are problems that we need to deal with. Labor, like everything else, is an ingredient

into this enormous enterprise that we're undertaking, the greatest industrial experiment in history."

I nod.

"So, while we need them, they need us. And there are far more of
them than there are of us. This creates other problems, but the easiest one
to resolve is that *they just keep coming here.*" He laughs a bit at that, not
nervous, not evil, just bordering on something else, as if he can't cynically
believe his own good fortune. He shrugs. "There are some in the community that seem to worship our newest additions to the country, and there
are some who detest them. I do neither, sir. I merely recognize them as
another part of our undertaking, a part that has its own set of problems
that are best dealt with in a way that is most expedient. They are like the
ore for the metal, the coal for the coke."

It all goes for the furnaces.

Finally, he reaches for his bottle and puts another finger of liquor in
my tumbler, gesturing for me to take it. The pour is not as generous as
the initial one. I take it and pause, holding his gaze in an effort to mock
polite company.

"Which brings us to you, Mr. Houghton. This task of yours that I've
heard about, this Istvan Magursky?"

"Yes."

"Hmm. Magursky, I am sure, has been here, though to my knowledge
he has not been seen of late. There are others too, of course, followers or
perhaps fellow travelers."

I take a more delicate taste of the whiskey this time, rather than just
tossing it down my gullet in bulk fashion. "Mr. Ferguson," I say, taking a
deep breath, "you do not work for a coal concern, nor Cambria Iron, nor
the Pennsylvania Railroad."

Ferguson nods slightly, returning to my questions with a wan smile.
"Mr. Houghton, I'm sure you understand. I am but a humble banker."
So that's one answer, from the horse's mouth.

He continues, "But while I am indeed not employed by any of the
local concerns you mention, at its heart, everything and every person in
Johnstown, in some way, works for Cambria Iron."

"I already suspected nothing less than that, Mr. Ferguson." I control
my temper, grinding my teeth. This is a waste of time, an intentional

distraction of some type, and one rapidly exhausting my patience. I'm beginning to wonder if the monied types in this town actually have information pertaining to a wanted criminal, yes, a Hungarian, but also then doing nothing but condemning them in general terms without pointing in a specific direction for me.

Ferguson nods, folding his hands across his midsection. His eyes take on a different gaze, as if looking far into the past.

"People around here prefer to make their own way, Mr. Houghton. We are connected to Pittsburgh, of course, and even Philadelphia and all other parts of this glorious Commonwealth, not the least of which is due to the able efforts of your own employer. Cambria has been losing ground against its brethren—or its competitors, depending—mostly from Pittsburgh, but from other areas as well. It is still a very big fish compared to many others, but no longer the biggest fish in the sea. Still, the town is booming because of the mill. Men work in coal mines, but if they can get a job in Cambria, even as a helper, they will abandon the work in the mine and come to the mill. How could you blame them?

"So you see similar things occurring in many places, all over the state. I'm sure you've seen it as you go from place to place, and we are indeed similar to what you might find in Pittsburgh. But the hills separate us in many ways. This does not always make for easy politics." His eyes shift outside to the rain. "Upriver is the bigger problem, in the form of the Pittsburgh types that cluster there in the spring and summer."

"I'm not following, Mr. Ferguson. I'm sorry, sir. You have to forgive me, as this is my first time in this town, as you've pointed out."

"Daniel Morrell . . ."

"The Quaker," I say.

Ferguson smiles just a bit. "The one and the same. He was able to treat his workers well, or at least, better than the standard conditions. Still far better, most likely, than where they came from. He was adamantly opposed to unions or any organization of labor, of course, but the worries about it kept him and Cambria occupied. But he was also involved everywhere; where there was Cambria, there was Daniel Morrell. He ran Cambria, but he was not the baronial type you see growing elsewhere." He moves his eyes vaguely to the wall squaring the corner of his office; I realize it's in the direction of Pittsburgh.

He moves in his chair, picks up his tumbler of whiskey again, and leans back. I wait. Of course I wait; give it long enough, someone will grow uncomfortable with the silence, and the odds are good that it will not be me. I try not to dwell on the weight of my weaponry and the temptations it elicits.

"Daniel Morrell had his flaws, to be sure. But he was a veritable engine of hard work and non-stop action, all patrolled by a pretty strict ethos of his own making. The same cannot always be said of other grand industrialists, I'm afraid. But along with this, Morrell got a bit behind the times during his last few years and some of the competitors downriver have overtaken Cambria in terms of profitability, income, and the rest. Now, a lot of those types are upstream from us, at a very exclusive Club of their own making. They put enormous houses—cottages, they call them—all over the banks of this lake created from damming the Conemaugh River. Mr. Houghton, I can assure you that each one of these cottages would dwarf any home in Johnstown, even my own. They spend their summers here in the highlands, at their *cottages*, and stare down the river at the poor hill folk in Johnstown. I tell you this because I feel you must understand the politics of the area, and the city in particular. To understand the politics is to understand the people here. Because that is where the power is. And it *must* stay here, in our own little city."

It sounds like a case of sour grapes, listening to Ferguson's tone and inflection change. With each word, he bites off more of his syllables, and I can see the tension in the corners of his eyes, the knuckles of his fingers. On the other hand, this description of the politics is similar to everything throughout the Commonwealth. There is nothing new here.

"I don't hew much to this myself, of course, Mr. Houghton, but I can tell you that Morrell was more than just annoyed with the Pittsburgh types. Well . . . and any other types not from this area and not understanding of this city and what Cambria has done. He had a complicated relationship with them. Like them, and yet not like them. Accepted by them, and yet not a part of them. So much so that while he was alive, he too had a membership at the hunting club upriver. He never said much about this, but it is a firm belief around these parts that his membership was as much to keep an eye on his rivals as it was to be a part of their circle."

"I see."

Ferguson holds up a single finger. "Not yet, you don't. You see, upriver from us is death for this city, waiting behind that dam. Morrell knew it. He even sent people up there time and again to do an inspection of the dam." He sighs, then points outside. "As you no doubt have seen by now, this city floods enough as it is.

"At any rate, there were concerns about the dam, but nothing has been done about it and, more to the point, there are plenty of others who say that the dam is just fine and that there's nothing to worry about. I'm more in that camp, to be honest with you. If it was going to break, it would have done it already, and, besides, what's another foot or two of water when you already have this outside?"

He throws up his hands and then waves them as if telling it all to go away.

"You had mentioned Mr. Morrell and labor."

Ferguson shrugs, noncommittal. "Yes. He was no friend of labor unions, or, in fact, any type of organization of workers. That is true. But . . . *but*, he paid his workers a fair wage. Didn't try to squeeze them, again, like the Pittsburgh types that are now overtaking Cambria." He finishes his whiskey. "I suppose there's some sad irony in that fact.

"He also made a point of hiring those who fought for the Union." He stares out the window and shrugs. "Served in Congress, too. The man did everything. Some day it seems like it was all for naught. This is what I'm telling you, and why I'm telling you, Mr. Houghton. It's not because of my love for any hunky. Quite wrong on all accounts. But I wonder if the people at your employer actually know what the root of the problems might be."

Ferguson hadn't seen my eyebrows go up when he had mentioned Morrell's support for the North during the war. After all, the Governor himself had worn the uniform of the GAR. Again, nothing new, but something that helped me prioritize my thinking and to whom and to what I will be listening.

"This is very helpful information, Mr. Ferguson. Especially well-tuned for an investor or possible man of business other than what I'm about. David Morrell died years ago—"

"Four years ago," Ferguson cuts in.

"Four years ago," I allow. "But the industry's changing even faster now than what it was. I've no doubt he was quite successful and probably worked himself into an early grave." *I've seen plenty of early graves, though not as many by office work.*

Ferguson waits, his eyes slit. I know something of what he's about. He seems to both admire Morrell and envy him. I suppose the two could be the opposite sides of the same coin, but rarely have I seen it so obviously and earnestly displayed.

"Times have changed," I say. This is as tactful as I can be. "Problems are different now. They've escalated. The mills themselves are much bigger. Many more mines, many more people getting pumped in every day from places where they don't really know what it means to be an American. I can do nothing about that except look after the interests of my employers as I am paid and instructed to do. What I can do is address one small element of the greater problem. And I am telling you that Istvan Magursky is the biggest of the small problems, the thousands of small problems that will be seen about these parts. Some problems are already obvious. I'm a state constable, nothing more. I know nothing of politics, sir, nor the larger powers that may be at work."

"I understand you had some facility in handling the Molly Maguires a few years ago."

I realize I had edged forward in the chair, so I sit back again, re-crossing my legs and folding my hands.

"Yes, although not as much as some of my colleagues."

Ferguson nods. "You won't find anything of that sort around this city, Mr. Houghton. All the hunkies around here don't have enough brains to even try to organize."

I give him my own best thin smile. "I think many have that impression, including your own local constabulary." *It's hard for the king's court to see the restlessness among the serfs, after all.* The book of Daniel said something about that. They drink the wine, and praise the gods of gold, silver, and iron—especially the latter here, especially in the world made and paid for by that ore and what it releases with fire.

"By all means, by all means. They'll be happy to assist you, I'm sure, if they haven't already."

"I'm sure as well," I reply, holding the same thin smile and not making any effort to make the first move, thinking about my visit earlier to Chief Clay.

Ferguson's frozen, it seems, then something finally rouses him, and he stands, stiffly, offering his hand. "It's a pleasure to meet you, Mr. Houghton, and I, for one, am happy to be of service to the Coal and Iron Police. Anyone from such an organization who has the ear of the governor in Harrisburg is an important man indeed, and we don't want Johnstown to give the appearance that we're a hive of labor insurrection. We'll do whatever we can."

I take my time getting to my own feet and take his hand. I hold his eyes through my own narrowed gaze. "I'm going to look around and some of the mines."

"Bring back memories of the Maguires?"

You'd ought to hope not. I don't answer him as I pull my hat down atop my thinning hair and exit his office.

I feel fortunate for a few minutes as the rain slams down, just in the sense that it carries away some of the feeling of gloomy and uncertain politics in this city, cast away in favor of the gloominess of this late May sky. Is Decoration Day not supposed to be the celebration of a new warm season? It seems, at least in these highlands, the warmth has been forsaken in favor of the cold deluge, but the politics . . . well, the politics are the same no matter where I go, even if the names are different. You'd have thought I'd be better at it, or at least more used to it, but I harbor no illusions. I'm a dog, an attack dog with a surname that makes my betters feel comfortable. The people remain the same, as is the poetry that they read to me, the words they've recited well to everyone but most especially to themselves. Words of prosperity and abundance, production and building, creation and re-birth into a new country, a new time. That hasn't been my experience, not exactly. My poetry is one of a world of brutality and the destitute, filth and mud, and destruction and death.

The difference is not one of my life's path or the path of anyone else's. The difference is one of fantastic dreams and that of reality. One is truth, demonstrated by daily events and the circumstances surrounding all of us.

The other is horseshit.

I know that Strickland and Ferguson alike were non-plussed by some of the things that I noted, the way I said them, what I observed, and the ways in which I related my opinion on such matters. There are many to whom I'm indebted for being able to engage in this manner; an educated man like Strickland or Ferguson or that ilk are just expecting what they see when I darken their doorway for the first time; an older man, laden with scars and with a reluctance to talk niceties. That much certainly is true, and it is also true that I do not readily demonstrate literacy until I absolutely must. For me, it is a power best kept secreted close to my breast, much like a hidden stiletto or single-shot conversation-ender.

My grandfather had been an educated man when he fled England with his parents, seeking some type of new start in William Penn's colony. They were not Quakers nor, as near as I could tell, a part of any other sect which would have been an immediate point of attraction for the Commonwealth. That has been lost between the generations. What my grandfather did impart to me, however, before he died just after my own 9th birthday, was an ability to read and his own willingness to spend time showing me the words in the books. My father then sold the books promptly after my grandfather had died, but of course, the damage had been done.

Later in life, when I courted Mary Elizabeth, I think she and her family were astonished by my ability to recite poetry that I had learned by rote and they had been impressed with the recitations from Horace and the ancients and most impressed of all by the statements from the Bible. Still—the poetry, told to Mary Elizabeth on blue and golden days of summer before I marched to the beat of the Grand Army of the Republic's war drums. At that point as well, I had been thrown together in a defile at Antietam and made the acquaintance of a schoolteacher from New Jersey, who had volunteered to serve with the First New Jersey. He had studied a number of things. Always thought he would be a minister, and then a schoolteacher, which is what he had become, even if for a short time. He knew Homer, the Bible, and a number of other things and was beside himself with joy that there was another man nearby who had read and understood these things as well.

I have never really had much in the way of friends, at least since childhood. One of the realities that I have had to face is that people don't last, and neither will I, so it is indeed difficult to see the point of any such thing, at least when one has had the itinerant life that I've had. The would-be bloodstained chaplain from New Jersey would have been the closest thing I had to a friend, and I saw what was left after he had had his jaw blown off at the Wilderness during the Overland, the meat grinder that the men got fed into by General Grant. What was left of him while he still piteously clung to life was another one of the scarred visions that I keep sequestered between my ears but comes back to visit me when I try to rest my eyes. He competes with the many other similar visions, but he had been something like a friend . . . which of course tends to make it that much worse.

I held a chloroform-soaked rag over what was left of his face until his struggles stopped. It took a few agonizing moments; he clutched at my forearm, something burning and glistening in his glaring eyes, even the one that had popped partly out from its socket and had been turning cloudy. I never have been able to deduce whether it was fear, hatred, or gratitude. Perhaps all three. I had said, "The dust returns to the ground as it was, and the spirit will return to the God that gave it." The war had its own way of prodding men into the words and deeds of Ecclesiastes.

I wondered then and still have occasion to wonder now where his God had gone. By 1864, of course, and the Overland Campaign, I had long known that there was no God. It wasn't clear to me that there never had been one, but it was obvious to me by then that he had long-ago fled this country and this world. Tens of thousands of men died, sometimes pulverized to bits by cannon, sometimes shredded with grapeshot, sometimes struck clean through the head with a Minie ball, sometimes crushed by a wagon, sometimes wounded and lingering for days or even weeks as pestilence sought purchase in their flesh and would eat away at it with the noxious smell of decay. Those men, still alive, could smell that they were rotting to death.

My own self-educated literacy could do precious little to help then. And it has left me to wonder, all these years later, why and how I had been spared when so many good men perished, sometimes in the most gruesome and horrific manner, beyond imagination, beyond description. I had turned to the Coal and Iron Police as a path to make my way in life when the battlefields closed their operation; I found new operations instead and turned them into battlefields.

God helps us all find a path, is that I've heard. What God wrought a path for a man like me? I know that the common thing held about me is that I had been somehow damaged by the war, and that I came out the other side of it this changed man, a bastard, a scoundrel. Truth is, the war did change me, but only as far as it changed anyone with my disposition and humors; it made me into more of what I already was, which was a bastard and scoundrel. It wasn't anything about CIP that made me this way, or any of the other men who darkened the doorways on their behalf; our betters wanted men that cut a certain jib. I was able to do that, as was Jimmy Welsh, or any of the other of us carrying that badge. We had no reason to expect redemption, nor truly any desire to find it. We are who we are, and we carry the knowledge of our own character quite comfortably, with eyes wide open. As Tacitus said, great empires are not maintained by timidity.

There are no excuses for me. Only a road to damnation, paved by God's busy hands.

Chapter Five

The mine, like everything else near Johnstown right now, is a sodden, muddy mess. Donkeys and mules stare glumly into the distance, bearing both the weather and their condition in life with a resigned dignity. The mine itself is a typical example of order mixing with chaos. Several warning signs stand about the entrances and any equipment, warning of danger in seven different languages, just as I'd heard from Strickland and Ferguson alike. I stare at the sign: English, German, Polish, a couple different brands of Cyrillic, and . . . there it is. Unmistakably Hungarian. Where there are Hungarians, Magursky will either have made the stop, or it will be on the list.

"Hunkies," says the helpful foreman, a man named Roberts, nearly an identical twin to Fritz but with a Welsh accent. He grins at me, which is also fairly different from Fritz.

"Hungarians?"

"Oh, at least them. Then there's the Polacks, the Ukrainians, the whole lot of 'em. They're all hunkies, at least in this spot." He grins, eyes twinkling as if the absurdity of the whole situation is just too much, and one shouldn't spoil it through overstatement.

"Hell," Roberts continues, "they named the whole county here after my homelands, and we've got nothing but wogs. Hell, the English would have and probably still would call *me* a wog." He grins again, shrugging. "There's gonna be a reckoning."

"How so?" I watch a line of men leading a similarly put-out line of donkeys to wait their turn as they will descend into the mine, riding one pair at a time, in a steel cage slick with water, mud, and donkey shit. Not to mention all of the coal dust and general slimy slag and gravel littering the landscape.

Roberts just shakes his heads, lifts his arms, and lets them fall back to his sides. "All this. It's not going to keep going like this forever."

I pull my hat brim down lower over my eyebrows, wondering how much he knew about the Molly Maguires—not that they're the only ones.

Coal mines are a bit different than the expectations one would have for a foundry or mill, judged in different technical ways than what one could witness in a metal worker. Mining had its own terrain of assessment, mostly in terms of death and injury. Not that these didn't happen routinely in the mills as well, but there's a very good reason for the hiring lists for the mills to be filled with names trying to escape from the realm of coal. The pay was better, for sure, but there was also a certain freedom to be sought in not living in the constant fear of firedamp or collapsing walls and roof.

This is why when I see the mines and the mills, the coal moving out on rail and wagons and the red-hot steel poured into its shapes and run along the machines, I feel a hollow place in the center of me. I wonder why this might be, but I mostly recognize it for what it is, which is an appreciation for what these elements can turn into, that which gold and silver might drive and transform. It turns soft, rolling farmland into cratered and smashed earth, fertilizing with blood and bone. The gold and silver turns into smoke and fire, noise and hot, flying lead. It turns things and people alike into rubble, and can turn a man with a heart into a cruel bastard.

And that fact is another *why* if someone asks *why* the interest in Magursky. My glance shifts from structure to structure, the long lines of telegraph wires and the mining house, the rails and machines. Water sluices down the steep hillside, almost as if it too were trying to burrow its way down through the trees and rock to the valuable mineral hundreds of feet below. Steadily and with marked efficiency, cartload after cartload of soft black coal emerges from the tunnels, being moved from cart to track, loaded onto larger cars to take their cargo to one place: the steel factory below, to feed its hungry furnaces. I rub my nose; I can smell the gases driven out of the mining vents and see the waves of heat driven by the mine's own furnaces emitting from the vent stacks. I've never quite been able to get away from the idea that the vision is one of a colonization of hell itself.

"Do you know any other languages, Mr. Roberts?" I ask.

He guffaws. "Not a scratch. No, I depend on the crew leads. All of them have some English, just enough to get by in a mine, anyway. For the most part."

The mine itself is a place that I hadn't first considered a possibility, but given the lack of interest from those in officialdom, I had little choice but to continue to pick around the various fertile pockets that could serve as a landing point for a shit-beetle like Magursky. The mine had been inconvenient, as I actually had to go *uphill* to reach it; I could see the area where the mine operates from outside of the Capital Hotel, but getting here was not a terribly easy task. The mine was sunk into one of the western hills above Johnstown, a place of irony where a deep coal mine has an entrance higher than many parts of the surrounding enterprise.

"We've got hundreds of men here, Inspector," Roberts continues, "from places where there are all of those languages and a bunch of places where they aren't. Shit, when they aren't here they're building some damnable church of theirs or shooting dice and drinking." He shakes his head. "You'd think the money would be more precious, as dangerous as it is around these types of places."

"Gas?"

"Yes, and plenty of it."

I brush the water from my face, only to have it replaced instantly by more driving rain. I think about this for a moment. The gas, what the miners call firedamp, is readily found in just about every soft coal mine in this part of the state. Always a danger when coal mining, the hard coal areas on the opposite side of the state don't carry the same risk. I stare again at the sign with all of the languages, and Roberts's admonition that there were some immigrants from areas for whom the languages were not even posted.

It's a wonder these places didn't blow up every day. *Of course*, a number of them did. I watch as the fireboss from earlier in the shift re-arranges his equipment; his life and those of others at risk unless he completes his inspection quickly and well—otherwise, an explosion and grim, flaming death.

Of course, sometimes they're wrong. I've seen the remnants of some of them pulled out in roasted pieces. Some other times other miners have paid the price of error.

I catch Roberts eyeing me. "What?"

"Well, you're a fairly big fella."

"And?"

"I was thinking ye might be a bit too much to squeeze down in these places. You might find it a bit . . . confining."

"No doubt." I had to agree with Roberts. *No space for me, not to crawl, not to fight.*

"See, even me, I'm a bit thick for the spots. But these wiry little fellas from the Old Country, they're half my size and can squeeze down with a pick and some blasting powder and knock some chunks out for us."

My turn to eye Roberts, who is well under six feet tall but every bit barrel-shaped himself with layers of muscle. The lumpy and heavy clothing did little to obscure that obvious fact. I had every indication that Roberts, even more than Fritz, would be capable of carrying more than his weight in a fight, and perhaps well above it. These men, out here in a mine like this, would have likely been even more difficult to persuade. He'd need all of that muscle.

"Have many new men working?"

Roberts nods, inclining his head. "Every day, Inspector. Every single day I get new ones. Got them lined up for the work, six days a week. Twelve hours a day. Good living, better than you're going to get at a lot of other places." He shrugs. "Except maybe in the mills themselves. That's where I lose men to as well, but down at the works they tell our bosses to tell us that there's plenty more labor coming in. So not to worry overmuch about losing men to them." He pauses. "Or to accidents. All tragedies, of course, some avoidable, some not." He shrugs.

I scratch my chin. I should show him the picture of Magursky, but not in the rain; it had enough damage already and wasn't going to last much longer even with gentle care. Perhaps made even more foolish by the fact that four out of every five men could be mistaken for the depiction anyway. I wonder whether he's thinking about losing men to things other than a better-paying job in a place where you don't have to spend half the day squatting or bent low into an unnatural goblin's crouch. Even the donkeys don't look to be terribly impressed.

The rain soaks through every layer; such is life, especially in this city. The conditions of these poor bastards are far worse than what I endure. Perhaps what they do is even more dangerous than my own. The politicians in Harrisburg a few years ago made it mandatory that operators report mining accidents, but the willingness and ability to file those reports with any type of accuracy and timeliness varied, as one might imagine. Men come to work in a place where they've never been before, at a job they don't know how to do, and try to learn with other men that hopefully but don't always speak the same language. Names that are unknown or unpronounceable, or turned into something ludicrous like George Miller or John Smith when the original name has far more syllables and letters jammed together in a way that makes no sense in English.

I couldn't really imagine how it would be, and I'd been doing this job for a long time: crossing an ocean, packed like salted cod, no money, no words, some vague family directions, and then a few weeks later you're hunched down in a hole deep in the earth, breaking off chunks of rocks for hours a day, every day. Within days, you're starting to cough, and your sinuses burn. If you're lucky enough to go for a few years without dying, your lungs turn to stone, and you die young anyway.

I don't see how this is worth it.

Of course, if it wasn't, I myself would have a different job. I look past the structures again, down at the massive steel facility below, belching out smoke and steam.

All in service toward the purpose of progress.

"My suggestion, Mr. Houghton, is to come back in four hours or so, closer to the shift change. That way we can gather the gangs together and get some of their translators to see if we can get some of the news that you're going to want. You never know."

"I may have to talk to them individually, Roberts."

Roberts shrugs. "It's your world, Mr. Houghton. Or rather I suppose it is the world of the Coal and Iron Police."

I nod. "That certainly seems to be true." *Or we make it such.*

"The shift change then. You'll be able to get a lot of the crew chiefs at the same time, as they head out and are coming in."

Ignoring this, I have more questions. "How well are your mines drained?" I ask, pointing to a couple of pipes churning water out from the hillside, further down from where we stood.

"Well enough, I suppose." Roberts stares at me for a bit and then his eyes drift off my face. Miners are in enough danger from gas and fire and collapse. Mixing that in with the potential of a flash flood that drowns them seems to be gratuitous and cruel. "There is a man in a hospital room if you want to speak to him . . . and if he's up to speaking."

"Why's he in the hospital?"

"Got knocked right out. Guy was prying at an overhang and the dumb hunkies weren't paying any attention to each other."

How many thousands have lost their lives in these stinking pits over the past fifty years, I wonder. It could be just enough to make a man callous; certainly, I am there, and it sounds to me as if Roberts is there as well, which is little wonder.

Remember Avondale. Oh yes, remember Avondale, and who could forget, although it seems as though it was forgotten even by the men who worked close by. I was still a fresh face, at least as far as the Coal and Iron police would go, and with my War scars still pink, when Avondale burned and collapsed in 1869. All in the hopes of ease and targeted toward efficiency, the mine had one entrance, which also acted as the exit. Any structure at or near a mine entrance represents danger. The anthracite mines out east all had breakers, and the Avondale mine was no exception, with a breaker on top of the mine mouth . . . which caught on fire, after some support timbers across the ceiling of the mine ignited. When the superstructure of the breaker and its coal too began to burn, the whole situation turned into an inferno, a tornado of hell's own flames and exploding gases pouring out in every direction, the wooden supports in the shaft itself collapsing and the only exit to the mine now blocked by raging flames. Such a fire is not like a fireplace, or even an ordinary structure burning; instead, the mine itself is a contributor to the conflagration with temperatures so high that anything even within a hundred yards of the center will be burned. Any closer, it would be reduced to wind-sifted ashes.

Every soul on the day shift perished, trapped by the design of the mine, trapped by the efficiency of the operation itself, undoubtedly powered by men like Roberts. It would have been far too expensive, of course, to dig a secondary exit shaft. Why have two when clearly one would suffice? The cost had been dozens of lives, and the lives of the families depending on the miners, their next step invariably to the almshouse or the street.

The Molly Maguires staked claims to the injustices of Avondale as well, and not without reason. The devil's trap of the dying miners stands as a stronger symbol of the careless view of the cheapness of life than anything else the Maguires alone could have possibly conceived, and the Nanticoke Coal Company had brought it entirely on themselves. Even as I was new to the Coal and Iron crew, I thought I had grown callous to the realities of life and death. Go through enough battles, see enough field hospitals with their piles of amputated, bloody limbs, carry shrapnel and scars inside and out for decades, see enough men die, fast and slow alike, and you start to think you're there already. Until you see the remains of a burned coal mine and think about the hundred-plus men who were trapped and turned to ash. Your only hope, upon this realization, is that they suffocated as they were overcome with gas and that their end was fast and painless. If you start to think too much in the other direction, and picture those men trying desperately to find a way out while the walls burn and roof collapses around them, screaming, choking, and blistering, you get an entirely different direction and the goal of such thoughts is not clear, except to relive and emulate the torture that those men had suffered. You stand then as a remaining witness, other than to realize that even that is a lie, that the true witnesses are the men who stepped forward to take their new places in the mines that haven't collapsed or burned, and that your goal in life is to ensure that those who do so are well-acquainted with the truncheon and the ways of industry.

We strung the Maguires up all right, and every single one of them died with a fire in their eyes, a reflection of that hatred. Those Avondale flames.

"Fine," I tell Roberts. "I'll go see this man in your hospital. Is he lucid?"

Roberts half-shrugs, half-nods. "As lucid as could be, I suppose." He motions me to follow, and we trudge through the mud toward the tumbledown building.

"English speaking?"

Roberts barks a harsh chuckle. "In some ways, yes, I suppose it could be said." He pushes the door open for me and rolls his eyes as I walk in.

The room is painted white, at least in one manner of speaking. A pair of rickety beds, mismatched and each with a thin mattress, protrude from the far wall, with a small bookcase and what appears to be a handful of dusty and ill-used technical volumes on the single shelf. I scan the titles; build lists, plans, geological study compilations. I narrow my eyes, imagining that at least one of them I can recall from my time in the war. A single yellow oil lamp hangs from a center rafter and gives the room a dim, strange light augmented by the paltry gray, twilight glow coming in through the grubby windows, coated with coal dust, filmy oil, and God alone knows what else. There's a man in a fetal position on the bed, clutching his head, rocking slowly back and forth, a strange keening vibrating out of his body. My eyes flick to another shelf where I see a bottle of clear liquid—some type of hooch—along with bandages, a couple of ill-used blunt surgery instruments, and a brown jar that I assume contains either chloroform or ether. It looks to me like the poor bastard writhing on the bed could have used a shot of either one, or both.

"Anything been done for or to this man?" I ask as I approach the cot.

"Wouldn't really let us touch him."

The injured man huddles away from me, clutching his head as much as he can, seemingly attempting to turn into a turtle, to bury his head under some type of hard shell.

"Can you hear me?" I ask, looking down at him.

There's little response other than the same actions and motions that he has had. I narrow my eyes, peering a bit more closely. Dried blood sticks to the side and back of his neck, staining his shirt collar, mixed with the grime of coal dust, mud, and smoky stains. A slight tear marks the angle of his shoulder, but I can't tell if it was from simple wear or from the collapse that injured him.

"Hey," I say again, a bit louder. Roberts leans against the side of the open doorway, arms folded across his chest.

I noisily drag the rickety stool closer to me, the drag slow, the pro-nounced scratching and thumping unmuted. I hope with only two beats of hesitation that it will hold a man of my mass. "My name is Houghton," I say as I settle onto the stool. "I'm a member of the Pennsylvania Coal and Iron Police. Do you know about us?" I pause. "Can you understand me?"

The man groans, his only movement being that of pulling his head further downward, blood smearing on the thin sheets.

I look over at Roberts, who looks back at me. He shrugs. "Hopefully the poor bastard's going to be fit. We sent a runner, just before you got here, to fetch someone from this man's family to take him back home, elsewise he's going to have to wait for one or two of his butties here to maybe drag him back home, if there's a shred of Christian charity to them."

"Uh-huh," I say, staring at the groaning man and thinking of what form that Christian charity might take. Other than the vague nod toward the occasional church or crucifix, the cursing by taking Christ's name in vain, and the loose change falling out of the pockets of the industrialists and the bankers, I've not witnessed much in the way of either Christian or charity. I've seen more of it on the battlefield than off it, come to think of it.

I reach forward, this time shaking the man a bit more roughly. "Wake up!" *If his skull's cracked it's probably better that he stays awake anyway.* The man groans, jerks his arm from my grip.

I bite back a degree of frustration. I cock my head, imagining that it must be the way that I'm looking at it, but the man's head appears misshapen to me, flatter on the left, moving to create a crest at the top of his skull. He opens one eye, just a slit, just enough for me to see the white of his eye shot through with red and purple and bulging too far out . . .

I'm sure it must be my imagination. *Must be.*

I stand. Roberts looks at me, uncertain; surely once again it's either the fast informal communication network in a compressed city such as this one to let him know that I wasn't shy with my methods of persua-sion, or the ever-present reputation of the Coal and Iron Police alone. I suppose I could have beaten an unconscious man, but today's not that day. Roberts appears to relax as I turn away from the groaning, injured worker and stride toward the door.

I look around at the interior of the hospital room again, then look to Roberts. "I need to find Magursky," I tell him. "Send word if you hear anything. I'm at the Capital. For now, anyway."

Roberts nods, just once, a curt tug downward on his chin. I move back out into the driving rain.

———

I slouch in the saddle and lean backwards as Amos descends the road back down into the valley. Johnstown from this vantage is almost completely obscured by smoke, mist, rain, and low clouds, gray sheets and curtains strung up hiding the view from any watchers. I made no mistake about it, however, that even on the brightest of days, the city would still be obscured by smoke from the mills and the buildings burning coal for light and heat. As we enter the summer, with that heaviness already attendant to the moisture all around, there would be less of the latter, of course, but still, there would be some. I tried to imagine what is must have been like in this quiet, pitched valley prior to the English settlers.

Mills and mines, mines and mills. I tighten the collar of my coat, a sudden uphill breeze blowing more of the cold rain into my face and my throat. *But even the most crazed operator realizes that the human body can't work twenty-four hours of the day. They always go home, even the single men who might swap cots from shift to shift.* I look at the clusters of homes hugging the hillsides and crowding around each other and the smaller supporting businesses around the mills and its many buildings and yards.

Where I'm looking now, as the mist and the curtains of rain furl and twist and cause the vision of the city and the steel to come into and fade out of sight, the city has carved the valley more deeply than even the rivers could have dared. The Conemaugh, escaping town, curves around the two banks of the city on either side, swooping south past the sprawling works. The hillsides, razed of trees of any size, serve as stages for stacked housing, smoke rising from chimneys and fireplaces and mingling with the far vaster output of the steel plant itself, the coking ovens further downriver, the steam and smoke from the locomotives hauling materials in and out of the mines and alongside the mills. The powerplants downriver belch more smoke into the air, with the blankets of rain and fog bringing oils and dust to collect as mud atop the hats and shoulders of the passersby.

The clusters of houses balanced and trembling on the hillsides and closer to the mills are one example, yet there are other homes that have small yards, surrounded by fences. Still very much the same victim of the smoke and the water as the rest of the city, but the very fact that they're there means something different. Certainly, it means something different to the fifty or one hundred people that tumble into the town from the train depot every day, something to look to as a goal, a signal that they took might truly arrive into the America promised to them in the Old Country. Perhaps it comes as even more of a signal than the American flag flying over the fresh Central Park of the city, a green square with paved paths acting as a stay between the bank buildings, social halls, and other architectural cues of this age . . . bank buildings, that is, streaked with soot and grime and having been built just a handful of years before but with the crowded re-creations of the Romans and Greeks and their architectural touches glued onto the outside. It's almost as if the capitalists want to give people the impression that their ilk had been in power and in charge of the world since Socrates . . . with almost all of them having been here for barely a handful of years. Even more, I'm sure the red man would have something else entirely to say about the style and sight of the edifices.

I hardly needed to wonder at it; I could see it, as plain as day, in any number of little shit towns and company cities all over Pennsylvania. One didn't really need to consider things too much, except of course, for the refusal of my employers and their businessmen allies to see what it was doing. Nothing lasts forever. Certainly not banks, as this century has proven out on many occasions. The same is said for the whole of society. These betters, these in charge of the industrial concerns, they bat their hands at the stewing and frothing ferment unloading daily at the docks in Philadelphia, New York, and Boston. They scoop into this boiling mass with both hands, taking out everything they can ladle unto themselves, never mind that which spills out and splashes on the ground.

There are, after all, plenty of those of us around with brooms and mops to clean up the messes that come about as a result of such rough handling.

I have no idea what to make of the notion that these lands had been inhabited only by the red men for an eternity prior to that of the English and the Irish. I had grown up on a farm, with woods and fields, and blood and sweat. To know that everywhere had once been like that—even more with the woods and less with the farms—could not be but some type of fever dream like the type droned on about by the transcendentalist flower-pickers. When one looks at the meaning of what has been made of that state of nature, into the artifice of man, one wonders what we will all be in store for in the next hundred years. Perhaps a century from now, none of the artifice will be here and things will have simply returned to the rivers and the woods. My betters among the ranks of those in command of the Pennsy, and the Carnegie mills, and the mines, and all the rest . . . all of them assume that what they have built is nothing but permanent, with the grimy slaves pouring steel and busting black rocks.

I slow Amos to a halt, staring at the shapes of the houses through the rain and mist. It would likely be a mistake to go to one of the boarding houses. I'd have to talk to someone who considers himself a family man, and it's probably not going to be him that does most of the considering of that nature, as much as it is going to be the packed hovel that the entire family of a dozen more squats, sleeps, shits, eats, and breathes in.

I scratch my chin, considering a cigarette if I would be brave enough to attempt it in the downpour.

Indeed. Not brave enough for that, but perhaps enough to see if I can set a few fires in the hay to see Magursky come slithering out.

I renew my grip on Amos's reins and spur him forward, clicking my tongue a couple of times as he picks up the pace back down the hill, back down toward the office occupied by Mr. Strickland and his many consorts of officialdom, politics, and power.

Couldn't really have expected things to be much different. This thought travels through my mind as I trot Amos back to where I needed to meet this approximation of officialdom. The middle layer, as always, is the thickest and ofttimes the easiest to grease, but given the lack of time I've had to work with on this particular trip, it's turning out to be nothing but tar. Others would be more effective at this type of thing than what I would; the reaction I see on most peoples' faces when they see me is mirror enough into my appearance. And yet, the Pennsy sent *me*, and they know what they're going to get when they put me in as a remedy. If they'd wanted a talker, they'd have sent a Pinkerton. The Pinkertons, of course, are expected to be brutal and there are many of them, many more than us. But for any conversation about what the Pinkertons will do, someone will mention the C&I and the conversation stops.

Couldn't really have expected anything to be different. Nothing's ever different, not really. I suppose the politicians might think they are, but what I do is the same since the ill-starred day of my own birth.

It's then that I notice the figure waiting for me at the bottom of the path. A trail of smoke exits from his mouth as the rain pours off the brim of his hat. He leans against a gate entrance to the steel plant, flicking the final bit of his cigarette into the rain-surging gutter as he barks a greeting, "Houghton," his voice rough and rumbling coming from a body piled with muscle and sinew and scars, none too dissimilar from my own.

I bring Amos to a halt and swing my leg over, hopping down and extending my hand. "Funny to see you here, Jim," I say.

He takes the proffered hand and shakes it. "Thought that you'd be here," James "Jimmy" Welsh replies, a wry grin on his scarred face. Another Union veteran, though it'd have been easy enough to find any number of scrapes he'd been in that can cause a star-shaped blood mark on the cheek and temple. "Any time I hear that there's a lead on Magursky, I figure you're going to be showing up sooner or later."

"Mostly been later," I say, lighting a cigarette that he declines from me.

We huddle under a roof corner and watch the heavy raindrops falling from the sky, puddles and ruts brimming over and venting their own tiny rivers into mud-clogged gutters. One can hear the machinery of the mills in the background, the furnaces roaring and the clanking machinery turning over and over and over, the trains coming in with ore and coal, the trains going out with rails and billets.

I smoke and look at him, thinking of the telegram from Harrisburg. "What brings you to the half-famous Johnstown?"

He gives a sheepish grin, shaking his head and turning to look upriver. I can see the traces of his burn scars at the side of his neck and running along his jaw line. I seemed to recall the story about him being caught in a fire and explosion in an ammo train somewhere in West Virginia. Kessler's Cross, maybe, or one of the other early ones? I couldn't be sure.

We all have scars.

"Same bullshit," he says. "They've got me on these message deliveries, and they've got you on the interesting stuff."

I grunt, raising my eyebrows. "I am here to deliver some messages as well." I drag heavily on the cigarette.

He laughs at that, a wry smile forming on his swarthy features. "This is what we do."

"This is what we do," I agree. I pick at a piece of tobacco from my lip. I tell him about the journey uphill to the mine, and the conditions there.

"I'm sure that everyone's eager to help."

"If you can get anyone who speaks fucking English." I pick at the tobacco again, realize that the sensation is an illusion, get disgusted with myself for falling prey to it, then pick at it again anyway.

"This town's quiet, though," Welsh says. He shakes his head. "Of all the places you'd think in this state . . ."

"This is why Magursky's here," I insist. I have no idea whether he knows about the telegram or not. Chances are that he knows that someone in the boss's ranks wants me to clean this up, one way or the other, and they told him to find me and assist. "Cambria has apparently handled a lot of the issues themselves. They've got a good set of ears everywhere already, but Magursky's going to feel pulled to address that challenge. That's why it's so damnably difficult to try to find him. Everyone's already shut out."

"And those that aren't are already very cautious."

"Smaller numbers."

"Smaller numbers," he agrees. He straightens up, a look of interest passing his craggy face. "You know about the Sons here, though?"

I had heard something about this, of course—the note being but one of them. The Sons of Vulcan were the progenitors of all of these problems although, if one looks at it correctly, I have my job because of them. The Sons had started by organizing the iron puddlers, then moved on to bigger and better things which also made them into purveyors of the difficulties that the Coal and Iron Police were paid to sort out. I'd sorted a few in my time, but the cancer spread ahead of where we could have gone over the past two decades. Now, the Sons of Vulcan were but a memory. Now they called themselves by the supremely more impressive title of the "Amalgamated Association of Iron and Steel Workers."

Immigrant scum. At least for the most part. That is, until I was forced to recognize the fact that without them and the troubles they have brought to this state, I wouldn't have a job.

How odd is it to find oneself on the opposite side of so many. Tens of thousands worked in the mills and mines, and more every day, while the CIP was a small force.

It doesn't take too many of us, though. Especially when one has the force and might of a government agency that holds a reputation for violence, one that has cleared many paths for us in advance of our arrival. As one might suspect, that reputation had to be constantly reinforced. Ever-present escalation seemed to be the orders of the day, and it was only a matter of time before something even bigger than the Maguires would happen. Things had been too quiet for too long. Carnegie's mills around Pittsburgh were fanning the flames themselves. It was only a matter of time before things caught in Johnstown here as well. Cambria had been trading on its isolation in a couple of ways for more than two decades now, but with all of the immigrants and the ever-aggressive Pennsy building more and more tracks and running more and more trains, bad ideas followed bad people with nothing to lose.

Still. The Sons did have an early appearance here in this city, even if their cancer had not taken root. It would only be a matter of time until it would, though the Sons are long gone—just like a cancer can be long gone. Hack off the limb with the tumor, the tumor reappears in the body, the head, the eye.

"Some of those types are still around, you know." Welsh shrugs. "Unbelievable but a lot of times they seem to get held up like they the great-granddaddies and they get paraded around like some damned pasha or something."

"Where?"

Welsh laughs, shaking his head, rueful. "There's a couple down in the almshouse past the brewery." He waves his hand in the general direction along the road on which I'd come into town. My eyes flick in that direction and Amos whinnies an agreement, a sound almost enough to bring a smile to my face.

"Where else?"

"A farm a few miles south of the city. Apparently, he got married to a farmer's daughter and she rescued him from the mills enough to spend the rest of his life covered in cowshit."

I chuckle. "How do you know this, Jimmy?"

"Came up a couple of years ago. Steger wanted me to come out here to settle a score with them and then I didn't do it. I caught up with the farmer but he was already in such a pitiable state and undoubtedly as stupid as the day is long anyway."

Steger—now that was a name that I recognized. He'd died more than a year ago, right behind the desk that he so astutely and adamantly manned and never left. He'd been sitting behind it, dead, for two days before anyone thought to ask or to check on him. He had this remarkable ability to scream with enough force to turn his face some strange hue occupying a space between blue and purple. And yet he could do this without seeking any greater leverage than what he could do from behind that desk. I never reported to Steger, elsewise I think his end might have come a bit sooner and I would be among the many buried in the potter's field at Eastern State Penitentiary in Philadelphia. Other lore connected with Steger's death had been that a couple of my colleagues from the Coal and Iron rank and file, so to speak, dangled him from his ankles out the window of one of the top floors of the Capitol Building in Harrisburg. CIP officers were all over the state, employed by any number of mills and mines, but Steger had placed himself in the position of being a "broker" of sorts and had, over a decade or more, accumulated enough dirt and gossip to enrich himself at the great expense of many others. He had never had to roll up his sleeves or get his hands dirty, but had managed to capture a ring of CIP all to himself as a sort of subcontractor. Then Steger had forgotten the old adage warning against biting the hands that feed and those same hands dangled him for three solid minutes a few dozen feet from the walk below. Passersby ignored his screams. That's a long time to hang upside down and stare at the pavement yards above you while the only thing stopping you from hitting it is the ill manner of the people dangling you over it. After thoroughly soiling himself, they'd—whoever "they" had been, though I had a reasonably good idea—dragged him back inside, slammed him down in his chair, slapped his face a few times to wake him up, his combed-over and well-greased hair splaying out in enough different directions to rival the crown on the Statue of Liberty herself, then told him to "shut the fuck up" and then they left.

"So what am I looking at here, then? Magursky's here or no?"

He blows air out of pursed lips, the rain coming out in a spray. "If there's one thing about that guy, is that he's here. He's there. He's everywhere." His hand traces out gentle circles in the misty air. "He's everywhere, Houghton," Welsh repeats. "That's the problem. He's your ghost, and you're seeing him around every corner of this godforsaken state. Why didn't you move out west with the rest of the boys twenty years ago? You could be running a saloon and whorehouse right now and weigh about 350 pounds and picking silver nuggets up off the ground."

It was my turn for the spray of disbelief. *Something might have to be said for actually running the saloon and whorehouse, rather than just working in one.*

"I aim to kill him," I said.

There it is, right out loud. Not that it was that much of a relief; it hasn't been the first time I uttered anything like that. This is what the CIP has given me license to do. I can kill with impunity and be justified for doing so. That will be my body of work on this world. It does come with its own type of overarching release of pressure, however, in that it is only another killer from CIP that would do as Welsh did: an acknowledgment with a grunt and then he said, "Maybe there are a couple of doors we can knock on together. Lest you want to take this whole damn town on by yourself anyway."

There's one thing I do know more than anything else about this city: Johnstown has tripled its population in fewer than the past ten years. The housing on top of houses on top of hovels here catch the eye, more so than they would in just about any other circumstance. In a city like Philadelphia, one is used to seeing the growth of the new peoples arriving; in a smaller area such as Johnstown, that tends to be the *only* thing that one can see. That, along with the mills and the mines.

A train whistle lights up the air, searing through the curtains of rain. *Ah, yes, the ever-present and ever-loving siren call of the Pennsylvania Railroad, the world's largest company. Stick that up your ass, Carnegie.*

That couldn't have been too much of a surprise for old Andrew, how-ever, considering that he named his burgeoning steelworks after one of my former bosses, the biggest of the big and the best of my betters, J Edgar Thomson, given the sweetheart fondling and handholding that the latter man was able to accomplish in leveraging the formation of Carnegie's steel company nearly twenty years ago. This is nothing new to me, this daisy chain of men with hands in each others' pockets, searching for funding, searching for succor, searching for attention. Whether the jostling of elbows and greasing of palms occurred in the banking house, the tavern, or the privacy of one's own bedroom was none of my affairs. Indeed, the sole result for me would be a manifestation of barely two coins to rub together in my own pocket and the occasional horse so they could still call us a "mounted" force.

Jimmy Welsh sees the same things I see now; he's seen the same things as I've seen before. He was there with the Maguires, and I know that he spent most of the past few years in the southwestern-most part of this state, aligning with the borders of West Virginia in the bituminous country, fast overtaking the anthracite region as the center of gravity for the world of coal. And if this isn't the world of steel, it must only be the world of coal. At this point, however, I just couldn't tell if he was looking for some extra loafing time just for me to play a clown and for him to get his jollies by watching me on some type of snipe hunt.

On the other hand, I've known Jimmy Welsh for years and I've never known him to be uninterested in cracking some skulls. It is a good thing then, for both of us, that we found our calling first in the Army, then in the Coal and Iron force. Welsh is right; I had known plenty of men who spent time on the battlefields and who then moved to places far west to start again.

Why did I never?

Then there was the idea of abandoning the ghosts, the ghosts of my brethren at Gettysburg, the gossamer ghost of Mary Elizabeth some-where along the hills and valleys of Fulton County. I've never felt like I needed to run. Not, at least, until after I had Magursky sorted one way or the other.

"So what did you have in mind?" I think about the almshouse and mention as much. Welsh shakes his head.

"Not going to be in an almshouse, not unless they're interested in making some type of public spectacle. No, they'll have the rights to visit each other somewhere else, somewhere they can control who comes in and out and so they will also know that if there's an unwelcome guest, it'll be there in plain sight rather than a rat sticking its nose into someone's privy."

I raise an eyebrow.

Welsh looks me up and down and gives a wry smile.

"How are your boxing skills, Houghton?"

———

"These Coal and Iron types . . . I gotta tell you, you clowns get bolder every fucking day."

This was an inarguable point, I suppose, and it also goes to my own state of mind; just how very unconcerned I am with walking into a place like this. The voice is well-spoken enough, barely with an accent, someone who had been in my country for a while now. *Let's just see.*

The man who says it to me is one of three men at a table, a hat pulled low over his eyes and a mangy beard around his mouth. Call him Thin Beard. One of his companions is a man who nearly matches him in age and beard, but with a prodigious whiskey gut—call him Stomach—and then a third man with a skin of mottled and shocking pink, without a single hair atop his head or adorning his face; he had been burned, either in the war, mines, or mills, and somehow managed to survive years looking like a boiled pink worm. Easy enough to call him Burns.

I sit in the chair unbidden and stare directly at the speaker; my pulse feels strong, regular, a bit higher than at rest but not at an extreme rate. I am paying attention.

And I'm enjoying this. Let's not forget that.

"You guys going to deal me in or what?" I ask, pulling a cigarette out from my case and lighting it.

"What the fuck do we get out of sitting at this table with you right now? We ought to be cutting your throat. It's our own goddamn generosity of soul that has you talking right now rather than gurgling your lifeblood out through a new neck tie on that crisp white shirt of yours." This from Stomach.

I have to laugh at that; none of my shirts were ever white, not anymore. This one is covered in coal dust and steel dirt, the same grit I have in my teeth and in what's left of my sweaty hair. It's also ground into the wrinkles in my knuckles, where it mixes with blood—not all my own.

Same thing with my shirt, which is something that the gentlemen sitting around this table would have also been very much aware of and a sign that I'd been intending all along.

This squalid social hall is about what I would have expected for something like this. The room is low and smoky, filled with the haze of tobacco and opium and hashish, along with the strange scents of their odd cooking and food preparation, the smell of raw water and sewer close by. The din and jabber, some in English, some not, fills the spaces between the curls of smoke. The participants set up a variety of gaming tables, scarred wood, scarred felt on billiards, scarred walls, scarred paintings to suit the scarred skin and scarred souls. One picture given pride of place is a reproduction of a painting of the Forge of Vulcan, at least 300 years old or more.

The reproduction looks even older.

"I'm looking for Istvan Magursky."

They all shake their heads at once, not even attempting to feign actual interest.

"Don't know anyone by that name," says Thin Beard, not raising his head from his cards. "I don't even know the names of these guys at this table with me. Or even my own. And I don't give a shit about yours."

"He's not doing any of you any favors. At all."

The second man speaks up, announcing his intention to do so by producing a storm wall of coughing and wheezing, giant stomach twitching with effort.

Coal. Steel. Who knows?

"Seems to me," says Stomach, after his fit settles and without bothering to look at me, instead observing his playing cards, "that you're not doing us any favors either, Yellow Dog. So why would we give a shit about any of these things you mention?" He coughs again, a bit more gently, but when he removes his handkerchief from his mouth, I can see the ruby rasp of blood. *Maybe coal, maybe steel. More likely consumption.* He seems rather unconcerned about it, as do his friends. And also more than a bit of a trace of an accent from somewhere far abroad.

As do I. If he was expecting something other than my indifference toward it, he's likely to be disappointed.

My presence in this hall is not without precedent; my presence in it without anyone else accompanying me would have to be seen as unusual. I do not take the previous large-shaped absence of reported problems as being the same thing as problems themselves. Judging by the trio seated with me at this table, there have been a fair lack of reports as to the problems here and there is no question that the fires here are burning, but underground.

As they have been for quite some time.

My eyes glance upward toward the ceiling, so completely obscured by tobacco smoke, lantern smoke, and smoke from the outside that it would be difficult to tell the last time it had truly been visible. A group such as this, in rooms such as these, operates in the same number of shifts as the mills themselves.

"Fuck it, I fold," says Burns, laying his cards in their graves. I drop my gaze to him.

"Great, then there's room for me on the next hand. Or are you too lordly to deal in a Yellow Dog?"

Burns rolls his lashless eyes and ignores the rest of the notion. It's clear that these three won't take any type of bait—or anything else—from anyone known to be from the law, the company, or, in the case of an outfit such as the Coal and Iron Police, both.

"There's a few fights tonight," Thin Beard says, lifting his eyes to mine as he shuffles the cards. "You want to deal yourself in on a real game, big man, why don't you deal yourself in there. Maybe you can beat everyone into telling you something that not a single. Fucking. Soul. Is going to tell you about right now."

I lean back in the chair, interlacing my fingers over my stomach. This is a temptation for me, as a good fisticuffs session so often is.

I look at each of them, studying their faces. Burns glances at me, then back at his discarded hand of cards. This lack of eye contact is not any sign of weakness; indeed, it's just the opposite. It's a powerful sign of them knowing exactly what could happen to me and the crowd at any moment.

How many times do outsiders stroll into a place like this at all, let alone one with a badge? That answer is simple as well—they're interested. And probably savoring the notion that my life is within their mercy, and only that.

"A few fights tonight," says Stomach. The first one nods. "We could put you in that ring, see what you can do."

"Who says I'd like that?"

"Who gives a fuck about what you like? You're the one who came in here, swinging your cock like it's the biggest in the city. So this gives you a chance to prove it, cop."

"What do I get out of it?"

Stomach lights his cigar, looks at me, and says, "You might be able to leave under your own power. Or not. I don't know. Your balls are definitely bigger than your brain, having yourself walk in here like this. You've got balls. I'll give you Coal and Iron types that much, anyway."

I stare at him. "I think I'll be able to walk out of there just fine." My voice is quiet, as is my direct gaze into his own eyes. "And even if I'm not, there is a very open question of how many motherfuckers will have to be carried out with me. I'm just one guy. But I guarantee you I'll put a dozen or more of you in that shit-eating hospital of yours, and some of you I'll put in the goddamn mud. And if you don't believe that, we can fucking dance right now."

The first man, Thin Beard, raises his hands a bit. "No need for such hostilities. We may hate each other here, but that's no reason we can't get along."

I look over at Burns, the man that I'm learning has the most credibility among the crowd, the man that literally bears the mark of the work. "What say you? Throw the dice on this one too like your ratshit fucking dunce friend next to you."

Stomach shifts, as do I, resting my right hand on the hogleg on my hip but also pointing my left hand directly at him, revealing the single shot pointed directly at his forehead. "I'll drill one right through your brain bones, my friend. Not sure that would inflict any damage on you, but it'll for sure at least slow you down even more, you jackass."

"Well, this is uncomfortable," Burns says.

I stare directly at each of them, and they each stare back. "We're just jawing a bit," Stomach says, his own voice even and icy. "I already offered him a match. Can walk out of here with more money than he'll make in any year of knocking innocent, hardworking folk about."

That's a fact. The only thing that might change is whether my desire to knock folk about is the least bit quelled.

The second man's eyes drift back down towards his cards. "It's not a match without a little bit of talking," he says. His tone is not that of either mocking or making an excuse; he simply states the facts. The other fact, that he's got a Coal and Iron detective across the table and leveling a single-shot palm pistol directly at his forehead seems to be a situation that he's unconcerned with . . . perhaps an experience that he's had before.

I relent, withdrawing my hand and placing it back down at my side. I tug on my coat as if to smooth the lapel, but it also announces the badge to that much broader of an audience. The rolls of silence spiral outward from around our table. I cock my head for a moment, and I can see the dark shape of Jimmy Welsh straightening up from next to the doorway, a shadowy figure about whom no one else would gather.

"If'n ya fight," says Burns, "and we take a little bit of a taste of something, maybe then you walk out of here and forget a lot of what you see."

I don't respond, not right away. "I am looking for Istvan Magursky," I say, the words coming slowly. "If I am to find him, I won't need to report on anything else." *At least not right now.*

Thin Beard speaks, "I think you're missing the point of all of this." He twirls an index finger about the side of his head, indicating the entirety not only of the room, but of the city itself. "You may know this, you and your bastard head-busting cop cousins, but there's a bond that's forming throughout all of the people. Hellfire, you might even join up one of these days."

I light a cigarette and wait, conveying my skepticism through my pointed glare.

"You may not think so, Yellow Dog, but you are the muscle in a system that eats itself. The mines. The steel. All run by snakes that are eating their own tails. You got drawn into that snake for some reason, and some day, you're going to eat yourself too. Or be eaten by whatever's at the mouth. So when you're out doing your thing, you don't even see where things are headed. But there are many, many more who can. Those that are staring down into that molten iron, baking the sweat and the life right out of their skin, and the loose caps around that are pulling down all the fucking mountains on top of everyone's heads."

I look at the cards laid out on the table among the three men. There's a metaphor here, I can feel that much, but there's not enough sense between my ears for me to be able to tease out a meaning right away. The face cards, the royal family, the flush, the numbers, the spades.

The diamonds.

The diamonds should be black; they certainly are in this part of the world.

"Yet more and more come every day," I say. I flick the cigarette ashes on the floor, picking another stray fleck of ash from my trousers. "It says something about that, don't it? Seems to me like everyone's pockets get lined." *Except for mine.* "Says something about where people are coming from, that they flee here, and then making the steel and digging at the rocks isn't good enough, and then it takes the likes of you to rile them up, to make them believe some type of other highfalutin horseshit. You got 'em snowed." I jut my chin at the pile of coins, a couple of crumpled paper notes strewn in among them. "This looks like any table I'd see in Harrisburg, Pittsburgh, or Philadelphia. Not much daylight there between all of you."

Now, their turn to fall silent occurs.

"If you think you're better than I am, that's why you don't deal the likes of me in your little game." I draw on the cigarette again. "Not that you've even embraced the least little bit of hospitality. You've proven your point. But here's the thing . . . I'm not really interested in doing anything else other than finding Magursky, and I have to tell you that there isn't much else in the way of activity elsewise and as near as I can tell, this is the most likely place where I'm going to find answers.

"I'll also tell you what you don't know. You don't know whether I really am here by myself. Or if there's anyone on the Pennsy payrolls in this room, or if there is a whole team of CIP outside, just waiting for a signal. You don't know any of those things, elsewise you wouldn't be sitting here on your fat asses making threats to the likes of me. You'd have just done it. But you haven't, which tells me a couple of different things. You could be yellow shits. You could be fucking about. Or you could have answers. All three of these options are interesting to me and what you do *not* have is any real way to get me out of here without giving me answers. And that makes you really uncomfortable, and that makes me into someone who's really enjoying that."

A small bottle of rotgut appears at the center of the table, delivered by one of the staffers.

"Ah," says Stomach, eyes alighting on it. "You're right and wrong, Mr. Coal and Iron cop. But what we have here is something special for the likes of you. And the likes of us."

"And why would I drink a goddamn single thing that you offer to me?" This is not some type of negotiation; need they be reminded of this?

"Because if you drink with us, and you come out okay in your bout," answers the second one, "we might see our way to helping you."

I raise an eyebrow and something approximating a laugh erupts from my throat. "Is that a fact?"

"Yes, that is a fact, as much as anything your own masters will tell you, you as their own white-skinned slave."

Dross. I think this, just as I also think back to what Welsh had said— this is where the action was, with a bit of fisticuffs in a hard-edged town. This wouldn't be the first time I'd done this, not by a long shot. It would, however, be the first time I had done it for an audience.

I look at each of them in turn. "You say that's a fact, but I see nothing but slavery. I see it in the fear of the rich men and the sadness of the poor. I see it in the faces of all of you too, deep envy and greed carved into all of it. You're just like those rich, fat suits."

I take the bottle and pour three fingers of some rank-smelling piss into a glass for me, and then do the rest for them.

Thin Beard looks at my drink, then his. The other two just hold their gazes where they had been set; Burns, at me, Stomach, at his hand of cards. There's no question in my mind that Burns is the most senior of these three—not because they give him the most deference, or that he even acts as if the most deference should be accorded to him, but he's the one that's been hardened by fire like so much in the mills. Not so much with Stomach, the softest around the middle. He's older, he's eaten more, and, what's more, there's no one in his life commanding him to do anything other than be soft. *He'll tell me.*

"This person you're looking for, this Magursky," says Thin Beard, raising his eyes to me. "He's worth something, even if he is just a legend, a dream, a hope that some may have. The costs of finding him might be high, too high for any of us, even if we have to pay from different tills."

"I've been with the CIP for more than twenty years," I say. *Twenty years in the CIP, and still on the beat. If they take me at my word, which they have ample reason to, they know that you don't stay in the CIP for the money, and if you want to stay in the CIP for any length of time, you get good at cracking skulls. That's what keeps you around, both for the higher-ups and for those who work. That, and there's nothing else for me to do, either.*

"Twenty years," I continue, "and I will find him. Everyone's run out of patience. You all should think of me as a Good Samaritan."

I say this just as Burns sips his drink, which he sprays out onto the floor, blinking his hairless eyelids, laughing out loud.

"How is that, exactly?" asks Stomach, unable to suppress his own crooked teeth in a grin.

"Well, if I am not successful in the next day or two, they're going to be sending a lot more of *me* your direction. Everyone runs out of time eventually."

It's a bluff, but only of a sort.

"I'll drink with you," I tell them. "But I'll go to hell before I think of you as any lesser fools than the assholes that direct me to whip you."

Chapter Six

They put something in my drink.

It always had seemed to me that there were two diametrically opposite mindsets with regard to how things worked in the world. One was, the religious, sober one . . . to the extent that religion could ever be called anything sober. This was the milk-drinking, prayer-sending, glad-handing group of joy that I found utterly unrealistic in anything that they did. The other was the group that lost their own soul amidst the battlefields, either that of the politics of the War Between the States or that of the group that gets so lost in the drink of so many that any resemblance, indeed, any *trace*, might be found of what you do.

They also act as if this were the only time that anyone had ever thrown anything in a beverage of mine.

Truth is—I prefer water after having had something else to drink besides that. And yet, here we all are in the same mass of mistakes in which we would have found each other before the fancy language and sanctimonious imprecations, before the reminder from Roberts that I actually might owe his men something and before the idea that I might have even been on the side of right during the War.

And though I prefer water, it doesn't mean that I have no experience with other things that one can consume. There were shares of things passed about the tents at the Union encampments that would have made any Chinaman blush. I was not so self-righteous so as to think that I should not share in this; I felt no regret in doing so.

The single difference, as near as I could determine, was that most of the men I served with did these things as a way of escaping their world of musketry and cannon, smoke and blood. I reveled in it. I took the poppy, the homemade moonshine, anything else not to escape, but to *intensify.* It would start with the tobacco and move from there on to other fields of trial.

I have enough awareness to know that someone else, probably most everyone else, would have regretted being in the situation I'm in right now. Challenging the gang leaders' best hunky to a bare-knuckles fist-fight? Check and underway, and thanks to Jimmy Welsh. Now, we're in a building not far from a set of coking ovens, where you can see and smell the coal getting loaded into hearths at all hours. The rain and mist blankets the smoke close to the ground, so the smoke comes into this building too, a social hall built by some of the same hunkies, next to one of their Papist churches, the walls already stained with their liquors and beers, the tobacco being smoked and spat. It's a big enough room to hold a couple hundred people, a couple hundred hoarse, shouting, shrieking voices yelling at me, at each other, at God. Stacks of money or scrip, shaken in fists like a rat crushed between the jaws of a terrier, make their way around the room. I can smell the coal, the sweat, the blood, the booze, off myself, off everyone.

I clench my fists and flex my fingers.

I watch Jimmy Welsh, an anchoring shadow most of the size of the wall he leans against. I can't see his eyes, his hat pulled low over his brow and casting his entire face in darkness. Still—they were there, and the only thing that would be a problem is if Jimmy Welsh were on the take. But Jimmy Welsh is too much like me, not nearly smart enough to produce a betrayal. No . . . Jimmy Welsh is motivated by one primary force, and that is the same as mine: always happy to turn water to blood.

I inhale deeply, the fumes of the stale beer and shite gin and smoke and God alone knows what else growing heavier with each passing moment. I feel the sweat on my skin, pausing there as if to sample the air itself. I taste something metallic on my tongue, on the roof of my mouth, at the back of my throat. Something like metal, something bitter, something that could be traced above and beyond that of the rotgut booze itself.

I can pick out some voices from the blathering roar in the background, the jabbering of the strange and foreign tongues, as they would have said in the Book of Corinthians. Some I can pick out just because it's in English, or something that passes close to it, and some I can pick out just because my hearing fades and gains in cycles, reeling to the front of mind and the receding once again to the back.

"—the scars, Jesus, will you look at that—"

"—the man's a walking corpse—"

How true. Just ask any number of my colleagues now long under the grass among the mud, soil, clay, and worms.

"—fucking knifed him—"

"—or something, maybe shot?"

"—maybe needs shot again—"

How true. Though the first few times didn't take.

I look at my opponent, a bruiser of a hunky half a foot again taller than I am, with me standing well over six foot. He's not carrying as much around the shoulders as I do, but he's not carrying as much around the middle, either. To look at me is to look at a grappler, a wrestler. To look at him is to see a ropy and rangy fighter. His enormous, drooping mustaches complete the effect of reinforcing his hunky ancestry, obscuring not just his lip, but most of his mouth and chin as well.

He smiles at me, eyes half closed as if in boredom, water and sweat dripping from his swarthy face. His mustache parts far enough for me to see what was left of his dentition, a black hole of rot and a green, empty smile.

If only this were Magursky.

I squelch the thought in the back of my head, the words smacking of doubt; *you don't need to do this.* That's true, in a way—Magursky isn't here and the likelihood of me impressing or beating someone into disclosing his location are vanishingly small. No—I recognized this for what it is. A show of force and the ability to stick my foot in the door, wedging my way into somewhere where I would, eventually, get some answers. I'm under no illusions that this is going to be anything other than a grind.

He is Magursky, in a sense. They're *all* Magursky, in a sense.

I will bring a sword down upon you, just as in the book of Ezekiel.

Whatever they had thrown into my drink, it was likely it had the opposite effect of what they'd been intending. The lights burn brighter, the din roars louder, the smoke smells stronger, the metallic taste at the back of my tongue tingling with the resonance of whatever it was. It felt like the world had slowed to a point where I could move and flit about like a housefly evading the swatter, the buzz in my brain the tether anchoring me to the tasks in front of me. I imagine that I can see concerned faces looking at each other, wondering whyever it was that they had put it didn't seem to be making me stumble. The reality was, even when in the closing days of the war and converging on a shrinking and collapsing Rebel army, there had been plenty to find and scour in the fields; yes, there was the opium and the hashish, but in the rich springtime Virginia soil, in the fields cluttered and uncluttered alike by artillery shells and bodies, there was also the Jimson plants and the foul-tasting mushrooms plucked from the cow patties in the many pastures that had run red with blood.

I sit on the corner stool, wrapping my own knuckles and palms in preparation for this.

I could hear the roar of the crowd.

The cigar and cigarette smoke hung heavily in the air, pressing and pushing against the stink of bodies and manure, leather and garlic, steel dust, and coal smoke. I keep my face impassive, a mask of scarred rage. The smells and the sounds here, however deafening the tumult of the raucous laughter, the shouted, hoarse curses and snarling insults, are nothing compared to what I had seen, heard, and smelled as a younger man.

I wrap my hands, and I think about the stink of the blood and guns at the battlefields, the ear-splitting deafening clatter of the rifles, muskets, and cannon.

I can hear the voice through the cacophony of the roaring crowd about the ring and surging explosions and reports in my memory. I can see the sneering faces around the ring, superimposed over the ghostly faces of the dead that I had left behind at the scenes of the battles. I close my eyes, slowing my breath. My pulse echoes in my ears, hard enough to make me question its origin, as it seems to be echoing up and down my body in different manners and at different times. *That's good*, one of the voices says to me, *that's good because this is how you know you're still alive.*

And that you still want to be.

It's true. Even with everything that I had seen and done during the war, everything that I had seen and done as a part of the Coal and Iron force, I still felt the little tickle of excitement at the bottom of my stomach and coursing through my veins. The lamps strung up around the room gave off light, but my vision sharpened the relief between the shades and the shadows, the lights and the darks. *You still* want *to be alive.* The voice comes with no edge of irony, no subtly sneering seed of doubt planted deeply in the words. They had slipped something that they figured would make me panic, but the opposite settles in.

The light and the shadows move about, the edges crisp. Sweat glistens on the faces of those around me, spots in their mouths gaping where their teeth are missing. I look down at my own bare forearms, corded with muscle and veins, the left one covered in scrawled scars, pink and white against my skin.

I take a deep breath through my nose, feeling my heart pound in my chest. *Steady, steady.* Absolutely, it's steady; faster than normal, but steady.

I wonder if Jimmy Welsh is ready for this. Almost certainly, he would have loved to have been on this stage more than I. The fact that I'm the object of attention, scrutiny, and derision are the facts that, for me, ameliorate my discontent with being in the position of being seen and recognized, something that I would try to avoid under any and all circumstances.

Sometimes you have to smoke the quarry out. The quarry is all around me; this much is true. They made a mistake by spiking my booze with something that stoked my boilers more than normal. I feel the cold, shimmering sheen of sweat on my skin, my muscles knotted underneath as they tense with readiness for action. My heartbeat is steady, just a little elevated, even with the coffee and the ramp up to sudden violence; if it does, I know I'm in for a good scrape and I'm about to dish one out to even greater effect. My heart pounds blood through my ears, the sides of my throat.

I smile and stare out at the three Sons of Vulcan, seated in the front row and off to my left. I give them a curt nod and a wink. They stare back at me, faces of stone. Burns and Stomach exchange glances and they lean close to each other, speaking directly into the ear of the other. Thin Beard just stares.

It's loud for me here in the ring; it is probably even louder for them, surrounded by the jeering and jawing of so many around me. I can't read lips, but I can tell from their deportment alone that they aren't joining in the mad-dog air of the rest of the crowd, which wants blood. They want blood as well, and they tried quite hard to make sure the circumstances align such that all of it comes from me, and me alone.

I also want blood. *I'm going to get it too, more than they can even imagine.*

And then I turn back to my quarry of the moment, bashing my taped hands together and curling them into fists.

"Okay, old son," I call to him. I roll my shoulders and bounce on my feet. "Let's dance."

I stand, stalking to the center of the ring, flexing my fingers against their bindings, the weight of the roll of coins secured beneath the wrappings. My opponent grins at me, a leer as he comes from the opposite corner, his thick mustache doing little to hide the contemptuous turn of his mouth. The crowd howls at my appearance, cheering him on. His corner man does the same, staring at me with a greedy, intense hatred, a smile wriggling on wormy lips, his own sheen of sweat meeting the condensation from the water bucket.

I feel nothing, except a damp and cold ball of hatred and anticipation in the bottom of my stomach. I dangle my arms, putting the full map of scars on display for all to see; the magnificent tears on my shoulder, my side, my left forearm, the ragged talon's claws of pink shreds at the base of my throat and around the top of my right collarbone and down to the shoulder blade on my left. In polite company, perhaps, the marks would have been remarkable; here, they are nothing.

To me, these scars are nothing. They chant with the voices of the dead. Those are the only ones I have manning my corner.

It is insane for you to do this, comes the voice of reason in my head. Where had it been for a few hours? It is correct; I'm here alone, with perhaps one or two of the town's police here as a representative of order and government, and it is indeed highly doubtful whether those particular brethren of the law would help me if there were some type of situation to emerge where I had to do more than box someone.

You're going to have to do more than boxing.

They put something in my drink, so there's more than boxing already.

The hunky grins at me as the referee holds out his arms to each of us. My opponent—the name is something like Boris or Istvan or some shit—holds his grin ahs he bends his elbows straight out, presenting his fists. *No razor blades.* I'm heavier than he is, for sure, and that's going to make him think he's faster than I am. Maybe he is. But I don't think he's spent the past twenty years making sure some shite for brains doesn't get the drop on him. The only thing that matters is that Welsh is watching my back from the crowd.

Can't think about that. Can't consider the vulnerability of that reliance. I stare, impassive, my heart thudding in my ears, clenching my jaw, my own arms dangling loose and free, all the while with me thinking, *there's no way in hell this is going to be a fair fight so why would I even—*

And there it is as Boris throws a quick right toward my solar plexus.

And here it is as they truly realize the mistake they made by raising my temperature.

The quick right is in slow motion. I step to the side, not avoiding the blow entirely but taking away most of its force. I feel only a slight sense of the sickly sensation that one gets from such a punch, and he takes nothing of my wind, his second punch already being thrown wide to my left, missing most of me just above my shoulder where my chin would have been.

Going for the knockout on me just like that, I think as I throw a right cross into the jaw of the referee.

The man's jaw gives a wet snap as my fist hits him. His sole blessing is that he's already out like a snuffed candle before his pain reflex hits. He crumples like bumwad, knees hitting first and totters to the side and rolls, splaying his arms out.

Boris, distracted, glances down and I hit him with my left, directly in the center of his face. I don't have enough reach so he doesn't get all of the force, but its enough to pulp his nose without fully breaking it, streams of crimson blood and snot coursing down his lips and chin as he reels backward.

I step in, throwing another right as he blocks and I follow with a left to the body. I feel the surge in my wrist, elbow, shoulder as I get him a bit too high with that one. It's a good punch, but not enough into the body to cause much damage. He twists and spins away, shaking his head to clear it and bouncing on the balls of his feet, clapping his hands together a few times, regaining focus.

That was my advantage, I think. I step over the crumpled referee, rolling my own head around on my neck, feeling a soft click and pop against the steady drumbeat of my heart. I flex my shoulders, get my guard up, knees bent, angling my hips a bit toward him, getting ready.

Here we go. Now we can fight.

The crowd howls—they've been howling, since before I even stepped into the ring, but now there's a roar that seems merciless, impossible, rising to heaven itself, since I had dropped the ref. I don't even think Welsh anticipated that one. I can't see him now, but he'd better be out there, lurking somewhere. We can deal with the required paperwork of him knifing someone; the one thing I cannot afford to deal with is the opposite.

"You are tricky, old man," Boris calls, his bloody smile and bloody teeth a harlequin's leer. He bites off the ends of the English words in the way so common for his type. "But like I say, you are *old*."

"If that's the best you can do, I'll finish you off fast and burn your shithole to the ground along with all your motherless cousins."

His cornerman shouts a string of something in the usual gibberish. I can't hear it over the crowd or the thumping in my ears. Drops of spittle flap from his lips, sparkling in the smoky yellow and orange light of the room. The fine strands of thread erupt from the ropes circling the ring. The fissures in my own knuckles burn around the taped wrapping as I flex my fingers.

I look back up at Boris and wink.

His grin widens, and he throws back his head and laughs again.

I rap my knuckles together and say, "Now, are we going to do this or are you just going to prance around like some goddamn sodomite?"

He nods amiably, rolling his shoulders and coming at me once again, light on his feet, his guard high. He tries a 1-2, then backs away, and I step too close, and he raps me a good one under my left eye, a lightning bolt streaking across my left field of vision, ringing my ears a good one as he follows up with half a haymaker. I duck it, his fist glancing off the top part of my head, and I thump him hard in his stomach once, twice. He checks me again as he shies away from the blow, and I lean back, barely avoiding a sneaky hook to the jaw.

I throw another right, which he parries, but I lean into it with a left to the body. It opens me up for an uppercut, but I twist my head and push him. His punch goes a bit wild but still gets me with a good shot to the mouth. My lip cracks and a hot surge of blood rolls down my chin.

The crowd roars its approval.

Though the blows connected, my head is clear. His fists drew blood but took little toll.

I step back then, feeling a new issuance of sweat squeezing out of my skin. *He's fast*, I think. *Getting faster as he feels my pace.* He's big enough to have weathered my first round and he had underestimated me; he won't do that again. He knows he's in for a fight and what's more, is that I now know that I am in one for sure too.

Money changes hands.

The crowd's jeers, taunts, and shouts increase, a dull roar growing into a regular thumping like the steam hammers in the mill. My heart takes up the same rhythm and I feel the sweat coursing down my skin. It turns the corner into a constant, deep braying of noise that drowns out individual voices and screams.

It reminds me of the battlefield, only there are no screams from the wounded and the dying. I can hear them only inside my own head.

Boris comes at me again, rolling his shoulders, still grinning his mad grin. He thinks that intimidates me, I'm sure, but I just keep my stone face and my guard up, balancing my weight, knees bent, hips open, ready.

Let's go, I think. *It's time to bring this to an end and see if the three Sons will honor the word that they so fervently preached about.*

I step over the still-crumpled official, my motion easy and relaxed even as the blood and the crowd rages in my ears. It's like I hear it from a distance, from the bottom of a barrel but through soft pillows the likes of which I've never known. If this is the intended effect of whatever compound they dosed me with, I'd be quite surprised.

Then again, the battlefield hardly agrees with everyone, or barely anyone. I'm one of the lucky few, I suppose, because I embrace the nightmares.

There's no bell here, no refuge.

Boris makes his move, stepping toward me. I feint to one side, dipping my head. He anticipates it and adjusts but I take another half step closer. He goes to headbutt me, but I feint again, this time to the left and it's just a graze; a hard enough hit for contact but not enough for effect.

He twists round to have another go and I grab his exposed right forearm with both hands, jerking him close to me, almost as a lover would.

And I bring all of my two hundred fifty odd pounds down in my right foot, stomping atop his. And then again.

His entire frame goes rigid, and he howls; I feel a crunch under my foot but I couldn't be sure of the lasting damage.

I whirl around, knocking my right elbow into his cheekbone. *That* crunches.

Boris reels back, wincing, limping, one hand clutched to the side of his face as he holds his right foot off the ground.

I could just shove him down, but we need a firm ending to this. The referee has yet to stir—not that it would have made a bit of difference anyway.

Time to make a point.

I stalk closer, still holding my guard up. Letting one's guard down is a sign of arrogance, foolishness, and a death wish. I have none of those; I do have apathy, perhaps, but that is a different breed of nothingness. But it's his guard that's down, however, and that's just going to be the end of things.

I don't bother with a roundhouse wind-up or anything like that. Instead, I come in, still ready, guard still up, weight still balanced, searching for an opening.

And I find it, my left hand flashing out, fingers stiff and held together not as a fist but as a wedge, and I connect with the center of his throat.

Crunch.

His eyes widen—his mouth opens wider—he can't breathe—panic . . .

His cheek forgotten, both of his hands clutch to his ruined throat. His eyes water, tears spilling. I have a moment as he reels backwards, into the ropes, bouncing and he staggers toward me, and I've got him lined up. I throw a right hook. He drops at once in a meaty heap. His knees slam to the floor and he slumps to his side, clutching at his throat, with his ruinous rattling and gurgling.

The noise of the crowd subsides, slowly at first, then all at once, a cacophony waterfall suddenly ebbing to nothing. There's only a murmur now, shifting feet, most everyone suddenly still. I walk back to the center of the ring, making a show of ignoring both Boris and the ref, slowly unwinding the tape from my hands.

I do that for a moment or two, then walk over to my cornerman-less corner and throw the contents of the bucket over my head and torso.

The racket slowly begins to pick back up as I climb out of the ring through the ropes. Welsh approaches me, his face pale and drawn.

"Nice fight," he says.

"Let's collect on the information I just earned," I said. "Good idea to get me onto the fight card, Jimmy. Good thinking." I want a cigarette, but business is going to have to come first, as it always should.

He doesn't respond but with a puff of his cheeks. "I'm thinking they're thinking—"

Welsh doesn't get a chance to finish his sentence as the roar of the crowd returns, not with a bloody rage but instead a shrill tone, a panic. I glance up as a crush of blue uniforms pile in through the side door and down the steps.

"*Stay where you are! This is a raid!*" someone declares through a bullhorn, probably a brass rendition brought back from the Indian wars out west.

Welsh moved his lapel back, exposing his CIP badge. I'm covered in sweat and water, my shirt already half-ruined by the grime, filth, mud, and rain here in Johnstown but I pull it on my torso, smeared with blood, both my own and Boris's at the same time. As if reading my thoughts, Welsh hands me a towel of some sort—I've no idea where he got it—and I dab at my face while also pulling on my coat, my weapons, my badge.

Chief Clay himself waves his baton about, a mad, incompetent, and energetic conductor to a concert of chaos over which he has no authorship, occasionally love-tapping one of the hunkies on the wrist or fist. He glances at us, giving us a look as if to convey *you'll get yours in due time* but glances back and stares at each of us in turn, recognition dawning on his purple and jowly face.

"You . . . you . . . *you* . . . :

"Let's go, Welsh," I say. "Time's a-wasting." I spy Stomach veering off through the kitchen.

I throw a curt nod to the Chief, despite his importuning us to stop. Given his station, this is something ordinarily complied with, which I can see from the uniformed force accompanying him. He also draws himself up short because he knows his jurisdiction ends where ever it is that *I* want to make the border.

I brush past him, the looming shadow of Welsh just behind me as I tear off to the right after my quarry. I catch up to him just as he exits the door, and I don't bother checking to either side of me as I grasp the back of his shirt collar, whip him around, and slam him into the brick foundation of the building we'd just exited.

It still rains, of course, and the cold, heavy drops pelt downward. The glistening drops blow about and twist in the wind, the spire of the closest church pointing to the dark sky painted with roiling black clouds. It's like the church itself is an accusing finger toward the sky, pelted with the rain and glistening with the glow of the lamplights from the windows and the red blaze from the nearby mills. All of my vision sparkles with it; my skin tingles with it. A buzzing chant and prayer are in the center of my head, between my ears. My breath surges faster and faster, almost as if I were still in the same boxing match; the absurd coldness of it blows onto my hands, my skin still hot from the combat and the rage. And whatever they had fortified my drink with.

The man grunts as he bounces off the wall. I spin him round, pressing my elbow into his throat. His eyes go wide, cheeks puffing with the effort of breath, but that's not his biggest problem. His biggest problem is in my left hand, a cold blade that I had produced, sliced through two buttons on his shirt, and pressed into the skin taut over his whiskey-bloated midsection.

"I'll empty your fucking guts right here and right now all over your shoes. Give me an address. I won that bout. I drank to your terms. I expect the deal to be fulfilled."

"Houghton," Welsh says, his voice low. I expect he's trying to urge me along, to hustle a bit. I can still see the gathering forms that we are attracting more attention again and it's not like the local constabulary is going to be keen to extract us from any difficulties.

I press the knife closer, twisting just a bit.

"*Address!*" I hiss.

"Ch-chestnut street," he breathes. "A family there with an old woman."

"Christ almighty, sir, I *will kill you*. Do you understand this? A family with an old woman on Chestnut Street. You must understand that I don't even know the Chestnut Street in this city, and I can assure you I will burn it all to the ground to find this one hunky. So, lest you want that on your conscience and what's left of your long and stupid life, I suggest you sink into the details a little bit more."

I mark the period on that sentence by an actual cut on his fat stomach, sinking the blade in, less than an inch, just enough to separate the flesh, for him to feel his own blood falling warmly down his parchment skin and the front of his trousers, all over my hand.

"N-no!" he gurgles. "Please!"

I move the knife to the side, just less than an inch, and I feel the hot, sticky blood trickling down the blade to my fingers.

"Third block," he whispers, his voice hoarse and quavering, "I don't know the number! On the right, half a house."

I shove at his throat with my elbow again, growling, teeth clenched. He turns his head, cringing.

"I don't! *I don't know!*"

I release him, pulling the blade away. I wipe it on the front of his soaked shirt. "The Pennsylvania Coal and Iron Police thank you for your cooperation," I say, turning away as I sheath the knife.

I look at Welsh, whose face is pale, lined, and somehow thinner, more deeply lined than it had been just an hour before. He looked as if he'd aged 15 years.

"Houghton," he says, his voice thick with phlegm. "I've taken ill—"

He pitches forward directly onto his face, his arms flat out at his sides. A deadfall like that is called that for that exact reason and seeing this happen before my very eyes, I knew that Jimmy Welsh was a dead man as soon as he hit the ground, even if his body would still draw breath for some time.

———

Jimmy Welsh was already dead, as near as I could tell. Sure—his chest still rose and fell, if unevenly, but the growing wheeze emanating from his throat holds the portent of certain doom. If that wasn't enough, however, dozens of sores had broken out over his skin. These are not the buboes of the plague or the pustules of smallpox. These are the burns of some goddamned poison that has come ripping him from the inside out, all within hours.

As soon as I'd gotten the information from Stomach and turned to see Welsh crumple, Stomach twisted away the moment my hold on him faltered. He grasped at his wounded midsection, blood leaking between his fingers as he staggered away, yelling for help, but with the entourage of the Johnstown constabulary surrounding me. Clay harrumphed and harangued until I again reminded him of my affiliation. Wordlessly, he motioned his men to carry Welsh to the Cambria Iron hospital.

"It won't be long now, I'm afraid," says the doctor, glancing at me as if searching for approval, and he quickly looked away as I stared him down. Why not me? Perhaps an aggressive formula of some type; perhaps it's just my same damnable luck as always. The same luck that earned me the medals rather than the holes.

"It's the internal injuries, you see," the doctor continues. He raises his hands, drops them. "Infection soon . . . poison burning him."

Dreaded words, of course, especially that of "infection" and it dates not back to the war for me, but to childhood. With one's mother lost in childbirth, one tends to grow up with it; the death follows one around, just as assuredly as the poison surging through Jimmy's body. I hold onto the grim reminder of how many times I had felt during and after the war . . . *that could be me. Easily.*

But it isn't. I flex my fingers into fists and relax them once again.

The sawbones continues, "Perhaps they threw something in his drink."

I close my eyes and exhale. *Of course that's what they did.*

They had given me the dose that further stoked my boilers. Whatever they had given to Welsh was something far worse. Had they mixed them up?

Or done this with every intention?

Someone with the local police, perhaps.

I open my eyes, exhaling slowly, staring down at the misshapen, diminished Welsh. If I hadn't known better about such things, I'd have thought of it as a curse.

Still . . . I had a street, and a block, and a description from the flabby old man. That is where the next steps will lead.

"Sorry, Jimmy," I say as I put my hat back on. I'm still cruising on the high from the fight; still cruising on the notion that I have even more targets than normal fastened to me; still boiling from the rage that they had courted by stoking my fire.

I give Welsh one last nod, then the same to the doctor. I leave the room without looking back.

Chapter Seven

I cannot help but think that what I see here is the end of the world.

"I know what you all think of me." I pause to catch my breath, feeling the sweat mingling with the rain and drenching the skin of my back, my shirt sticking to the flesh. "I'm the devil, that I'm some type of anti-Christ. Here, what you don't seem to factor, is that I'm just doing my fucking job. If all of you would just do the same, and not consort with the types like Magursky and his ill-fated friends, I wouldn't be coming up here and doing . . . this." I point down at the man, still spitting his teeth out. One tooth rolls into a crack in the floor and disappears. Everyone gazes at the disappearance, as if stunned something like that could happen.

I had come to this house on Chestnut Street, this structure fresh with the smell of glue and lumber, following a group of the most-mustachioed men to their neighborhood. I had sent another telegram back to Harrisburg, telling them of Jimmy Welsh and did not bother to wait for a reply. I had the scent, and this Yellow Dog was going to go after it, re-earn, and remind all of these types what the Coal and Iron Police was willing to do to get a job done.

I didn't blend in terribly well, being relatively clean-shaven and half a head or more taller than these new imports to the country. I followed as discreetly as I could, keeping the sap half-drawn from my sleeve and in my palm, one of the secreted in the other. I followed the man into the upstairs of the four-split house, him turning to face me too late, as I was already on him with the derringer pointed and the tip of the sap at his chin.

I pushed through the door and announced my presence, telling them all to sit. The man who had opened the door and who stood in front of me shouted instructions, a family of seven with a couple of cousins or nephews taking up even more room. And the older generation, too, as I now see a horrifically ugly old woman, the shape and hue of a corpse but still moving, staring at me.

The crone—so misshapen I could barely even look at her, more scarred than many I'd seen in the battles—just gave me a horrific, single-toothed grin. Her lips, etched deeply with the lines of age and cracked with dryness despite the pouring rain and sopping surroundings, draw back and give me a perfect view of diseased gums. "Oh, not the anti-Christ. Not you, certainly not you."

"I'm not sure who you're talking about, madam," I say. "Certainly this era has a plentiful amount of figures lacking morals and character, and more come to this country every day. As if we didn't breed enough of our own."

The old crone's clouded eyes bore into mine. Is she *truly* blind?

Her voice comes, quaking, cracking, creaking: "There is an evil coming, born on this year, not but a month ago. If only his own mother had strangled him with the umbilical cord and cast him away with the afterbirth, the world would be a better place. Instead, darkness will rule. For decades."

I can't help but to steal another glance out the window. If anything, the skies achieve an even deeper darkness, complete with ominous, jaundiced yellow around the edges. It's not sunlight, this much I can tell. Instead, it's the sick hue of clouds careening against other clouds, the lightning flashing and arcing from cloud to cloud, and not yet to the ground. Rumbles of thunder end her pronouncement.

She sits back then, smiling at me with her handful of crooked, yellow, and half-pointed teeth.

Even I can't go so far as to beat an insane and demented old woman who thinks herself a witch. It's been two centuries since that type of song and show occurred in New England, and we can do even longer without it now. This flashes as yet another part of the problem in trying to regrow the "old country" into the new.

I would give them some credit; they kept this tiny four-room home with the lot of them in here workmanlike and cleaner than what I had thought it would be. I glance at the kitchen woodstove, the rickety cylinder of the chimney poking directly outside; something was cooking on the top. The table was nearby, surrounded by the chairs, feeling the thin, dark planks of wood flooring yielding, ever so slightly, to my own weight. There are weapons to hand, but at least no hands near them . . . yet. I turn my gaze back to them.

"I need to know where I can find Magursky," I say slowly, although it's also perfectly obvious to me that the woman understands and speaks English without any difficulty. Accented, yes, but she has no struggles with meaning.

"He's long gone by now, Coal and Iron Police. Long gone in this time and in any other."

I rethink my reticence to not use the sap on her, but one blow would undoubtedly kill her stone dead where she sits.

"That's as clear as the sewage I see running through the streets," I say. Instead of the cudgel, I busy myself with rolling a cigarette and lighting it. I offer none to her, nor her silent surrounding Greek chorus. "Magursky," I say again. "I'll not stop until I burn every one of these flophouse hovels down to get the answer that I need."

She knows. I know it . . . she knows I know.

"I'm sure you have the will to do that, Coal and Iron Police. And your own bosses may expect that from you."

"They expect results. That's what I'm paid to get." *Paid,* I think. *Right.*

The man and his son and daughter gather some chairs around the room. Of course, there aren't even enough for all of them, let alone me as well. I tell them all to sit where they are. I go to the chair nearest a wall, an ashtray already there and half-filled with expended tobacco and ash.

"So you too are labor, then?" the crone's wavering yet powerful voice cuts through the dry, smoky air, this tinder of fumes.

I stay silent, exhaling smoke from my nostrils.

"I do not know this Magursky, Mister Coal and Iron. None in this house do. What I can sense however is that it might be that you should meet with him perhaps with a different intent than the one that you say you have. You may have more in common than you thought. He might even be, dare I say, an ally for you, as *you* labor."

I do not have time for this same trail of horseshit that's led me everywhere but to the man that I've been sent to apprehend.

"You are too stupid to see, Mister Coal and Iron. You look down at us, those that come to this country now. You forget how *your* people, the *English*, got it. They raped and tore and burned, as did the Spanish. As in the Old Country, so in the new. But in your stupidity, you do not see this. You do not see how things are *connected*."

I light a cigarette and stare at the old woman, trying to figure out the difference between burgeoning fascination and an abrupt collapse into boredom. It's not like I hadn't heard any of this stuff before, the Avil Oy from the fucking Irish or any of the other ridiculous shite that one encounters from the Swiss or the Germans. I throw the smoking match on the floor.

"Something sinister arises there, Mister Police, Mister English, Mister *American*. Something sinister over there *right* now which will mean that there are those of us in this room right now—" she casts a cloudy gaze around at us—"that will remember this day and will rue it. Now and forever, and the children of the children will too. Something sinister there, something horrible here. Time and space, distance and memory."

I'd love nothing more but to burn down these rabbit shacks with the occupants piled together in a rodent den. And take perhaps several into custody; I did have some more colleagues besides Jimmy in and around the area, and given the PRR's famous efficiency, it would be a matter of only hours, rather than days or weeks, before they would also be riding into town. And instead of a slow, leisurely horse's walking pace, it would be at the speed of the trains themselves that ran in and out of this town with such alacrity and drive. Such daydreams are wont to put a smile on my face, undoubtedly sending a further confusing communication to the old woman and her ilk in this crowded, boiling room.

I grind the half-smoked cigarette out in the rough clay ashtray, twisting the glowing end into a column of smoke, exhaling the last remnants of the same from my lungs. The crone just stares at me with her sightless eyes and nearly-toothless grin, almost the perfect parody of what the local newspapers would have undoubtedly described her.

I surge to my feet, knocking my chair backward with my knees. The hand had just appeared in my far peripheral vision, and I lurch to the left, spinning, reaching out and grabbing the wrist.

The man who'd been introduced as a nephew—who was now holding a derringer not unlike my own—has no time.

I jerk and twist on his arm at the same time, a crack so loud it could be mistaken for a gunshot.

It wasn't. It was his arm.

He screams, the derringer that had been pointed at my head tumbling to the floor. It didn't discharge, thanks be to Christ, because that would have likely been the perfect ironic end to one of us in the room.

I continue the motion, pulling the broken arm toward me and then spinning more, bodily throwing him across the room as he crashes into a too-small table laden with cheap dinnerware for a family of many generations sharing the room. The man screams, an eardrum-piercing animal shriek as he comes to a stop amidst falling plates and cups. He turns fetal, clutching his arm, face frozen in a rictus of agony.

I spin round again, drawing the twin .45 Colt Peacemakers, thumbing the hammers back on each one. My own derringer is in my coat pocket, the other still safely strapped about my calf and ankle.

"I've got enough in here to smoke all of you," I say. "You make one move and I'll be sure to send you right to hell."

The man with the broken arm still shrieks so I turn back toward him and point the left pistol at him. "And you, sir, can shut the fuck up before I ventilate you and make the arm the least of your worries."

"H-he won't be able to work now, not with the arm like that . . ." says another one of the younger men in the room, eyes wide and welling.

"Maybe he should have thought of that prior to trying to put a bullet in me. Exactly what were you planning anyway? You're on the third floor of this building. It's not like I'm easy to carry and hide."

After a pause, the crone says, in her blistered voice and strange, trilling accent, "You'd be easy enough once in pieces."

I narrow my eyes. I find a grin pulling at the corners of my mouth. "Old lady, I'm starting to like you."

I draw in another sigh, looking away from her. "I want to know where Magursky is. I know you people—" my eyes flash to the old woman—"know *something* about where I might be able to find him. Now, tell me, or I'll be breaking some more bones."

"He—" starts the younger man.

The old woman spits something out in an unintelligible language. The young man looks at her, eyes suddenly very, *very* tired, and he looks back to me. "I don't know for sure. But I did hear that he was in Mineral Point."

"Where's that?"

"North of here just some ways. Upriver."

More water. How can one possibly refuse?

"There are trains that run next to it all the time from Cambria, and Johnson Rail. You won't have any trouble getting up there to look around."

"Indeed," I agree. "And how do I know he's still there?"

The young man's mouth opens, again as if to say something, but he shuts it on his own this time. "I'm sorry, but that is all that I do know."

I take a deep breath, glancing back at the broken-armed man, still wailing and rocking back and forth, clutching his arm. "If I go there and I find out that you've sent me on some type of goose chase, I'll come back here *before* I continue my search for Magursky. And you'll like it even less than you do right now."

"Sir, I am telling you the truth. Mineral Point is the place where I last heard that Magursky would be."

I holster one of the pistols. "And how, exactly, do you know this?"

He breathes out. "One hears things . . . many things . . ."

That is almost certain, he sees, to trigger in me a desire to extract more information; I don't even need to take the step forward. He stammers out again, "This group said that he wasn't welcome here, but they also said not yet. They said to try a cousin up north, up around the mines there. No one was going to be sticking their neck out, down here, not yet. Not until they got some more interest growing where we wouldn't be seen so much." He shakes his head. "You think you're the only one. Cambria's got men in every crew, reporting back to the bosses, the bosses reporting back to their bosses, and so on. There's no way. Just no way down here, not yet."

The old woman makes another growling sound, peppering it with incomprehensible syllables that I assume are some type of bizarre cursing. Or even perhaps curses themselves. I wasn't sure if these people might have even been Gypsies, so little do I understand or care to understand about where they are from or what they do.

I stare at the young man. "Mineral Point," I repeat, as if trying the words out on my own.

He nods.

I hold up the wrinkled and spotted rendering of Magursky and point at it with the muzzle of the Peacemaker that I'm still holding. "And this man. This is the man that you know as Magursky and he is there."

He nods with less enthusiasm this time, but it does not seem to be one of evasion. It is one of resignation. I see now that their fear of reprisals, perhaps from Magursky or even from other workers around, is close to their fear of me and the companies. I slowly fold the likeness up and replace it in my jacket pocket.

"Thank you." I turn back around then and glance at the man still writhing on the floor. I don't know if I'd have apologized even if I'd needed to.

I close the door firmly behind me and take the stairs two at a time. I'm on the hunt now. I have the scent and I can trail it. The steps spring up to meet the bottoms of my shoes, and it's still early yet; I can make it to Mineral Point in an hour with Amos, maybe even less. With each breath I draw, I can still hear the crunch of the man's arm. I'm used to that; what I'm not used to is that it doesn't fade as the moments beat past.

"And I persecuted this way unto death, binding and delivering into prisons both men and women . . ."

———

Some thought that it was going to end when we hanged the last of the Maguires. I knew that it wasn't going to be that simple, and it wasn't just because of the fact that I was new at this whole thing when we just rolled them all up and I didn't want to miss out on all of the excitement. Truth is, the Maguires were what they were for the time they were there. But times are different now, the police are different now, and industry is different now. The people coming in, they make things different too, and I've certainly changed during that same time.

If the Molly Maguires were any lesson at all, it's that the movements and the supporters alike can spend decades, generations even, dedicated to their cause. Only some fools in Harrisburg and perhaps scattered around in different counties of the Commonwealth thought that it ended the decade before. Even when we hanged the ones we did, we at least were under no illusions. The words "Molly Maguires" just started to appear to people as being something from the past. Something too like the Sons of Vulcan, who never disappeared but instead just changed their shape and form. Johnstown and the mighty Cambria facilities might have been spared most of the discontent up until now under the steady and watchful eyes of a prudent Quaker for decades, but that didn't mean that the other ones had his abilities, much less the measures of generosity that tended to show. This was not a case of a single bad apple, but a good apple in a bin of rotting ones. Eventually there was going to be a soft spot and the worms would burrow their way in. Morrell the Quaker died a handful of years ago and it should surprise no one here that what was once admiration and affinity for Cambria will now change to something else, either because Cambria and the surrounding mines were going to be a bit different than what they were, or the fact that the rotten apples around this state and others would feel quite free to spread the disease to this isolated spot, transforming the lazy and hazy iron town to a set of restless hills.

I had been thinking a lot about the coal miners, especially given my experience with the Maguires out east and most of my roving workadays about the Commonwealth, along with the fact that so many men would run as quickly as possible from the coal mines to get to work within the mills if they could. The thing is, at least as I could see, working with the molten steel and iron wasn't any safer. Over the past few years in Pittsburgh, a bunch of men were killed: asphyxiation, scalding, burns, falls into the ladles of molten steel—a particularly gruesome way to go. One can't help but think of what that must be like, the last few moments on earth, as you lose your balance on the catwalk, struggling to right yourself and then realizing you've failed and you're tumbling, screaming, falling into the white-hot vat. The temperature of the air as you get close so, in theory, at least, you'll already have lost consciousness and even broiled and steamed your sweetbreads before you contact the molten metal; more likely still that you'll be on fire before you do anyway. It's all academic, as they say, after just a couple of seconds anyway.

Savor it, I figure, as those are likely to be the longest two seconds of your life.

I don't know how often this has happened in the history of John-stown, or is happening still. I stopped looking at the numbers when I started to realize that it didn't matter to get done what I had to get done. Given the rates of accidents in the Pittsburgh mills, the fact that it is common knowledge seems to be reminder enough that the men who take their risks, and the families who watch them do it pray for their safe return day in and day out; these prayers are not so regularly answered as many of them might wish. Mill or mine—it doesn't matter to me any more than it matters to the dead.

Nearby is the world's first railroad tunnel, a wonder that had never been seen before, and not a single life had been lost during its construction. The rest of the town, like so many others in the area and throughout the state, is the same: coal. The bigger towns now are steel, leaving the small company patches like this one to be the standard bearer for the fuels. This town, like so many others that I've visited over the past two decades, contains the home, work, and leisure of all of the residents. Sometimes even I had to go along with where they were on things like scrip money and the company store. Then again, no one asked them to come here, and no one asked them to mine for a living, any more than I had asked for what I had become either.

Such are the times.

Mineral Point heaves into view as Amos trudges along, as if growing resentful at the imposition that my repeated presence seems to cause him. Not that I could blame the animal. The horrific conditions beggar description. I've had roughly two hours of fitful sleep; some of it the lingering effect of whatever drug had been given, then Welsh's collapse, the encounter with the strange old woman and her family, and then the trek north of the city this morning to this little town, defying anyone's impression of what would be a hotbed of labor discontent. The cold water pelting us all from far above reminds me in some sad way of the grapeshot that ruined so many men on the fields twenty-some years before. As the horse trudges up the path next to the railway bed, my own body and head bobs with each passing step. We both try to push as close to the edge of the woods as possible, away from the trains trundling past every few minutes, and I think of the years that have passed since my birth in 1844. It's a different country, to be sure, and, more to the point, I am a different man. I like to think about it in terms of the war, especially when I'm feeling all of the bumps and scars in my forearm and other places on my body.

A sequence of squalid noises rolls through the heavy air, and I turn to look back down the way that we had come up, a section of the earth dissolving under the assault from gravity and the rain. The chunk of land drifts downslope, a muddy roiling mess, taking a section of trees, boulders, and ferns with it.

I watch, fascinated, as the land-island, now cut loose, spins slowly on its own axis as it travels just downriver to Mineral Point. It piles into the culvert next to the railroad bed; at first, it appears the saga will end there, but instead, it hits the telegraph poles and knocks them over, snapping their wires with a sharp blue spark. What was left of their communications is now gone, perhaps for days. The lines had already been downed; this was guaranteed to cut the town off for even longer. Given this weather and this landscape, the work involved in restoring it would be formidable.

Well, the fine people of the Mineral Point aren't going to be talking to anybody anytime soon anyway. More's the pity, given the fact that I have every intention of dragging a body out for all to see and to photo, put it in the papers, and hang the pictures from the walls.

I check my watch—nearly two o'clock now, the height of the afternoon, really, if only someone could see it as such. I sigh again, turn, pat Amos's muzzle one more time, and then proceed.

The rain pours off the brim of the cap, yet another funnel of it running onto Amos. We both ignore it, the best that we can. There had already been a couple feet of water running through the streets in the hotel as I left; the Conemaugh river looks like a red and purple rippling bruise flowing through the land.

I'd have quite a hard time, I think, attempting to replicate the effectiveness of some of the gentlemen who might be better at this job than I am. I, just like many others within the C&I, were charged with the tasks of breaking bones and hacking various pieces off various people. Allan Pinkerton, however, did a little bit more than that, not only trading on his favors in the War but also, God help us all, learning from it.

Allan Pinkerton, the famous man that everybody knows, who just shuffled from this mortal coil a few years ago after biting off his own tongue. I cannot say if that was ironic or not, except for the notion that perhaps he spoke out of both sides of his mouth from time to time. He also spoke frequently, and at great length, mostly about himself.

My own remembrances of him were, like everything else, what I heard about during his feats during the War, but more personally about meeting him and two others: Jim McParland, a spy that Pinkerton had somehow gotten into the ranks of the Maguires, and then Bob Linden, a man that I knew from my earliest days with the Coal and Iron Police.

The War made me, but the actions around the Maguires re-made me, just as it was remaking the Commonwealth and even most of all of industry and enterprise. They made the men like Pinkerton and McParland too, though on a different level than myself. Indeed, Pinkerton had some sort of major authorship role in the events affecting the nation. Friend of statesmen and presidents. McParland was able to do what I was never able to, which was to persuade people that he was their friend.

No one ever would have mistaken me for their friend, even with the commendations from the Army. That got me the job with the C&I, and then I did the rest to make sure that the C&I force kept me paid. That's what the world is; if you're not getting paid, you can't put food on your plate, you're lost. These new babbling waves of immigrants would have had better chances than I do. You can't go home again, as the saying goes, and that is doubly true in my case, my family and the family farm in Fulton County are essentially all but gone.

While Pinkerton sold his way into prominence by being good at what he did, McParland did what he could do by his own guile and charm, taking the role of being a part of the Maguires and, the whole time, sending reports to Linden and Pinkerton. And then the action came down to men like me, men with the guns and the clubs.

I didn't hate the Maguires, despite their violence and their mentality. I didn't feel envy or jealousy of much of anything, in fact, for Pinkerton, although, like most everyone, I did find myself admiring McParland.

I didn't even hate the Rebels, not really. I thought, and still think, that they're stupid and wrong and traitors, but to me, that's the same thing as blaming a rat for being what it is.

The first man I was able to really get a visceral hate for was a man named Franklin Gowen, a first-rate villain of greed who would have sold his own daughter and mother into whoredom for a halfpenny. He would pass himself off as yet another one of these goddamn titans of industry and he was nothing but a crook, swindler, and a first-rate son of a bitch. He conned his investors, he conned the government, and he conned us all. Such a businessman that he continually drove his own prosperous business into bankruptcy twice and had to have his rich banker friends throw him a lifeline, sucked from the government tit, and did everything he could to be like Carnegie and Frick. Those rich bastards are shysters too, but at least I'll grant the point that they've had success. Gowen was just a lucky, brash, incompetent, and greedy fool. I've worked for far too many of that type.

I've never really been one who would be able to suitably blend in, to move through others' ranks with nice-sounding puffery, never truly been able to ingratiate myself to anyone that might signal a display of trust beyond that of the merely contractual. In one sense, I suppose, it's due to my appearance—a big hulking fellow, to use one of the kinder turns of phrase I've heard in reference to myself, but that's just to start. Next would be the description of all the scars; it's almost like my own song that could be sung. I suspect that many simply assume that I caught the rough end of a brawl, which is true in more ways than one.

It is inevitably only for a short time that I'm capable of doing so; I reckon that these small bursts may be what keep me on my feet.

When one bothers to get past my monstrous appearance, one finds the person beneath isn't much different. I've never been someone whose company is sought after, only that my services be rendered and then my presence made scarce shortly thereafter.

This is not a reflection of self-pity; to the extent I would ever wonder about such things, I quickly reflect that I am glad to not be the type of man who can swim in such waters. I am unable to sell. I am unable, it seems, to pass as what would be known as the upper class, or even polite society at all. The reactions of the couple I first encountered in the hallway of the Capital underscored that most recently, as if I'd needed yet another reminder of it. My own role is not even that of the hired hand, the manservant, the butler, or the cook. I am the hand that grips and tears, the fist that pummels, the arm that shoves, and the person who separates the bodies of the masses from those of the elite. I am the opaque curtain behind which so many of my betters lurk.

I would admire men like Pinkerton and McParland but I also hated them for knowing that they were whom I could never be. Pinkerton defended the President, while I defended the Union. My name is pressed into some archive somewhere in Washington DC, buried beneath piles of papers bearing other names of the lost and forgotten. Pinkerton became wealthy and famous beyond his wildest dreams, the wildest understood American dream. McParland became less famous, less prosperous, but still cosmically more than anything that I could ever hope for. I never did want to be famous, but being rich, or at least having some type of money, wouldn't be bad.

And yet, when I look around, and I see these bedraggled men and women coming from faraway places, the stinking-garlic and gibber-ish-speaking nations of Eastern and Southern Europe and God alone knows where else, and I see myself far better off than they are. Who am I to complain? How many of them would get an account with which they can stay at a hotel like the Capital? No matter how many of them carry rocks and ore and iron, I must be a different type of force indeed. They'd have been used to being smashed like bugs by the so-called nobil-ity within their own country, and now they carry the weight that makes the nobility noble in this one.

On yet another hand, I suspect that none too many of them are carrying around the lead and iron inside of them the way they are, fired at me by traitors and those who want to enslave others. More recent days though I see that there are many different types of slavery. What trans-pired in the South was a disgusting and unholy mess, and yet the condi-tions I see around me is this old wine turned vinegar in stained bottles. This mass of humanity, crushing against the land itself, all in the hopes that anything here is better than what they left, is left like a simmering cauldron of hate left to boil. I shake my head. I grit my teeth against the bitterness I taste, which I recognize as my own servitude, pulling against a yoke of my own fate and consequence.

This is pointless. Even the Governor is carrying shrapnel.

It's difficult to believe my life has come to this, I think, wondering for not the first time what my family's old farm must look like now? Who owns it? What had happened to my parents and my grandfather, my brothers? I had not been home, properly, in more than a decade. I had not tried any letters. I lost them, and they lost me.

This too is pointless, I think, as I trot Amos across the tracks and then across the bridge over the swollen and angry river. With the steep hills not just in abundance, but everywhere, the amount of water running down their sides must be astronomical. I see branches and other debris riding downstream, bobbing in and out of view in the cascading waves.

I peer upriver through the driving rain. Despite the green leaves of what remains of the trees, everything is brown and drab. The mud courses down the hillsides, carving its own paths through the contours and dumping soil, silt, and worms into the river. The coal smoke from the stacks and houses alike, along with the smoke and steam of the loco-motives, painted the hillsides with black and gray grime, at least half the trees stripped bare from the black clouds clinging to the hills and valleys. The gravel bedding beneath the steel rails is streaked with grime from the same smoke, along with all of the brake dust cast away as the trains roll past. All of it then, eventually, gets to the river—rolling and boiling with a fury today, and likely most days—and then carries it downriver to Pittsburgh and then into Ohio. The tree trunks glide past, popping in and out of the confined and raging surf. They might end up at the next curve downriver. Or, it seems, they might travel down to New Orleans and float out in the Gulf of Mexico. I picture myself making that journey too, someday, or maybe even today. Just another thing floating downri-ver through the shadows of the mills and mines.

The town, Mineral Point, is a span of houses perched between the river—today as inflamed and angry and swollen as I'd seen a river to be—and the steep hillside. The houses defy the pitch of the land, it seems, the dirt tracks and roads just tributaries of mud and grime, making me wonder if they too will serve as greased chutes to channel the houses into the boiling river.

And this goddamn rain.

I tie Amos to a hitch in front of a railroad tower that houses the telegraph office, anything connecting the mines to the other mines up and down river. A train whistle screams in the distance. Despite the sight of the wires and the noise of the trains, I feel insulated and cut off, even as close as this is to Johnstown and probably other coal patches.

No sooner had I walked through the front door of the office, water streaming from my cloak, and produced my Coal and Iron badge, when the clerk starts to speak.

"It might . . . it might be a good thing for you to ride back down to Johnstown, sir. Tell them we need help up here . . . we've been cut off without any type of wires or word for a couple of hours now."

I stare back at the man, feeling the grim concrete settle into my expression. "I'm not a messenger," I reply. "I'm here for Magursky, period, and I don't give a shit about anything else right now."

"But—"

I grip the badge harder, thrusting it forward. "Harrisburg sent me to find him, and now I'm here in Mineral Point, finding him. He may be alive, he may not be. But there's no way in hell I'm riding all the way back down there, not in this shitting weather."

I feel a pounding in my temples—it was only a matter of time for this to happen anyway, I realize—and I study the clerk, a man of medium build and obviously someone who had been consumed with his worry about the events going on outside. The weather is, after all, probably the only type of excitement that one might get in a town like Mineral Point. Except, too, for the possibility of Magursky and his ilk that would be coming up through here, invading people's homes, and, in so doing, invading the homes owned by the company.

I take a deep breath and put the badge back on my vest, obscuring it once again with a judicious tug of the lapel.

A woman sits at the telegraph desk, one hand poised over the signal lever, another spread flat over a notebook. Every so often she taps the lever a time or two, studying the workings of the machine to see if anything comes back. She does it and then turns back to us, her eyes lingering on me just for a moment before switching to the clerk. She shakes her head and glances at the rain pouring down the windows.

I unfold the poster with Magursky's likeness and hold it up, the paper now weak with water, the ink running and the rest of it fading in spots. Still, it's enough.

"This is the man I'm looking for. Istvan Magursky. Hungarian and asshole. Likes to stir people up, likes to get people hurt. I'm here to either take him to Harrisburg, or hurt him, or both. Now, goddammit, I *know* he's here and I need you to tell me, right now, where I'll be able to catch up with him."

"Sir, you must understand . . . I realize that you're searching for this gentleman, and I know that the Coal and Iron force is the group charged with sorting out problems of this nature, but we would not know of something like this."

I swallow my frustration after a beat of a head-flooding fantasy of sapping this fool too. "You—" I point at both the clerk and the woman—"both work at the telegraph office and are aware of all messages conveyed in this area, and you're telling me that you have no knowledge of labor unrest in a town which is barely larger than your office? When everyone knows each other? When everyone is working in the same mine?" I lean across the counter, allowing my cloak and coat to open a bit and display my full armamentarium. "I find that damnably difficult to believe."

"They're not gonna be in any of the houses," the woman says, looking at me, and then returning to the silent wire set in front of her. "The Pinkertons and the company men make sure of that. They're rousing them up something fierce, probably makes your job a lot harder." She shrugs, still staring at the equipment. "It's like all of you are playing the same game. Just with different dice."

Outside, water drops beat against the thin glass and the tin of the roofs. Amos stands stoically in the rain, occasionally ruffling an ear or blinking away some water. *She's right.*

"Where about is there any shelter then? If not in a house." Not that I believe everything I hear, but from what I can see, Mineral Point is tiny enough and it's unlikely that someone with Magursky's profile is going to remain secret for too long. Unless I just got lied to. Which is perfectly possible, and which makes me aware that I'm going to have an hour or more ride back into Johnstown to savor what I'll do to that same family that sent me on this chase upriver.

"It's probably the tunnel," the clerk says, stammering, eyes wide and staring at me. Something had shifted in my deportment, apparently, the clerk picking up on it as I had considered the damage that I was about to inflict. "Some place where they could meet, talk, and plan things out, sir. That's the only place I can think of, the tunnel."

"The railroad tunnel?" I ask. I look outside, across the roll of the tracks to the upstream and uphill part of the tracks and the tunnel's plane.

"That would be as good a spot as I can think of, sir. I'm sorry," he continues, holding his hands up once again, "but I have no truck with any of those types, sir."

"I am sure that's correct." This man either hasn't had much in the way of hard labor or was chased out of it, judging by the spareness of his frame.

"I do know, sir, that there are camps out there, near the tunnel. Some say they're just typical people moving through on foot and looking for work. Others, more to the line that you might be looking for, officer. You and many others. Perhaps you know of it—it's called the Staple Bend."

"Indeed." I light a cigarette. "No word on when this might lift, I suppose?"

"No, sir, like we said, we've not had any communications for hours now. I imagine there have been some landslides, knocked a pole or two down. Word must reach Johnstown, sir. The waters *must* be cresting the dam at the Club."

I nod, thinking less about that possibility and more about the fact that Magursky could slip away amidst all of this confusion.

The woman taps out a few more attempts at her telegraph. She waits for a few moments and sits back, closing her eyes. "Still not a single thing," she says.

I sigh and nod, still smoking, not looking forward to the return to the elements. So close now, though, if that is where he is. Still, it's the only solid information I've had since coming into the city. If I didn't check it, I'd have left something significant hanging out in the open. If he's not there, then I'll have time enough to get back into the city and ask some questions.

Maybe I'll have to be more insistent on the answers that I've not been getting; I'll start with that horrible old woman in the tenement and then, just maybe, move onto Strickland or even Chief Clay himself.

"A campsite, you say?" I ask.

"Yes sir, a couple of miles around the bend you see on that hillside." The clerk presses his lips together into a thin smile. "Well, you would be able to see the bend on a day that isn't best suited for Noah and his tribe. You can see the campfires up there on some evenings. Perhaps hobos, perhaps not."

And Noah did according unto all that the Lord commanded him. *Staple Bend? So be it.*

CHAPTER EIGHT

Good luck getting a fire started in this shit.

I finally succeed, lighting a cigarette half-sodden from the wet and smoking my way through it the best that I can, letting it dangle from my bottom lip. I exhale the gouts of smoke from my nostrils, the same smoke mixing with the mist and splash from the weather. I've got two more. One more for the walk, and then after that, one more cigarette to smoke, either lit after my successful conclusion with Magursky, or that they'll be lighting up in celebration over my corpse.

The rain pours down as if it had no other nature in these stinking surroundings except to drive mud down the steep hillsides. I tie Amos to a tree that offers just as much shelter as possible, put the blanket on him, and pull it over the top of his head, between his ears, to give him just as much protection as I can. I stroke his nose a bit and scratch the spot between his eyes. I give him a handful of oats. He sniffs at it, looks at me with a tired resignation, and eats it out of my hand.

"Good boy," I whisper, rubbing his face one more time. "Stay here. I'll be back in a few." I pull the shotgun from the scabbard and pull the blanket down to obscure the rifle. I also rearrange a couple of the supply bags off the sides of the saddle to be in plain view, reading PENNSYLVANIA COAL AND IRON POLICE. "I'll be right back," I say again. With a body slung over my shoulder, with any luck at all.

I turn around, looking at the bend in the abandoned railway bed. Somewhere down this road is Magursky, the culmination of this journey. I check my pistols, dunking two shells into the shotgun breech and

snapping the action closed with a wet metal click. Amos blinks his eyes
at the noise. For some reason, I brush the rain from the barrels with my
bare hand, the water drops flinging from my fingertips and in an instant,
the rain has replaced the water that I had just brushed off.

The things that you do when you're about to go kill someone.

———

I walk the trail, the shotgun held at a relaxed port arms. As always
with such a stroll, I'm put back in the position of my boyhood home in
the hills and fields of Fulton County, awaiting the arrival of an ill-fated
squirrel or rabbit that I'd convert into some type of foodstuff for the family. I even thought about it this way, at times, when on a specific detail
in the war. Of course, the squirrels and the rabbits wouldn't and couldn't
return fire, unlike Magursky, but right now I am thinking that the word
I was given is as solid as any I'd ever been given in trying to find this
troublesome ghost. I know where he will be, but, with any luck, he won't
know where I'm coming from. He came here as a part of his rotation in
going around the state looking for sympathetic audiences who might buy
his charade of a better life.

He does, however, know that I'm coming for him. There can be little
question of that. There will be no strategic surprise here, but I have hope
that there will be a tactical one, and it will be in my favor.

The rain is even colder now despite the calendar date, my clothes
completely sodden and my boots and the bottoms of my trousers heavy
with mud. Every step I take squishes in the soft ground; with each lift
of my foot, the suction of the turf drags at it and releases it only after
a struggle and with a wet sound. I have two choices here, as I'm in the
middle of two paths. I can stick to the old railroad bed and have better
footing—and thereby be readily visible to all comers—or I can slip into
the woods. The problem with the second option is that the topography
of the woods, like everywhere else in this cursed, damnable spot on the
map, is that the hill again gets suddenly steep, with ruined wood and
dead trees from the smoke and stinking steam strangling them, the fallen
trunks slippery in the rain and littering any type of path. It would take
me three times as long to pick my way through that as opposed to even
struggling in the mud between the woods and the gravel.

I spit the remnant of the drenched cigarette from my mouth.

"Fuck it," I say aloud, my mouth and throat suddenly dry, an enormous irony considering the rain and the raging Conemaugh below me on the right, over the side of the hill.

I feel that a few minutes have passed, but I know it probably has been longer. My sense of distance traveled is probably better than the internal clock anyway, particularly on a dark and drenched day like this one, when the sky is etched in permanent twilight and weeps for the knowledge of it. I hear a faint train whistle over the roar of the river running below, but I can't be sure. Upriver a ways is what I know to be an engineering marvel, the Conemaugh Viaduct, a bridge spanning one of the deep gorges among these rolling hills and the main reason why the section of the track that I'm walking by now had been abandoned. I can still smell the sintered metal hanging in the air despite the rain and the silence—the stink of locomotives, the stink of the coal dust and mud in the soil and streams, the remnants of the smoke from the mills downriver still clinging to the remains of the trees, the bark, the rocks, the soil.

What time? How much time does he have to try to flee again?

It's after two, that much I know. With each step forward, my pace slows a bit while the pace of the seconds beating by stays the same.

I move with ease, a solid pace, keeping my movements smooth, deliberate, and purposeful over the longer spaces between the tree trunks, eyes watching in front of me and downhill to my right, watching the heavy fog wrapping around the trees, as a hunter watches for a deer. Days like today don't work too well when one is attempting to stick to the shadows; on the other hand, with this ongoing storm, there is nothing but a world of a single shadow. The rain and the mist cut my visible range to thirty or forty yards, automatically within range of the scattergun. The breezes blow currents and pockets through the fog, sudden clarity looming in front; another advantage of the shotgun was the speed with which I could wield it, bringing it to bear in an instant.

I stop again, also noticing the fog coming from my own exhalations. I slow my breath, easing out every cycle and slowing.

I'm not sure how far Magursky has made it into these woods; I cannot even be sure that he's back here at all, except for all of the testimony I'd gathered so far pointing that way. The staff at the telegraph and rail station had related the campfires and the Tunnel; I'm not sure how much I could trust that possibility, but it seems reasonable, especially today.

Given the lack of any knowledge, solid and complete or otherwise, that I'd gotten over the past couple of days, anything had to be acted on. I was wary of a trap, of course, as it wouldn't take long to set one up, but at the same time, it's not like I had a choice; the point of this entire excursion had been to retrieve Magursky, dead or alive. And if the latter, preferably physically destroyed to the point where he would not be traveling, mingling, conversing, or in any way communicating with the vulnerable masses and thereby encouraging them to rise up against their nobles and slave owners.

Assholes.

I spit the rain from my lips and stalk forward, the shotgun at the ready in front of me. What exactly has happened since the time when I would be in a forest like this in Fulton County, looking for the stray gray squirrel for the fry pan, until these days when I'm stalking a man like Magursky?

The rain is incessant, harder than it had been before over the previous day or more. Water had already been knee and, in some places, hip-deep downtown, dragging the smoke from the mill and dust from the coal closer to the earth and suffusing everything around it, the buildings and people alike. The same thing occurs outside the city as well; these small towns and coal patches are connected by rail where the roaring steam locomotives trundle the tracks and wind their way through the valleys.

There's something more about this rain; it's drowning everything else out, even in the broad and foreboding nature of it foreclosing all the sound except for its own and the occasional screech of a train whistle.

My stomach rumbles. Should have eaten . . .

"Fuck it," I say aloud again, exasperated. Fatigue seems to punctuate both the feeling and the realization at the same time. When was the last time I'd eaten? I can't remember now. I seem to recall having something shortly around the time I'd met with the Chief. I also remind myself that a man my size hardly had any indication of a need for nourishment, given my prodigious dimensions, especially in comparison to the usual wiry whippet-type of quarry that I would normally face.

I pause instead to take a drink from my flask; many might it loaded with corn liquor, but I found that impairing one's vision or balance is usually not a good thing to ingest when one still wishes to survive in an environment where one's enemies crawl and swarm like locusts. Still, it worked out well enough during my bout, I suppose.

Just ask Jimmy Welsh.

The roaring river below and the pelting rain above, along with the trickle of the cold liquid running down my throat give me the impression that everything is now water, that all were verging on melting away and rushing into some distant sea.

I see the flash and react before I even understand what's happening, throwing myself down and to the right, another flash from another angle. The crack of the Minie balls snap past me, feet above where I'm lying.

It's likely that one at least would have hit me.

So much for being ready for the trap. You just got ambushed, old son. The two solid *booms* roar and bounce through the wet woods.

The water flask tumbles away and slops down into the mud and I roll again to my left, putting more distance between myself and the shooter. I get halfway up, scrambling deeper into the woods.

Muskets. I'd know the sound of Springfields anywhere—an outdated weapon, but fortunate enough for me . . . for now.

The fact that there's a skirmisher or two out there equipped with ancient muzzleloaders was pure, blind luck on my part. If they had had a Henry or even an old single-shot Sharps, the chances are that they would be walking to find Magursky to tell him the good news right now as the rain washed away my own blood into the muddy forest floor.

If that'd been a Winchester like the one I left back with Amos, I'd likely already be dead. I curse my decision to not bring it, and I both curse and bless the fog.

Have to be more careful. My luck is going to run out. But still—how to do that? I'd been living on borrowed time for better than twenty years anyway. Perhaps even longer.

The .58 Minie ball fired by the Springfield is not a particularly fast round, especially by comparison to what's available today. Now, these two also have to go to the trouble of a manual, powder-centric reload, which isn't going to be an easy thing, not in this downpour. The fact is, despite everything else, the Springfield was a pretty accurate gun, particularly at less than 200 yards which, given the contour of this part of the country and the situation I'm in, any shot will be at least that close.

I scramble a few yards back down in the woods, again cursing that I left the Winchester. Bad decision, I think. Dumb. Especially for all of the reminders to not underestimate Magursky, you just did.

I check the breech of the shotgun, making sure it's closed tight against the rain and the elements. I'm on my side, and I peak above the side of the log I'm lying behind. I can't see anything through the squalid gray curtain of the downpour.

Two things in my favor right now—one, the length of time that it takes to reload, and now, since I somehow managed to get just lucky enough, they'll be in a hurry, so things won't go as smoothly as they'd like. Even trained and practiced soldiers have a similar problem. I learned early on that the best way to reload a muzzleloader quickly is to do it as methodically as possible. You don't gain much by rushing, and the chances of making a mistake are magnified.

The other element in my favor *is* the elements themselves. *The downpour works against them more than against me.*

Counting on the other side to be incompetent or to make a mistake is a recipe for a disaster. I've seen firsthand what those Minie balls can do to a human body. They tear open huge, gaping wounds, smashing and largely blowing an arm or even a leg completely off. Getting hit by one is pretty much a death sentence no matter where the errant round might land because the best-case scenario is that the second one is used to finish you off quickly after the first one cripples the target.

I regulate my breathing, turning my face toward the rain falling from the sky, the larger collected drops cascading from the half-bare branches and wasted leaves. Some of the trees further uphill haven't been as affected by the smoke and soot as the ones here, where it looks like an eternal charcoal November.

Thirty seconds.

I inch my way down the length of the log, rolling over and then moving forward, hunching down and carrying the shotgun in my dangling arms as I run, crouched, from tree to tree.

Fifteen seconds.

I press into the rough bark of a big cherry tree, swinging around again to my right and shouldering the shotgun.

Nothing in front of me, except for the swirling mists and pouring rain.

Have to get closer.

Closer.

Closer for me, for getting within range of the shotgun, but if I get closer to either of them—assuming there are two of them, and I don't have a third stalking me from behind—the Springfield's accuracy is going to be far better than my own. The one thing remaining in my favor is the horrible visibility.

Of course, it does mean that they also were able to see me before I was able to see them. And it was just blind, stupid luck that I was still moving, vertical, and breathing right now after the initial encounter.

I zigzag, lurching to the right and then again to the left. Both closing the distance and staying in motion were the only other ways I could get the odds in my favor.

What are the chances that it's Magursky? My heart skips a beat even more quickly as the thought flits through my head.

Chances are none at all. What I can tell is that the echoing, rolling booms of the muzzleloaders will also be a warning signal to him, made more so by the time I get around to the time of returning fire.

I switch directions again, spying a big maple. The ground's getting steeper, my feet sliding in the mud and pushing against the forest floor coverage: the sticks and twigs and rotting leaves. The scent of autumn hangs heavily over what should be a late spring air, a miasma choked deeply with the stinging smoke and metal that never fully goes away.

The clock in my head strikes its chime.

Time. The muzzleloaders are ready again if they're any good at all.

The woods are quiet except for the sound of raging nature all around. The rain gives the low drone onto the sparse leaves and the forest floor. The river crashes below me, angrier, it seems, with every passing moment. It's not just Johnstown that is going to have knee-deep water if this keeps up; everywhere else connected by these same streams and rivers is going to have to be digging away at the piles of mud once this finally clears.

I peer around the tree again, risking the right side of my face. I can see nothing in the fog other than the ghosts of my own that I've carried with me for more than twenty years. I see the ragged blue uniforms, the figures carrying their own Springfields, sometimes charging over the wall or running across an opening or even a field, but always cut down by a murderous spray of lead and fire.

Ghosts from both before and after Appomattox. Some ghosts just stop their haunts frozen in 1865, and I bear that year forward with me, and now each year comes with new haunts.

I ignore them as they swirl about.

There.

A shadow of a shadow, presaging movement. *Another mistake.* These gentlemen are definitely not experienced in this regard, but blind dumb luck also flips the dice on occasion. This one has moved closer to me, evidently too trusting of his own senses and not realizing that I had covered enough ground and come back uphill. I wait, and I listen.

I blink away the cold water running in my eyes. I can see an arm, I think, jutting out strangely from a tree trunk less than twenty yards away. I regulate my breathing and I slowly descend to one knee. I watch.

Yes.

He shifts position again, marked by the long and artificially straight shape of the muzzleloader as he tries to maneuver it.

I would certainly appreciate it if you would get just a little bit closer.

I draw a breath in and let it out slowly, holding my mouth wider so I can stay quiet and the steam from my exhalations won't be noticed. It's not a lot, admittedly, in the heavy rain and fog surrounding everything and all of us.

My right knee finally touches the soft ground. A third of the right side of my body is exposed, but my entire shape is broken up by the lower position, my silhouette interrupted by the shape of the tree.

My eyes scan yet again, even further limiting my motion, depending on my vision roving slowly over the woods around me.

He moves again. I can see the Springfield, its shape and shadow. I understand his trouble, trying to keep the rain from running into the powder.

He's going to get impatient. Or he's going to have to clean the pan and reload it.

I slowly turn my head to check on any motion behind me; nothing, other than the constantly shifting curtains of fog and rain.

I blink away more of the rain. I can no longer tell any difference between my hat, my scalp, and the rain-sodden air and woods around me. My coat and shirt cling to my torso, soaked through to my skin and scars alike. I flex my fingers on the shotgun's forearm, then around the grip with my right hand.

Come on, man. Get a move on. If you're going to panic, now would be a fine time to do exactly that.

The figure doesn't move, though, seemingly content to expect me to come directly at him from the direction that he had fired.

There's a time to unleash a more aggressive pathway, and a time not to. This is not yet the time.

I sink lower, pushing myself more into the trunk of the tree.

A wave of my hunger moves through me again and I close my eyes in annoyance, the drops hitting my squeezed eyelids. I open them and blink away the rain.

Another figure moves, from left to right. The first one, next to the tree, doesn't raise the rifle—I can see that the other man has something that looks a lot like the Springfield too—and holds one hand over the caplock in an additional effort to keep out the rain.

These are the two assholes I'm looking for right now.

Choices: continue to wait where they are, perhaps redeploying and spreading out a bit more; think that I am wounded or dead and move away from here in the direction where they had last seen me, although it looked to me like the second man had already done that and could not find anything; they could move to the right in an effort to cut me off, believing that I was able to get around them; or they could flee.

Fleeing would have been the smartest thing for them to do.

I squat, moving smoothly to the next tree, five yards ahead of me and to the right. I watch them as I do it, the noise of the storm and occlusion by the fog more than enough to hide my movement.

Being five yards closer, when already within shotgun range, is a very handy thing to have.

Patience, patience, patience, except that at some point, there is a clock ticking, with Magursky somewhere ready for his getaway and now thoroughly alerted by the rifle fire.

He's about to be alerted again.

I slide back upright, pushing into the tree trunk. In one motion, I shoulder the shotgun and step around, bringing them both into view.

"Hey, jackasses!" I yell.

Both of them freeze—one whirling in one direction, the other turning right toward me. The fog and noise of the rain had obscured the direction of my voice.

The first one, the one who had turned toward me, fumbles with his rifle, his eyes wide, his mouth opening in a silent shout.

I touch off the first barrel, the shot pattern lancing into his chest. He staggers backward, dropping his weapon, clutching at his chest, rosettes of red and pink blossoming through the shredded fabric of his shirt.

The second one turns round, just in time for his face to be met with the full charge of the second barrel. He drops like an infant's thrown toy, his face a tangled mess of flesh, blood, and bone.

I step forward, breaking the shotgun open, the spent and smoking shells arcing through the air over my shoulder, and I easily drop two fresh rounds into the breach.

I take another step, training the shotgun again on the first man, who still staggers backward, staring down at his chest, the ragged and bleeding holes cleansed by the rain and the welling crimson blossoming from rosettes into a deep purple bib. He raises his gaze to mine. His mouth hangs open and his eyes widen in shock, watery blood dripping from his fingers.

Why, doesn't he look familiar after all this?

It's Thin Beard, one of the Sons of Vulcan, one of the three who had dosed me before the so-called boxing match. And the guy who killed Jimmy Welsh.

Holding his unbelieving and shocked stare, I fire again, hitting him in the same spot.

I turn around just as the wet noise of his body collapsing to the forest floor comes to me. *That's for Jimmy.* I take a deep breath.

Magursky, I think, breaking the shotgun open once again and reloading.

CHAPTER NINE

Time presses. There's going to be a detectable difference in the noise of the shotgun compared to the Springfields. Now, Magursky's going to know—he'll know from the two evenly spaced shotgun blasts rather than the big hollow *boom* of the Springfield—that his men are down and I'm still vertical.

Still, though, charging in is going to be quite a stupid thing to do. Be deliberate, watchful. I curse myself again for not bringing my rifle.

The quarry is close now. My heartbeat hadn't changed a whit when killing the two thugs, other than from the exertion of movement. Now, however, I can feel the blood surging, the tingling in my fingers and toes, the knowledge that the hunt is on. Closer now than ever before . . . far closer . . .

I recheck the shotgun, an overwhelming urge toward detail ensuring that it's loaded and ready to kill.

I should have checked on those men, made sure they were dead. I was rushing this, at least insofar as taking a risk that I would not have even taken a week before. Given the notoriety of Magursky state-wide and the sudden focus on *my* ability in Harrisburg, I'm making decisions that I never would have before made. What is wrong with me?

I pause in my hurried creeping, lean against the tree, and force myself to come to a complete halt and *wait*.

There's one surefire way I can slow down; a smoke. Not much tobacco left. My hat is soaked and sodden to the point of absurdity, as is the rest of my attire. I take a rolled cigarette from my tobacco tin and hunch over against the rain, my match flaring and adding the smoke to the

surrounding fog. I breathe the smoke deeply into my lungs, dropping
the match into the mud and leaves and pressing into the tree behind me.

I straighten, the stinging vibrations of the tobacco leaf cascading
through my body. I exhale slowly, thinking of a dragon's breath. It's
another way to stave off the hunger as well, though I had to just get on
with this. It's too late in my life to make notes about how I live it and can
improve; my chances at improvement ended more than twenty years ago,
blood soaking into the mud. *One single job to do.*

I pad forward, the shotgun ready, as I spit the remnant of the cigarette out onto the mud. Pieces and piles of industry abound; mountains
of abandoned railroad ties; ruined, rusted, and twisted old rails cast aside
as the PRR had abandoned this route and picked it over for both spare
parts and for storage. Overgrown grass and low shrubs had covered most
of it, the break in the cover of the woods overhead spelling out the gap
that had been created by felling the trees for the railroad.

Cautious step after cautious step, I move on, the weight of the pistols
rocking and rubbing through my shirt, chafing my torso.

A bit of water never hurt anyone.

This mist, however, just might, as is the fact that visibility is virtually
gone. Like the heavy smoke of the battlefields, the only guide being the
detonation of the cannons and the flash of the muzzles and fire . . .

Here, there is none of that, but for the roar of the river and the last
of the ringing in my ears from the gunshots.

That's when I see a figure lurching toward me out of the mist,
charging uphill, swinging the outlines of arms. My breath stops, just for
a moment. My heart, finally, beats faster in excitement.

Can't believe it. Just cannot believe it.

I raise the shotgun to my shoulder and settle the ivory bead between
the barrels in the center of the laboring, lurching figure.

"Greetings," I say, my even voice loud in the fog.

He draws up short. He had been looking over his shoulder, as if someone were pursuing him, but I see it even through the obscure curtains
of vapor, the perfectly Hungarian-mustachioed face of Istvan Magursky.

The depiction on WANTED poster had been, unbelievably and
uncannily, a near-perfect likeness of the man, with his heavy mustache,
his hollow features making him look even thinner. I had seen it before,

though never this close. I'm reminded of it—this man's face, without question, had been seen around town and the flickers of recognition I had seen in the faces of those I'd questioned were not my imagination.

No time for puffing up and strutting now.

I pull the trigger, detonating the right barrel, and a cloud of lead rips through the fabric of his right sleeve. He spins and tumbles face down to the ground.

"Don't move a fucking muscle or I'll blow your goddamn hunky head right off."

I step closer, the shotgun still on him.

He groans, rolling over onto his back. "The famous Cossack," he says, laughing a bit, coughing and spluttering against the water and the mud sticking to his lips. "You've been after me for a while." He coughs again. "The curse of Turan, the curse of all my people. With me, it is you. *Te barom*, you bastard you."

"Stop with the gibberish and get on your feet. I should just cut off your head and march it out of here on the end of my scattergun."

I step still closer, wary, and then draw back with a single motion and slam the point between his ribs.

He cries out, shying away, trying to roll away. I had hit him hard, but you can't trust his type.

"*Menj a pokolba . . .*" he breathes.

"I said, *on your fucking feet!*" I shout, my voice hoarse, my body jangling with excitement. I've waited so long for this moment.

He lurches upward, to one knee. He hauls himself back to his feet, teeth gritted, blood soaking his sleeve. I had aimed away from his arm, only catching him with a part of the pattern. He knows this. He's trying to gauge me, what he can of it, anyway, and what I will do. Still, if he knows enough about me, he knows I'd just as rather do what I told him than try to get him out of here as a prize still breathing.

"Hands up. Reach for the Himmel, or whatever you Huns call it in that stupid pig Latin rubbish that you're always babbling like a fucking ape."

Magursky watches me, his hands high above his head. His right hand and arm are a bit lower, his sleeve mangled, blood coursing from his curled fingers and twisted hand, the rain diluting it and turning it a muddy rust color. He tries to smile at me as well, but even for him the pain is having its effect on his deportment.

I notice the revolver tucked in his trousers at the waist, the handle cold and black against his pale shirt.

"Well, officer, what do we do now? You gonna take me in, huh? You going to parade me around in front of all your capitalist masters to show what a good puppy you are, huh?"

I sigh.

He narrows his eyes at me, the grin still etched in place. "Oh, you've heard this all before. I understand." He attempts a shrug, still holding his hands up. "So many out there like you. Not just the cops and not just the servants, but everyday workers. You're no different. I see that. You've got a job. So you're doing that and yes, you've heard all the words before and you're tired of it, huh? I can understand that too."

I have one more shell in the left barrel of the gun. He knows this.

"You do not understand this, despite all you have seen, despite seeing the hell that is the mines and the steel making."

"You came here for that, you stupid son of a bitch." My trigger finger itches. "No one forced you to."

"And here, you are, mister policeman, the arm of the rich, no one forced you to do that. But here's where we *both* have landed." Careful to keep his hands above his head, he twirls his fingers, gestures with the direction of his glance. "A ruined land. A flood, so much death."

I'm not going to have some type of political debate with this fool.

"Someone," he says, "*someone* must speak for the worker, the poor. Someone must speak for the hopeful, because it is not *you*."

I am not sure if it was some subterfuge of movement or just luck that came next. Just as I open my mouth to provide my final warning, Magursky collapses, sliding face down again and tumbling to the ground, gravity taking him faster than I could follow.

I don't even have a moment to curse as I see him disappear, pulling the shotgun aside. He slides down and rolls, lurching to his feet and scrambling toward the close trees and closer mist.

The ground had given way.

He rolls and somehow extricates the revolver from his waistband, firing a snap shot at me as I juke to the right, an angry hornet buzzing past my ear and a searing pain across my scarred left arm. He flies to his feet, half-running and half-sliding, careening from tree to tree.

I shoulder the shotgun, adjust my aim in an instant, draw down on Magursky's fleeing form, and pull the trigger.

The shotgun fires once from the left barrel. The incline of the woods, the heavy rain, and the rushing water combine to quiet the sound.

I watch as the group of shots hit Magursky, peppering him and pitching him forward as his topcoat blistered in a dozen or more spots, his torso, hindquarters, his left leg, a shoulder. He stumbles, wheeling and windmilling his arms to keep his balance. I take another step forward and touch off the other barrel, only to have the hammer fall on a spent round.

"*Shit.*"

Still, he runs.

Cursing, I break the shotgun open, dunk two more shells into the breech, and snap it closed. For whatever reason, that's the sequence of movement that burns my arm. I glance down at it, seeing my sleeve soaked brown with blood and rain. The shirt cuff around my wrist is crimson paisley now. I curse again, surging forward after him, index finger on the trigger guard.

The bastard shot me. Not by much, perhaps, but enough of a reminder not only of the situation but my own poor decisions in pressing this without a clear advantage.

Harrisburg is doing this.

Magursky dodges behind a tree just as I'm about to hit him again. I put the gun back up, rushing to close the distance. He's too far for a shotgun to have much of an effect anyway, other than to spur him on and keep him running.

I need to get closer.

I expel my breath, water flying from my pursed lips as I bring the gun back down and run forward. I count on the fact that Magursky is still armed and not hurt too badly by the latest from the shotgun.

That leg wound looks especially bad though it had not apparently hit the bone. The blood pouring from it paints his trousers the same rust and ruddy color as my sleeve, except that his wound looks to be pumping out.

Just need to keep him running. One way or the other, I'm going to get him. Either through his own blood loss costing him his consciousness or even his life, or slowing him down enough where he either gives up . . . or just gives up the ghost.

I move forward, in pursuit now rather than a stalk. Hunched over and carrying the shotgun at the ready, my hands freeze with the temperature and slick with the cold rain. I've had worse. I've always had worse.

I move quickly, but the footing is perilous, the soil and leaves and branches on the forest floor loose under the assault of the weather and gravity. Each step I take is a prelude to sliding down the hillside and into the boiling, raging cauldron that is the great river. I glance up at the sky; it seems to be getting dark early, if that's even possible, though it can't be but around three in the afternoon. I blink away the rain in my eyes again, the bowler soaking through my thinning hair, its fabric saturated.

I move from tree to tree. *Method, method, method.*

There! I bring the shotgun up just for a second, then put it back down. Maybe it had been him, maybe it hadn't. The darkening shadows of the passing time, the rain, the mist, the trees all combine for the eyes to play tricks.

"Fuck!" I yell, ducking just as Magursky steps out from a tree to my left. I throw myself backward and to the ground, rolling away and keeping the shotgun pointed up. I fire the left barrel in his direction and roll to a muddy stop at the base of a failing, rotting oak. I cough, catch my breath, spit the water from my lips, rivulets of grim running down my face.

I quickly scan my body to see if there are any new holes that hadn't been noted before.

"Lucky police!" Magursky bellows, receding in the distance.

Cursing again, I struggle to one knee, peering around the trunk of the tree. I break the shotgun open to reload.

I scramble uphill, throwing a glance back over my shoulder as I can see, through the curtains of mist and rain, the raging torrent. Black shapes tossed to and fro course by—I can make that out through gaps in the weather. Jesus, it's really getting bad.

I pause, looking forward and to the sides, my back pressed against the rough bark of a massive cherry tree. I flex my fingers wrapped around the shotgun, the bone-chilling cold threatening to freeze their stiffness into numb sluggishness. I blink away the water running into my eyes and lick my lips. My face feels as frozen in the cold rain as anything else, absurd against the knowledge that this is coming up on the end of May.

I hunch, stalking forward, shotgun at the ready. I spy a movement to my right. I glance in that direction; something other than a person running had drawn my attention. I return to my normal scan from right to left and back again as I slowly place one step after another, easing in the direction that Magursky had fled.

I reach the point of impact about where I had hit him with the shotgun blast; there are a couple of scattered shreds of clothing, one of which looks satisfyingly blood-stained. Any blood trail on the ground, however, would be nigh on impossible to discern. If a shot pellet had cracked a rib or, better yet, popped a lung, this could be a short chase. If not, it threatened the possibility of losing him.

Again.

I had a brief flash of annoyance in thinking through what such a scene would entail: me sending in a telegram, then with a long journey after that back to Harrisburg to savor the feeling of failure. Next, after that would be the walk to the offices of my superiors within the Pennsylvania Railroad system and then the inevitable oral delivery of the same report of complete failure. My position as a C&I cop attached to the railroad, rather than to a mine or set of mines, would be in jeopardy. As a consequence, they could ask for my badge, putting me out of work, or at least this line of it.

I think back again to my fantasy of floating down the river to somewhere else. It could be the other side of the Divide too, back East of here, floating down the Potomac or the Susquehanna to somewhere else. I could have a new name, a new history, a new everything. There are no attachments, no real reason to stay. I have no wife, no children. I grew up alone on the farm, fought on my own in the War, and now I travel the state the same way.

That won't happen. *Mary Elizabeth . . .* it's the strangest moments when her name comes to me. She represents the false peace of my past, that which never was and never could be. It's better to be realistic.

And reality is that they won't demand I return the badge, either. They'll do something entirely within the character of the system itself. They'd just take me off the trains and put me in one spot, probably a spot that's out of the way and either totally recalcitrant and boiling with violence—the new works and burgeoning steel enterprises in Pittsburgh, for example—or a place that's essentially endless boredom. Some godforsaken mine in either northeastern Pennsylvania, in anthracite country, or some other singleton mine where nothing ever happens in the southwestern part of the state, in bituminous country.

Or, worst of all, I could be moved to an administrative setting, scratching out my initials on an endless parade of papers covered with inked characters telling stories of heroism and other horseshit.

I tap my nearly-empty tobacco tin, annoyed.

There might not be another chance. Another man might tell himself that he was stalling, that he was afraid. Anyone who doesn't have fear in a gun battle is a fool and a menace to himself and others; I hadn't yet given up on so much that I would succumb to that degree of recklessness.

I light the cigarette, and I wait. I close my eyes, thinking once again of the hills of Fulton County, this complicated landscape of mud and blood. The memories of other hillsides, obscured by smoke, the grounds shaking with cannon fire, ears ringing with the musketry push, as they always do, my own version of the boyhood fable.

I finish the cigarette; or, more accurately, the weather finishes the cigarette for me as it becomes sickly sodden with its own tobacco juices before I'm even past the halfway point. I throw it, extinguished, to the forest floor. I look down at the shotgun breech, once again obsessing over the closure of the barrels, and as I look back up, I see the flash of motion.

Well, goddamn.

The motion of me tossing the half-smoked cigarette away in disgust triggered some type of movement, not but seventy yards away from me through the woods, downhill to my right, and moving quickly.

Is it him? The question cannot be answered. While it is indeed hard to conceive that there would be anyone else traipsing about in this weather, one can't rule it out. It wouldn't be the first time that someone innocent got caught in the middle. Under the Constitution, both in the Commonwealth and of the Union, one has a right to a jury trial, and this also includes a presumption of innocence; that presumption is significant, however, and very few deserve it, particularly when many serve a purpose of nothing other than incitement and disorder.

Magursky is the finest of this example, moving to this country under the auspices of seeking liberty and fortune and doing nothing other than struggling to attack and kill the system that so welcomed him to the shores. I realize not everything is exactly like paradise in the mines and the mills, but things were also hardly like paradise on the muddy fields of Petersburg and everywhere else, where the blood bubbled up from the rutted and stomped soil along with the water soaking the loam. Life was even harder for the Negro and not made any easier even after Mr. Lincoln gave his famous speech on the Hallowed Ground.

I consider having the last of the tobacco. Something else rumbles more deeply in me, worse than hunger. I know that feeling. It's a prompt to get aggressive and do more to author this encounter rather than just reacting to it.

I take a deep breath.

"Magursky!" I yell. "Magursky, give yourself up! We're Coal and Iron Police! You are fucked!" Not to put too fine a point on it. But I'm not exactly here to read poetry to him.

There's one other thing he knows—we will always be there. He's not going to elude me, and even if he could, the C&I isn't going to fold.

No reply, but as with everything else, it's hard to hear a single thing over the pelting rain. I hold the shotgun across my chest, my back pressed into the tree and my head cocked to the side, throwing my voice to a different angle.

"Magursky, I know you can hear me! Give it up! I'll walk you back to town and we'll get on a train. Just come out!"

Then, a reply, either quieter or far more distant than what I anticipated, "Fuck you!"

Despite everything, I chuckle, shaking my head. *Every time. Every Godforsaken time.*

I creep forward, then lunge to another tree. I'm unsure as to his ammunition or even his ability to do anything with it, but I have to assume that he has plenty of ammunition and more than enough ability to fight this out. I cock my head. I hear a distant thud, a *boom*, in a way.

Must be thunder.

I take another step forward, the shotgun held upward in front of me, the cold metal of the pistols strapped about my torso pressing into my chilled flesh.

Must be thunder, I think, again. I lunge to the next tree. *Boom!* And then, with a snap going past the tree, a bullet flits by, a murderous wasp. He still has some ammo left, then.

But here's a virtual certainty: I've got more guns and ammo. He'll run out of both, long before I do, even with the previous engagement. I crack the shotgun open and double-check that both shells are ready to fire. I snap it closed and doff my cap, flipping it once from behind the tree, to the left and then to the right, and back to the left. I drop to a knee and spin around the side of the trunk, shouldering the shotgun and touching another round off directly in front of me.

I surge to my feet and run to the next trunk, the thundering *boom* of the report bouncing through the soggy woods just for a moment before the water and mud again soak up the echoes. Still, the roaring in my ears grows louder, something that I can't trace.

Another flash of motion, moving away from me, sliding again, sliding downhill toward the current. I jump again, moving directly toward it, breaking the breech open and putting a fresh shell in. My knees bend, ready to leap again as I crouch, reducing my profile and staying in motion.

Magursky tumbles forward, pirouetting twice before going down again and then scrambling to escape gravity and the mud sliding him toward doom.

Magursky spins around, looking at me with surprise as I touch off the second barrel, the blast of the shot hitting him squarely in the chest. As it sometimes happens, time slows down and I get the impression that I can see the blast of the shot blowing out of the barrel from my eye lining down the length of the gun, the shot bursting into his soaked shirt and clothes in a dozen or more places,—blood already gouting and seeping red through the fabric in an instant.

Without thought, I drop the shotgun to the ground and pull two pistols, one in each hand, bringing them up and training them on Magursky, clicking back the hammers. Magursky wheels backward, spinning his arms like windmills as he tries to catch his balance down the steep and slippery hill.

I fire one, then another, the pistols bucking in my hand, the detonation of the powder blasting sparks and smoke, and the sudden heat and expulsion of gas mixing with the mist and obscuring my vision even more. Clicking the hammers back one after another as I walk forward.

While my first shot had missed, the second one takes him high in the right shoulder. He finally staggers and falls, rolling quickly down the hill, branches, leaves, and even more mud clinging to his clothes and even being spun off by the movement.

I slip then, one of the pistols sailing from my grasp as I hit the ground in a sitting position, my tailbone sparking a pain shooting up my back and around my hips, a numbing and icy clutch around my testicles. I grit my teeth, leaning over to my right and hissing in pain, curling my legs up.

Impossibly, I hear another gunshot from below, a sharp singing buzz of a bullet snapping just inches from my head. I continue my own roll to the right to the partial shelter of a young maple tree, not enough to cover all of me, but just enough for me to collect my bearings.

"Fuck," I mutter, shaking my right hand. I look down at it, my index and middle fingers wrenched and already turning bruised. Somehow the fall and the tossed pistol had twisted my knuckles. I wince again at the pain, sucking in breath through clenched teeth, more concerned about function than the pain itself.

I push myself further down the hill, the roar growing louder.

"Fuck you, you Cossack *Police*-man!" Magursky calls. I can't see him; I can just hear his voice coming to me from just below a shallow dip in the contour of the hillside. His words spit toward me, along with his coughing. The thought of frothy blood spraying from his lips makes me smile, just a little.

I slide on my hip, taking as much cover from his shallow trench as he was. Problem is, I'm on my left side facing in his direction, but with my injured right hand, it's difficult for me to shoot. I curse myself for having dropped the shotgun. That had been a mistake, a classic tactical error that exposed my overconfidence, which grates and claws at my mind. A voice tells me to wait, that it cannot be long now; he must be bleeding out. All of these are fine thoughts indeed, but as I knew, from hunting as a boy even long before the war or any of the deeds I've done since, bullets can do strange things, and animals and people can do things that are even stranger. I've seen men die of fright from a flesh wound and small deer running for hundreds of yards and lasting for hours with a bad wound in a chest cavity . . . having followed a trail of frothy pink lung blood for what seems like forever, only to have them again flee from me when we lock eyes.

I slide down some more, keeping my eyes on the misty "distance," as it might be called, from where Magursky had last sounded.

The weight of the shotgun shells jump in my jacket, a taunt from the abandoned shotgun and, hence, better judgment, now also abandoned. It's almost as if those small bundles of lead were dragging me further earthward, a reminder of both ego and stupid choices.

I flex my fingers on the grip of the pistol, rolling onto my left elbow and propping myself just a bit up, hopeful that the contour of the fallen tree providing my cover was also enough to obscure my movement; my sodden gray and muddy clothes would blend in with the sodden gray and mossy bark of the fallen tree trunk.

My eyes dart to each pocket in the fog, in the meager cover that might be offered to Magursky as well.

Got a bullet with your name on it, you son of a bitch.

And then—the world came to an end sometime around three in the afternoon.

The noise that accompanied it came before the onslaught of the waters, a horrific cacophony of groaning metal, raging water, breaking trees, and screams of people, as I watched the water move from flood stage to apocalyptic.

In a second or less, the water surges from the riverbed over the banks and explodes up through the woods. The waters have everything surging and bobbing and crushing against each other. Houses, structures, and even massive train cars tumble end over end and twirl around.

My eyes widen. The wall of water surges towards Magursky and me alike. I don't hesitate. I shoot again and then run for higher ground, my hand thumping in agony.

I slip and fumble forward, the water surging through the tree trunks. I look up and see nothing other than a rolling mist. More structures and trees tumble out and scatter to the sides as if God himself was splashing the waters with his hands. My breath comes in hitches as I'm winded, and the pain of the grazing wound reminds me of my true place in the world.

The mud makes for treacherous footing, and I slide back a foot for every two feet uphill that I manage to make.

I'm coughing now, and I stagger and slip and sputter some more as I struggle to save myself.

The water surges around my calves and then my knees, ripping the ground cover from under my feet. I fall to the side, splashing, panicking, arms flailing as I scratch and claw my way back to my feet, the water dragging at my coat and trouser legs.

I climb again, my hands reaching for the tree trunks in front of me as I charge up the hill, the water rising, rising, rising.

I glance over and I see Magursky clinging to a tree trunk himself, watching the waters rising around him, and then back at me.

Another angry buzz burns just above my head. Magursky's laughing, his mouth wide open, blood running down the corners of his mouth. He raises his revolver again, but I shoot two more times, still running. I see one of my shots strike a tree, spraying wet bark and splinters. The other shot doesn't seem to hit anything.

He fires then, the report of the shot hollow and too loud.

Holding a pistol in my right hand, I scramble more, hunched over and pawing at the ground with my left, my feet slipping and sliding against the water and muddy grounds.

I fire blindly, the revolver kicking in my hand as I angle uphill, trying to close off the top of the radius. I know he'd been hit, hard, by the shotgun and a couple of the revolver bullets, and the fact that he's still alive and fighting is a source of boiling wonder and frustration to me. I'd seen it before, of course, men struggling ahead through the mud and their own blood, no leg, no arm, blood flowing like the Ohio from every hole in their body, and yet not only clinging to life but continuing the fight.

Magursky carries on in this spirit.

Yard after yard, breathing heavily, I fumble to reload the revolver's cylinder, splashing through the water surging up the side of the hill.

I get to another tree trunk, pushing into it and hiding my profile perpendicular to Magursky's view. I refill the cylinders of both revolvers and ready them. I glance down. The water still rises around my feet even though I'd moved uphill considerably.

I'm wondering about Magursky—

"Fuck you, Coal and Iron! Nothing but slavers, all of you, and you're the caretaker of the slavers! Do their bidding, you dim bastard!"

I can hear him screaming, his accent tinting and curling every syllable of each word.

He fires again—I can hear the *boom* of the gun, but that bullet doesn't come anywhere near me.

Magursky's gunfire doesn't sound right to me; for a horrible second I think there's a bullet in my skull, scrambling my hearing or something else, but instead, I realize that it's the weather. Between the rain, the dampened ammunition, and the water surging around us both, it's a wonder the guns fire at all. The roar of the water and the debris slamming and booming through the trees overwhelms everything; I don't know what's happened upstream, but I'm already banking on the fact that it's those fat rich bastards' private fucking lake seeking a new location for the fat rich bastards' giant houses.

I sweep up and to my right, continuing uphill. I watch as box cars and pieces of houses tumble by, rolling and tumbling in the surging, muddy river. I think I can hear screams, but the roaring in my ears would put the lie to that. Between the roaring of the river, and my own pulse and ragged breathing burning through my ears, I realize that the chances of me hearing a goddamn thing are vanishingly small. Still, somehow, I think I hear something more—the distant shriek of a train whistle.

I press into another tree trunk, giving myself just a few more seconds to steady my aim. I cough, clearing my lungs and spitting out a gob of phlegm. I watch the river, water rushing around the trees just yards away from me.

A section of trees a couple dozen yards downhill and to my left, an entire swath of trees sway to one side and then the next, the ground underneath them tearing away from the hillside, spinning away. I watch, suddenly with a renewed sense of horror, as the trees fall and tumble away, one after another, like some children's game.

The entire hill is collapsing.

How much longer is this going to last? Is it going to wash all of the mountains away into mud running downriver, all the way to Pittsburgh and beyond?

I capture control over my breath one more time, then lurch out from around the tree.

I raise the revolver again, Magursky furiously fiddling with his own as he clings like a monkey to a swamped tree.

"Magursky!" I scream.

He glances up, a grimace on his face, before fumbling again with his handgun.

The revolver jerks in my hand, and I see a geyser of blood spurt from his other shoulder, excitement surging through my gut at the sight of it.

Magursky looks down at his shoulder, the latest of the wounds looking to be the worst of them all yet. He stares at it for a moment, his own ancient revolver falling from his grasp and tumbling into the water raging around the bottoms of the trees. The water still surges higher. I draw the hammer back again. The water won't stop—it keeps threatening to swallow the rest of the world.

Again, the water wraps its embrace around my already-soaked feet and calves, and I stumble backward and slide forward. Gravity conspires against me. Cursing, I turn to run uphill again, and I lose my footing, falling and splashing again to the muddy ground.

"*Fuck!*" I roar, flailing my way forward on all fours, knowing the ridiculous target I'm now presenting to Magursky. I scramble uphill, clawing at the mud and the water. I reach the tree again, shaking the revolver free of the water. It could be filled with mud—firing it now could mean blowing up a bomb in my face and hand.

I turn around to see Magursky leaning away from the tree, clinging to it with one arm and both legs, then just his legs as his grip slides away. His pistol is gone, swallowed by the water. I want to take another shot. He hangs, mostly upside down, from the tree with his legs wrapped around it. For a sickening moment, he reminds me of a squirrel I would have shot as a boy as it resists the pull of gravity with the last of its strength as life seeps from the holes in its skin.

I cough, sputtering mud and water from my face as Magursky falls, his plummet ending in a cratering splash in the frothing water at the base of the tree. The swirling waters engulf and cover him. A second later he springs up, breaking the surface, spluttering the water away.

No, it can't possibly be.

For a moment, hoping against hope, I see his floating body tumbling and turning like a maple seed on the surface of the water, and I believe him to be dead.

Then he picks up his head, and his arms and legs surge at the same time the current strengthens and picks up the speed. He bounces off a tree trunk and rights himself, sweeping along in the current but bobbing to the surface. The water's movement spins him around, none too gently.

My eyes widen, my own breath hitching as I draw the revolver's hammer back and fire again, and again. One eruption of water lands next to his head, and then the hammer falls with a dry metallic click, deafening over the roar of the current, and I scream in frustration, trying again and again, the hammer falling on an empty chamber each time.

The river wraps Magursky's path downstream and away from me as he almost taunts me from eddy to eddy. The force of the current and the gravity are inevitable as they conspire to move Magursky out of range.

He was already out of range.

I heave the pistol at him, fumbling for another beneath my coat.

He turns around again and his eyes lock with mine, a smear of blood across his mouth and dark grime and mud across his face making him into a leering harlequin.

As we lock gazes, he reaches up with a single arm—his left arm—and stretches out his middle finger to me. I think I can hear him laughing over the noise of the waters as they carry him away from me, downstream, to his escape.

Epilogue

I had seen the glow for a while now, silhouetting the tops of the hills as I steered my way down the valley, picking my way through. What has been strewn before me is unspeakable, even to these eyes having seen what they saw in the war. Mostly, it can be described as mud and pieces of everything: wood, wagons, homes, animals, people. It's as if God Himself tossed his drink in frustration, flattening and smashing and tearing everything in His wrathful path. I hadn't been able to find Amos or even the way back to him. I can't shake the vision of Amos fighting his way downstream in the raging current, his eyes wild and rolling as he struggled against the inevitable, swept downriver at twenty miles per hour, overcoming with the debris crushing and smashing into him and forcing him under the surface which bubbles with rage and toil.

I also can't shake the vision of Magursky looking at me and extending his middle finger, then swallowed by the same raging destruction. I tell myself that Magursky's dead. He *must* be dead. But without proof, it is as good as his making his escape.

I limp too. Blood has soaked my lower right pantleg, even more than what the water and mud had already done. My fingers still throb with agony from being wrenched, but the only thing I can do is stagger and stumble my way toward the glowing horizon.

My left arm feels singed, welcoming its newest slashing tear, a new scar to join its crowded company on what remains of my flesh, a Greek chorus of savagery and blood.

For a few horrible moments, I thought I would get hurled back in time to the battlefields, hearing the groans, screams, and cries of the wounded once again. Not here, though. The only sound I could make out was my own slow, ungainly, uneven footfalls in the sucking and splashing mud. I couldn't fathom for a moment that there were living things here.

But there were not. Nothing living—the flood had scoured the earth of all things living and moving, breathing and making sounds, and swept them screaming downriver. The only thing left behind was this horrible silence, descending like its own deluge of ruination. The trees weep but only in silence.

Such thoughts naturally lead me back as well to my last vision of Magursky, flailing and bleeding and laughing all at once, gouts of blood from his nostrils and his mouth.

Surely, he's dead as well, with all of the lead in him and the rate of his bleeding. The last vision of his smiling face and bloody grin returns to me, a single outstretched middle finger looking back at me.

He must be dead.

And yet he locked eyes with me, a knowing glance, almost a wink in a way which had said: *I'll see you again soon, Cossack.*

I cough a few times, shaking my head. I pause then, the throbbing in my leg unrelenting. If anything, it is worse for the sudden lack of motion. I grit my teeth against it. I'd love to have a bit of tobacco to fry the vision of Magursky out of my mind; when I think of returning without his body, or at least some piece of him, I already know what the big brass in Harrisburg is going to tell me.

If only they knew.

But they don't know, they don't want to know, and they sure as hell don't need to know. They're in the positions they're in if for no other reason but because of their ignorance of the world. Of *this* world, at any rate. No one would really be there to question my account, of course, and I think that I would have enough goodwill with my superiors for them to accept that the man had been swept away in a flood. Surely notorious Magursky cast such a long shadow that, combined with my own reputation and livelihood, they would realize the risks I would be taking by reporting the man dead and then suffering the consequence if he were to return to the living in days, weeks, months, or even years. *Surely,* they would realize that.

They would see that this was not an absurd claim: an enemy filled with lead and coughing blood, falling into a flooded river?

My head pounds and my stomach churns, reaching into the back of my throat with a sour acid taste. Even after this, I can still summon up enough inner stew to gather the beginnings of a red mist limning my vision. The one thing I can always do.

Dead *and* missing. No grave, unmarked or otherwise, for his followers to converge upon and use as a shrine. No place of remembrance for his followers, no shrine to pray toward. Just pieces of him around, covered in shit and mud, where he deserves.

Where we all will go someday.

The thought had been there. I know it as soon as I realize it. This is not new, but I think: *I'm not what I once was. I cannot do this anymore.*

———

I want to climb directly up this hill, but it is the middle of the night and as dark as it can possibly be; there are no lights, other than the dim glow of Johnstown above the ridgetops. The rain has relented. Making my way up an unfamiliar hill in the dark, with God alone knows who might be in those woods, looking for a straggling survivor, was enough to count me out from that plan. No, I had to go along the same cart and horse path as the other figures were, moving down the valley toward the city—shambling like a ghost trapped in some hideous veil, forbidden from entering the next world. At least the glow of the city was enough to give one some idea as to the contours of the land. I still had the derringer, the small pistol, and one blade.

I hadn't thought it would look like this; I began to think that the larger city had been spared, that the smaller villages upstream had taken the brunt of the wrath from the raging waters. What had been roaring and screaming was now nothing other than a dull trickle that one might strain to hear from a placid creek on a warm midsummer's day. And yet, knowing that Mineral Point was erased from the earth, scoured clean by the flood, posed a strange contradiction between one's senses in the present and one's knowledge from the recent past.

Breaking through the quietude is a groaning noise, ahead of me and to the right. I adjust my remaining weapons and continue limping forward, seeing a vague shape off the side of the road, a man severely injured and not long for the world.

"Water," he croaks at me. On my life, I can't tell whether it's a request or a statement of what had just happened.

"I'm sorry, sir," I say, moving closer. I grit my teeth as I squat down. I can't see much in the dim shape. "I've no water."

"All right." I see a movement of his head, an attempt at a nod. As I squint, I can see that this man's left leg juts out at an angle from the rest of his body, his hip, leg, and possibly his pelvis shattered from some twisting impact of the debris.

"I'm sorry," I say again. I, too, wish I had water. I think for a moment about moving down to the quiet burbling river, but I've no way to transport the water back to this man.

He doesn't reply. I just hear his breath weakly rattling in his chest. Not long then. But for him, it will seem like an eternity.

"I'll send help for you," I tell him, gritting my teeth again as I stand. Complaining about my own injury at this point seems silly after seeing the damage to this man.

Still no reply, just a groan and the rattling breath. Probably cracked ribs as well. God alone knows where this man came from.

"Your name, sir?" I ask.

No reply, so I ask again. Still no reply.

I take off my hat and scratch my head. "All right," I say to myself, breathing out. "All right." To whom am I speaking? This man? Myself? God? How could a God such as the one we've been told to believe and trust allow something like this?

I sigh and continue south and west, trudging with the vague dark and gray shapes shambling along, the march of the displaced and dispossessed.

It wasn't the glow of the city lights; it was the glow of the city itself. Psalms Chapter Five: *For in death there is no remembrance of thee . . . in the grave, who shall give thee thanks?*

That's enough of a thought to make me grunt a bit of amusement. Indeed, no remembrance. Not for me, not for Magursky.

I had begun to detect some whiffs of smoke not long after I encountered the man dying along the roadside, but it grew stronger as I grew closer. At first, I feared there was a forest fire that would have blocked my travel and forced me back north and east, the way I had come, and I couldn't be sure how much longer my leg was going to be able to take weight and how much more blood I'd been losing. The flow had seemed to have staunched, but I was unsure.

There were more bodies and more destruction the further down-stream I went. Some of the marchers I'd been moving with peeled off and sat down, perhaps figuring that their journey was complete, one way or the other, with the smoke growing too thick or their fatigue and injuries too much to continue.

I draw my jacket tighter around me, obscuring both the badge and what's left of my weaponry. There is that one blade clinging to my bat-tered person. I could have knifed someone for another cigarette though, a single dry bit of tobacco lit with a dry, crisp match.

The thoughts of it leave me when I see the truth—the city is on fire.

The sickening irony of it crashes on top of me in an instant; what wasn't destroyed by water is now consumed in flame.

I stagger closer, seeing the behemoth silhouette of the Cambria Iron Works against some of the glow of the flame, but seeing too that it's not the mill on fire; it's the rest of the buildings in the city which had been piled up against that strong stone bridge of the Pennsylvania Railroad, all of the homes, the stores, the trees, the people buried under millions of pounds of themselves. Several ruined railroad tank cars lay against each other, split open, spilling their fuel out and engulfed in flames. A fresh wave of heat blasts against my face.

Then something caused a spark and ignited it. The mud itself is on fire.

So is the water.

Whether from an oil lamp or lightning or an errant cigarette, it mat-ters not; what matters now is that all is aflame.

One of the railcars breaks loose from its brethren and bobs up and down for a moment in the thick, oily fire-waves—the enormous PRR logo in the center of the car, just as it splits and slides beneath the surface.

I cough, waving away a current of surging smoke away from my face. "Jesus Christ," I mutter, shielding my eyes and moving off to the right, still fanning away at the smoke. The main conflagration is far away, its own smoke tumbling skyward with the speed of a runaway locomotive. Numerous small fires burn all over the pile of floating debris. Indeed, that new, strong Pennsylvania Railroad bridge spanning the Conemaugh at the conjunction of two other rivers had withstood the waters. It became a new dam and in front of it, a new lake had formed. The mass of what's left is water, oil, kerosene, flesh, metal, lumber, nails, animals, people, and mud. Bodies float and smash against each other and the bridge, the flames licking around everything and sparing nothing. I hear the screams of those closer to me, trapped in the floating rubble. I see a plaintive face shining bright in the glow of the flames, before the waters and rubble consume it once again. Yes, the new lake for the social club of the poor and now destitute, happily removed from the wealthy upriver whose dam had done this and laid waste to the homes of thousands, with Christ alone knowing who might be dead.

I should have thought of Magursky; I should have thought perhaps of the members of the filthy rabble that I'd come to collect on behalf of capital, of long-gone Mary Elizabeth, of my grandfather, or the Fulton County farm. I think instead, as always, of the thousands of wounded and dead lying strewn about a battlefield, corpses, and near-corpses groaning and moaning against the inevitable.

Impossibly, I see a face floating there between two boards of a broken window frame. It somehow looks familiar to me, and I squint to resolve my vision against the burning smoke and the rancid fumes coming from the ruined floating and burning city.

How do I know that face? Is it someone from the C&I?

I step to the side, cocking my head in an effort to see the visage straight on.

"Ah, shit," I breathe.

It's Officer Eldridge, the young-looking and earnest chap I had met in Chief Clay's office.

What day is it, even?

I stare at the face, confirming to myself that it is in fact that young man, despite the bloody and bruised distortions of it. It was supposed to be his day off.

I stare a bit longer, shaking my head and exhaling in a slow and uneven expulsion.

My knees wobble, a new weakness cascading through me and I find myself falling, tumbling onto my arse, a sudden raging lance of agony splitting silent and raging through my skull. I squeeze my eyes shut tightly, my left eye wanting to explode. The pain surges through my jaw and the roots of what's left of my teeth. I bury my head in my hands, elbows propped on my knees. More agony now than what I'd ever had than when I'd been hit by any number of cudgels.

I keep drawing breath, slowly in, slowly out, and the pain in my face and head starts to recede. I pull at the back of my skull, trying to wring out more tension from my neck. I cough again as a new round of smoke from the burning city prizes its way into my nostrils and maw and explores the confines of my lungs.

I breathe out again, slowly lifting my head and staring at the burning city, this jumbled pile of flesh and wood and wire held firm by the bridge. The screams grow louder as my beating pulse subsides, just a bit. It's a chorus of the damned, freshly arrived in hell. There are no other ways of putting it in comparison, other than thinking that this must be what hell would look like, and yet these people had done nothing to deserve anything like this.

I sit stone-still and watch the flames. I realize I should get to my feet. I realize I am the easiest target in the world right now, back to the wide world that I'd just left, my gaze and attention transfixed by a slaughter. Any number of types from my twenty years or so with the Coal and Iron Police could want to nail my scalp to their wall.

My eyes drift down to the badge, the dull shine echoing the glow of the flames back out into the night. I pause, staring at it for just a few moments, and I find my left hand reaching up for it, my sore and injured right hand moving to assist, as I take it from my breast. I sit there for a moment, toying with it, staring down at it.

That is when, with one motion, I get to my feet and heave the badge into the night, into the debris, into the flames. I think of Virgil once more: *The descent into hell is easy.*

I cough again. For a moment, I dare taunt myself with the possibility of moving closer to the conflagration, diving into the waters amidst the bobbing debris and the dead. I can't bring myself to do that. The smell of the burned and unburned alike steers me away.

I think: *now is the time, if there ever was one.*

The badge is gone. I can do the same, even without the stupid act of self-immolation. I know where these rivers go. They head west, to Pittsburgh, and further south and west, until it reaches the Mississippi and then onto the Gulf of Mexico. Or I could turn right instead and follow the Missouri to the north and west. Or I could find an overland pathway . . . again, to the west. Washington, Montana . . . the Dakotas . . . all fully-fledged states in the Union now. An overland pathway to being forgotten.

To the West it is, my badge is gone. It is time for me to do the same.

I rub the literal two coins together in my pocket. There's nothing for me here, nothing for anyone. I think of a verse from Genesis: *"And God said unto Noah, The end of flesh is come before me, for the earth is filled with violence through them; and, behold, I will destroy them with the earth."*

I walk away from the sunrise, rejoining the shambling figures doing the same, some calling for relatives and friends, others silent. I wonder if the people I see around me are people or if they're ghosts. I am, in a manner of speaking, not a person anymore either. Just that badge, laying somewhere in the mud.

I too am a ghost, and I am headed west.

Author's Note

The Johnstown Flood was absolutely real and did happen; the events and physical appearance of the flood are much as I depicted, or attempted to depict, in this work. More than 2200 people perished in the flood and ensuing fire and, up until the time of the Galveston hurricane nearly 20 years later, the Johnstown flood was the greatest "natural" (though unnatural) mass-casualty calamity in the nation's history.

The question of whether the flood is a "natural" disaster seems to be settling, slowly, in the direction of "no." The malfeasance, negligence, and otherwise intentional ignorance of the South Fork Hunting and Fishing club with regard to the dam's maintenance were all legendary. It was, therefore, not a natural disaster per se, but a human-made one with little or no consequences for the rich owners, except for the loss of their fish and water. The human cost would be exacted upon the thousands of poor and not-nearly-so-privileged living in the shadow of the dam and the incomparable and incomprehensible wealth of the members of the club.

The Pennsylvania Coal and Iron Police were a real law enforcement entity within the Commonwealth. While Thomas Houghton is himself a fictional construct and it is unlikely that there would have been his kind of "free agent" roaming around the state cracking skulls at random areas of particular concern, the CIP were renowned for their brutality and inhumanity. The original strikebreakers, the Coal and Iron Police helped drive the Molly Maguires to extinction and caused untold amounts of mayhem, injury, and even death upon labor representatives, union members, and anyone else who stood athwart the objectives of the rich capitalists.

Some of those more free-market aligned in philosophy (and I count myself in that category) tended to look at the late 19th century so-called "Gilded Age" as some type of laissez-faire golden era. It was not. While there were unparalleled stories of economic success, the notion that much, or even most of it, was done by private individuals without government help stretches the boundaries of truth too far past the breaking point. The formation and institution of groups such as the Coal and Iron Police quite handily put the lie to it. The mounted force of the CIP was essentially the public resource to be deployed by rich, private individuals to shape their way in the world, with no consequence for the rights of ordinary people, Constitutional, or even those afforded to everyone by dint of the ancient history of the common law springing from the British legal system upon which the American colonial ones were based.

As a writer or a reader, it is difficult to put yourself in the position of truly being able to understand what it would have been like to live in a city like Johnstown in the late 19th century. There were no medicines like the kind the vast majority of us have access to today. Our 21st century society still stands replete with problems, but not along the lines of what a new immigrant would have encountered in 1889; even as much as systemic prejudice and racism exist today for African-Americans and other marginalized groups, one at least stands a chance at finding someone to help. That would not have existed in 1889; one's own family, perhaps extended family, would have been about the best that one could hope for. If one was extremely lucky, one might have been able to depend on some folkways and extended kinship and friendship pathways to gain employment and to avoid penury.

The standard of living afforded to immigrants lucky enough to find their way to work in a mine or mill was, by our standards today, hugely unjust and dangerous. At the same time, it was orders of magnitude better than what any of them would have faced in the "Old Country." It was, after all, not just that the United States was a beckoning, blinking, beacon of liberty, but that life at home meant only certain and early death. Nonetheless, there was an active exchange of people, things, and ideas throughout these times, with significant influxes of immigrant groups from cultures that had never before been to the United States. These successive waves of immigration continued for decades, largely in response to pressures at home and with the possibility of starting over, with a new life, in a new land.

The movement was not, however, unidirectional or restricted to certain times. Often, one or a small part of a family would make the move and send for the rest later; it also sometimes occurred that the separation would be permanent, either among siblings, cousins, or even spouses and children. It also was not uncommon for the travel to be bidirectional; sometimes, a new immigrant would make his or her fortune (or a nest egg) and return to Europe and use that windfall (however modest) as a new start in their own native land.

More often, however, the move would be permanent, and the kinship ties would pull more members of the family over from Europe. At the time of *These Restless Hills*, the large influxes of immigration came from the lands of central and eastern Europe, all of whom were derogatorily described as "Hunkies" (for Hungarians), irrespective of what their actual national or ethnic background was, which included many different Slavic groups (also unironically called "Slavish"). These people, already poor and oppressed and fleeing a land where they could, at least, be understood and not have to learn an entirely new language, headed into a maelstrom of a growing young country largely patrolled by those of English, Scots-Irish, Irish, and some German extraction. The latter established groups generally took the opportunity to maintain and improve their own socioeconomic positions and created both pathways for themselves and institutions that were of mixed effect on the new peoples. In such an environment, labor was still cheap and oftentimes treated as such, but labor was also often difficult to find in sufficient quantities to run the mills and mines in the way that circumstances of competition required.

The Coal and Iron Police were a special breed of enforcer renowned for their brutality and widely feared throughout Pennsylvania. The new immigrants would call them "Cossacks" as a way of describing their "conquering" nature and their unrepentant ability to revert to extraordinary levels of violence to break strikes and, indeed, harass and intimidate anyone who might be inclined to form or join a labor organization. First formed shortly after the Civil War, the CIP was a magnet for brigands, psychopaths, adventurers, and other assorted types for whom the idea of law enforcement would have likely been a laughable euphemism for their actual activities.

I wrote the character of Houghton to reflect this; a veteran of the Grand Army of the Republic from the Civil War, he is an old soldier with many physical scars and even more mental and spiritual ones. Like so many things, sometimes whitewashed and almost often obscured through some fuzzy and romantic soft-focus lens, the battles of the Civil War were horrifying, terror-inducing, deafening, blinding, and bloody. The amount of smoke obscuring the battlefields would have been enormous, coupled with the stink of animals, men, powder, kerosene, and any other number of bitter and toxic scents. The deafening crack of the rifles and thunder of the cannons would have caused great hearing loss among almost everyone. Everyone would have seen the carnage of torn and smashed bodies, dismembered limbs, great coppery pools of blood and offal, destroyed eyes and faces and digits.

The disaster that was the Johnstown flood was every bit, if not more, as epically destructive as what I tried to depict in these pages. Thousands of homes, people, animals, and things were completely smashed, annihilated, and burned in the mayhem. While there has been some dramatization in the various depictions of it over the past century and a half (taking license with, for example, the train captained by John Hess which, in reality, traveled *backwards* at top speed, with the whistle tied open, between Mineral Point and Conemaugh), it is nearly impossible to find the correct expressions for the enormous destruction and death that occurred. One need only look at the hundreds of unmarked graves in Grandview Cemetery above Johnstown to see just a small picture of the destruction; any apologists for the rich and their negligence of the South Fork Dam need not only a psychological examination but an overall intelligence test as well. The rich industrialists were clearly, convincingly, and overwhelmingly responsible for the deaths of thousands.

Several national changes occurred in light of the failure of the dam. Notably, a sea change occurred in tort law, under which none of the owners or maintainers of the dam were held responsible. (This is clearly an example of an instance where one might note the presence of the law being "a ass, a idiot," as told by Charles Dickens and subsequently retold by Justice Antonin Scalia.) Andrew Carnegie contributed to the flood recovery with the construction of a library (now, naturally, the Johnstown Flood Museum owned and operated by Heritage Johnstown);

Henry Clay Frick made substantial contributions to the recovery effort as well. Not all of them did, however, which further underscored not just the absolute callousness of the majority of the property owners of the hunting club, but also more emblematic of the times overall, that the event would occur, and some wouldn't even feel the slightest bit of responsibility to lift a finger to right the wrong in some form or fashion.

As a note, there were a couple of local historical characters encountered by Houghton. Patrolman Samuel Eldridge too was real and drowned in the flood while attempting to assist in rescues. He was one of the first police officers to die in the line of duty in the City of Johnstown. He left behind a wife and three young children when he went to work on his day off. Victor Heiser, a young man admiring the watches when Houghton encounters him, survived the 1889 flood that killed everyone else in his family. He later became an infectious disease physician, spoke multiple languages, and, through his work in setting up the Philippines public health system and leprosy control, is credited with saving more than two million lives. He was also a primary interview source for David McCullough's 1968 *The Johnstown Flood*, which still stands as the pre-eminent historical work on the subject. After spending time all over the world and living in New York City for much of his later life, Victor Heiser is buried in Johnstown's Grandview Cemetery, having died in 1972 at the age of 99. The steel mill buildings (called sometimes the Cambria facility, the Lower Works, or the rolling mills) and the mighty hammers were all as depicted in the story. The deep mine Houghton visits was later called the Rolling Mill mine, as it was nearby the rolling mill and a very productive mine. On a late morning in the summer of 1902, it was also the site of one of the worst coal mining disasters in Pennsylvania history, where there was a firedamp (methane) incident and explosion that killed 112 miners from asphyxiation, fire, explosion, and debris collapse.

I intentionally wrote Thomas Houghton with an eye toward his ambivalence regarding his employers. He's a farmboy from central Pennsylvania who would have grown up in a significant amount of isolation; I found him to have a more convincing voice if he had a close relative who gave him some degree of schooling, along with his wartime acquaintances. That said, his level of rage and PTSD from the war, the nature of his job, and his own shortcomings make for a brutal figure with occasional reverie rather than a contemplative person with the occasional burst of rage. Houghton is an unsympathetic character, but for there to be a member of the Coal and Iron Police who hesitated or had second thoughts about his expression of violence would have strained credibility. These were not men (as far as I am aware, they were all men) blessed with a significant degree of conscience or concern. Inspector Houghton is somewhat of a preternatural example of the character that it would take to carry on the mission of the CIP, their employers, and still be able to explain things to a reader.

The labor strife continued to grow in Pennsylvania and elsewhere. One of the most notable events occurred shortly after the Johnstown Flood, at the Carnegie facilities in Homestead, Pennsylvania neighboring Pittsburgh. The Homestead Uprising, as it was called, occurred in 1892 and represented an attempt by strike-breaking Pinkertons to engage in battle with striking steelworkers. Governor Robert Pattison sent in the state militia to rescue the Pinkertons who met with stiffer resistance than what had been anticipated. The strike itself failed, dispersing after several thousand armed soldiers surrounded the facility and its attached company town. Istvan Magursky is a fictional character, but he certainly is a composite of the early pioneers (perhaps bordering on guerrilla status) of labor action. The courage that these people would have shown in the circumstances of the Gilded Age is almost enough to beggar the imagination.

While not immediately successful, the Homestead event led to great awareness of and momentum behind the labor movement in heavy industry. Steel and coal companies would have labor strife for decades following and the Johnstown industrial network certainly had its share. There were significant coal strikes in nearby Windber, for example, in 1906 and 1922, and the Coal and Iron Police would have been in attendance for that as well. They were especially known for their mounted presence; Houghton's use of a horse would not have been unusual (though the mounted aspect of the CIP was generally combat-oriented, as so much of their work was of the strikebreaking nature.) In the steel industry, major strikes occurred in 1919, 1937, and 1952. The 1937 labor action in Johnstown resulted in sabotage and bombing of the water supplies to the mills; these were not peaceful times.

The scene with the Sons of Vulcan is entirely fictional, though I do not believe it to be a far stretch from the truth. This was more of a rendering of a mythological and trope passage than anything actual historical but what is vice today was vice in the 19th century as well. Underground boxing, illegal liquor, and illicit controlled substances are hardly new and limited to the current age; indeed, black market trade is as old as legal trade. The fact that Houghton is aware of it and comfortable there is also a reflection of the gritty times in which the book is set and what a man of his life and lifestyle likely would have experienced.

The Coal and Iron Police were disincorporated in 1935, four years after Governor Pinchot refused to issue new commissions. The end had been a long time coming, where the brutality of the force had even been recognized in 1902 by then-President Theodore Roosevelt after an attempt by the CIP to end the Anthracite Coal Strike; it had become evident that the CIP was far more interested in brutality for the stake of brutality, rather than mere intimidation to end labor action. In 1929, a number of CIP constables were held over after beating Polish immigrant coal miner John Barcoski to death. Two of the CIP members were convicted of involuntary manslaughter. A member of the Pennsylvania House of Representatives and later Pennsylvania Supreme Court Justice, Michael Musmanno, was infuriated about the incident and wrote and agitated extensively to put an end to the force, including the publication of a short story (entitled "Jan Volkanik"), subsequently made into a film and still later a novel, about the Barcoski incident. The era of the Coal and Iron Police was over, and not a moment too soon.

I trust you enjoyed *These Restless Hills*. I wanted to write a historical novel based on real events and real circumstances but also have it as a bit of a hardboiled mystery and the story of a pursuit. I also wanted to pull no punches when it came to the depiction of the challenges faced by people living in those times, and when it comes time to describe the grit involved, both the dirt and grime of heavy industry and its relentless expansion, but also the necessary sandpaper of the soul carried by people who could be successful in those times and under such circumstances. Yes, the CIP was tough. But the immigrant peoples who came to these shores and made a new life for themselves despite the long odds were even tougher, and it is they who built this country. We are not the legacy of destroyers, but of those who built.

And a special thanks to Richard Burkert, now retired, who was the President of the Johnstown Area Heritage Association (now Heritage Johnstown). Richard has devoted his career to the heritage and history of this part of the country and did his best to stop me from making any large factual blunders in this work—any and all mistakes or instances of "poetic license" are my own.

About the Author

Joshua Penrod is a native and resident of western Pennsylvania, which also supplies much of the setting of his writing. In addition to his writing, he is currently an executive for a global trade association in the biomedical sector and an award-winning adjunct professor at the University of Baltimore and Southern New Hampshire University, teaching courses in business and public administration. He holds a Ph.D. from Virginia Tech, in addition to law and graduate degrees from other institutions, and completed post-doctoral studies at the University of Pennsylvania and University of Florida. He has previously published books on topics of industrial history (*Johnstown Industry* and *Johnstown Waters*) and neuroscience's role in marketing research (*Ethics and Biopower in Neuromarketing*). He has also been an essay contributor to the *Northern Appalachia Review* and the *Loyalhanna Review*.

www.ingramcontent.com/pod-product-compliance
Lightning Source LLC
Chambersburg PA
CBHW011355010726
47494CB00008B/2324